PRETTY WORDS

Jordan Grant

BROKEN HEARTS

BRUTAL HEARTS

JORDAN GRANT

CONTENT WARNING

Dear Reader:

This book contains disturbing scenes that may be triggering. Please read the content warning below, especially the triggers of **self-harm, sexual assault, and rape,** which are EXPLICIT.

Your mental health matters.

-J

Triggers:
All are explicit unless noted.

Main Characters
- **Self-harm** — cutting; VERY explicit
- **Profanity**
- **Bullying** (limited)
- **Sexual situations**
- **Blood play**
- **Knife play**
- **Mental illness** — PTSD; suicidal ideation (limited)
- **Sexual assault** (NOT between MCs)
- **Rape** (NOT between MCs)

Supporting Characters
- **Death**
- **Mental illness** — agoraphobia, hoarding
- **Alcoholism** with alcohol-related brain damage
- **Sexual assault** (perpetration of)
- **Rape** (perpetration of)
- **Parthenophilia** — related to virgins only
- **Dacryphilia**

ACKNOWLEDGMENTS

Thank you to the following people who helped this story come to life.

Beta Readers: Edie, Amber, Melissa, & Danielle
Copyeditor: Owl Eyes Proofs & Edits
Proofreaders: Brittni Van and Roxana Coumans
Cover Design: Maria Spada

DEDICATION

This is for the estimated 1 in 3 women who are sexually assaulted in their lifetimes.

I was 11. He was 17.

If you can't get vengeance, I hope you find peace instead.

- Jordan

P.S. Fuck you, Chris.

PART I

DAWN

— Gil (Years Prior) —

I sit at my desk in my office, papers strewn everywhere. Balance sheets, profit-and-loss reports, accounts payable, accounts receivable, all of it bleeds across the hand-hewn wood and nearly hemorrhages down to the floor. Our business, our lives reduced to ink and paper and numbers that hang with a death rattle in the air.

Fuck.

"Good night," Eli calls to me from outside my open door.

"Night," I say reflexively, before I extricate myself from the proof of our ruin. I raise my hand and give him a little wave, though he's not looking at me as he strides toward the elevator, the motion sensors picking up his movement and following him with a trail of fluorescent yellow spotlights.

I snatch my mug, swallowing the corpse of my coffee that cooled hours ago in one gulp. Black and bitter, just how I like it. I set the mug back down on the table in front of me and bring my hands to my temples, closing my eyes as I massage small circles around and around, trying to ward off the migraine that's crawled up my spine and started to bed down for the night at my shoulders. The lamp on the corner of my desk with its levered arm swung toward me colors the world through my eyelids, curtaining the darkness in peach and coral.

Around and around, I go, pressing harder, my index fingers digging into my skin until it hurts.

I promised Eli I would find a way out.

I promised my wife.

I promised my family.

And I have failed miserably.

These past days have been replete with nothing but my discovery of even more debts and liabilities. I thought we still had equity in the Chula Vista properties to the south, but it's gone, evaporated to nothing with the ebb of the real estate market and the crash the Wall Street economists say is coming. It's not coming though, and it never will because it is here, staring at me in black and white, calling the time of death of everything Eli and I have worked for since college. In those days, we stayed up late, crammed into my tiny dorm room, watching the penny stocks and dreaming of making the big bucks. He came from money. I didn't. My father never had anything to lose, but Eli's could lose everything.

So we watched and waited, designed and planned. We were going to forge our own path, and we did, straight into the damn ground.

Fuck.

My eyes pop open, and I comb through the pages, my fingers skittering across paper that smells like burnt ink from the printer in the secretary's office that needs to be replaced. I find the right page, part of the receivables listing payments six months past due from Affinity Pharma.

The numbers bleed together on the paper. A quarter of a million dollars remains overdue, owed to us for Affinity Pharma's lease of the San Bernardino storage facilities. It would be more than enough to keep us breathing until the next quarter. But we'll never see a single red cent.

They ignored the letter from the lawyer Eli and I had hired, demanding immediate payment or else.

Not that there was an 'or else.'

Not that we could afford to hire him to file suit.

It was an impotent threat, all bark and no bite, and they knew it. There would be no chapter eleven in our company's future. It would be complete liquidation, shutting the doors and feeding the scraps to the creditors who loomed and waited.

I stare down at the page, blinking away the blur of the numbers.

Self-pity wasn't going to save our company.

I needed a miracle, and I would try my damndest to find it.

I reach for my coffee mug again, frowning when I tip it to my lips and find it drained.

1

LAYNE

*B*listering sunshine needles my eyes and goes in for the lobotomy.

It's too early and too damn bright for the hangover that's hovering over my head like my own personal thunderstorm. The ibuprofen I chewed dry like a couple of Tic Tacs in my apartment proved about as helpful as a brick to the face. So when a tall blonde —definitely a cheerleader—shrieks across the quad and jumps into the arms of an even taller guy, I imagine beelining for her, sawing her tongue off with the frayed shoelaces of my Chucks, and setting it on fire.

Now it could be said that I hate mornings.

Okay . . . it *has* been said that I hate mornings.

And sunny days.

And summer.

And beaches.

And all things happy.

I didn't use to, though. Well, for as long as I can remember, I've always hated mornings, but I didn't always hate all things joyful and glad. I used to be . . .

Don't go there, Layne.

The cheerleader shrieks again, and I sink my nails into the meaty part of my palms to quell the urge to stab them into her face. That wouldn't be nice. But, then again, no one has ever accused Layne Steele of being nice.

Grumpy, yes.

Sarcastic, definitely.

A stuck-up bitch—*abso-freaking-lutely*—though that one wasn't entirely fair. That fucker was an asshole who couldn't keep his gross, grabby hands to himself.

Still, I have to play nice or be expelled, and I do not want to be expelled. I can't be expelled, not right now anyway, not when I am exactly where I need to be at Arlean University. And that's what matters—that I am here, that I fucking survived twenty-one years of hell to get here. Not that it was all bad, it wasn't, but I count my first four years of life as hell too because they gave me hope when it would have been more compassionate to fuck it all up and leave my expectations at the starting line.

The girl shrieks again, or maybe it's a different cheerleader this time, but I'm careful to not react, even when it feels like somebody took a cheese grater to my brain and then lumped all the pieces back together and called it a day's work.

Stay. Survive. Settle the score.

After that, I'll find the cheerleader and do the world a favor by muzzling the bitch.

Maybe I'll set fire to the university too while I'm at it because this storybook shit isn't really doing it for me. The campus is sunny and warm, nestled in the mountain ranges north of Sacramento and even further, past Redding, in the middle of nowhere. I am in the land ruled by the sons and daughters of LA's rich, the plastic surgeons and corporate lawyers, the movie producers and lookalike Barbie dolls. This is a place of pretty mountain views and private waterfalls, where it's always comfortable—never too hot and never too cold—and only occasionally snows in December.

I'd prefer it to be rainy, windy, and gloomy—just like my soul—but at least it doesn't turn into a winter freaking wonderland every damn year like a rom-com puked its holiday-themed guts. It snows on top of the neighboring mountains where the ski resorts open in the winter, but not here in the low valley. It's like the land itself despises Christmas and snowmen, and that's fine by me.

Christmas can go fuck itself as far as I am concerned. Santa can too, the creepy ancient bastard. My mother loved Christmas, or at least she had when she was younger. She never missed a chance to tell me how awesome it had once been, for her anyway—not so much for me. And that's enough for me to hate the holiday forever.

Don't. Fucking. Go. There. Layne.

This year is going to be different from all the others before it. Hell, maybe I'll even get myself a Christmas present this year.

Unlikely.

This is the year I've been waiting for, when I can finally get justice for all the shit and suffering before it. It would've been easier to use a bullet, but I'm not that kind of girl. I want suffering for suffering, a modern-day Hammurabi's Code.

I spot my target, the pretty boy I've been looking for, walking across campus, his aquiline nose buried in his iPhone. I swear he's walked like ten feet with his ridiculously long legs since I spotted him, but he still hasn't looked up from the thing.

He's got a problem, obviously.

Not that I give a shit.

Not that I feel *any*thing.

He's Archibald Orson Blakely, son of Elijah "Eli" Blakely, majority shareholder and owner of the largest electrical conglomerate in North America.

The archetypal rich boy, though I guess he's nice to look at, if you can ignore the silver spoon that's lodged in his throat.

He's tall, even taller than the shrieking cheerleader and her boyfriend, and he's got the whole California homeboy thing going on. Bronzed skin everywhere I can see, sun-bleached hair that nearly touches his shoulders from where it falls out of his man bun, and blue eyes that could melt a girl's panties off like liquid fire.

Though I only know that one from his Insta.

Golden Boy posts his entire life online.

What he eats.

What he wears (or doesn't).

Where he goes.

Whom he's with.

But never here and never with her, which is . . . *interesting*.

For the past three weeks, I've watched the two-legged advertisement for the morning-after pill walk into one of the stone and marble buildings reserved for faculty offices. I had to join the cross-country team to get on campus early with the football players. And I fucking hate it, thank you very much. Two hours each morning, at the buttcrack of dawn, running around with a bunch of morning people?

End me now.

I plan on quitting the team after the semester officially starts, but until then, I need an excuse to stay on campus so I can watch him.

I've spent a lot of time watching him, waiting, biding my time. Today's the day, though. Or at least it'll count as my first attempt. Time to catch the mouse by the tail and put him in a cage.

I head into the building, following the king of Arlean University, the poster child for donations and the booster club. He's so buried in his phone, smiling down at who knows what, that he doesn't even notice me. A big-boobed alien with four tits, three eyes, in a crop top and a thong could fall from the sky and land right in front of him demanding a human sacrifice, and I'm like ninety percent sure this guy wouldn't even see it. From what I can tell, dude's the literal definition of smartphone addiction, and by the looks of it, he's going to need cognitive behavioral therapy and a metric ton of pills to break his habit.

So I follow him, keeping my distance, and remain utterly unnoticed.

Though the unnoticed part is normal, for me at least.

It's basically my superpower: invisibility. I can blend in anywhere, anytime, anyplace. It was a requirement growing up, how I survived. I either became invisible or paid the price. Trust me when I say with my mother, you *never* wanted to pay up.

I follow the reigning champion of obliviousness down the hall. No one seems to care who I am or what I'm doing. I've literally been following him for *days,* and no one has so much as said hello to me. Still, I manage a side-eye glance to make sure no one is watching me watching him. Then I continue to follow him as he walks down the hallway and goes straight into her office, closing the door behind him.

Honestly, it's kind of impressive how little he is concerned with being seen. But then again, that's typical for people like him. Rich people are always like that, especially those born rich. It's like they expect the world to fall at their feet and pledge fealty just by waking up in the morning, like they somehow know everything is going to work out.

Probably because it always has, for them anyway.

If Golden Boy was concerned about getting caught doing whatever it is that he's been doing, then he certainly doesn't act like it. Then again, when are rich kids ever accustomed to staying hidden? Never, not for this one, anyway.

The weirdo posts his entire life on social. I know what he thinks about the upcoming football season—that they'll win for a lot of technical reasons I don't understand and don't give a flying fuck about. I know why he thinks the dean might have a congenital stick-up-his-ass—have to agree with him on that one. I even know what food he was in the mood for last Friday night—shrimp tacos with sriracha mayo like *all the way, bro.* He isn't in this building for work— athletes are prohibited from working outside of the athletic department during their respective training and playing seasons. Not to mention, he's not the kind of guy who would ever work. If he could get away with it, Golden Boy would definitely be a trust fund baby for life.

This building has jack shit to do with his major—business administration, just like his father and his father before him until the beginning of time for the Blakely family, apparently. The lady he keeps visiting is a literary arts teacher, and none of her classes are required for his major, though he keeps taking them for the humanities credits, I guess.

According to the sole heir to the Blakely fortune, summer classes are lame, and his fall semester course offerings are guaranteed easy A's, including yet another one from this lady. Still, he has zero reason to be here now. The fall semester hasn't started yet.

Also, who posts their entire schedule online? It's like this rich fucker *wants* to be kidnapped.

My bet is he's getting his dick wet, especially since their meetups have that scheduled, clandestine feeling that always seems to be associated with fucking someone you aren't supposed to fuck. But if that's the case, wouldn't the twat at least try to hide it?

Then again, the Blakely heir has obviously never had to deal with anyone like me before, and I appear to be the only person who seems to have noticed where he's been going. It's not like all the students and professors are on campus yet, as the semester won't even begin for another week.

I look down at my phone and start timing, though on average their little meetups take twenty minutes, sometimes thirty if it's an especially long day. I get to five and I keep going until it's been eight minutes. If I'm going to get what I need, my best bet is to catch the University's favorite running back off guard. And I hope to God this works, because if it doesn't, I'm going to have to try harder, and Blakely isn't even my target. I just need to make sure he stays out of my fucking way.

I walk down the hall, and it's eerily quiet even with the soft footfalls of my shoes on the tile. I stop when I arrive in front of a wooden door placarded with Mel Givens's name, Professor of Literary Arts.

Unceremoniously, I fling open the door to the office, and *oh fuck!* It's worse than I imagined.

Ugh, nasty! I need bleach for my eyeballs.

Across the room, behind the desk, the blond pretty boy shifts his head just enough that I get a full-frontal view of this lady's no-no zone. It's like being part of a porno, only I don't want to be part of it, and I never asked to join. My stomach rolls with whatever's left of last night's handle of Jack.

Professor Givens has her bare feet, the nails of her little piggies painted fire-engine red on the desk, her legs spread wide like she's in the stirrups at the OBGYN, and Golden Boy kneels between them, his man bun bobbing as he . . .

I think I'm going to be sick. I cough and sputter and try not to throw up because what's left of Jack doesn't like the view either.

Arlean University's star running back turns around, swiveling just enough so that I can see her . . . her juices on his chin and smiles at me.

"Fuck," I say, feeling last night's bender skitter up my throat. "Fuckety fuck fuck fuck."

The lady says something, and my stomach rolls again. I do *not* want to see this bitch's cunt, but *all* I can see is her cunt, front and center.

I scowl at them and try not to puke. "Fuck. Gross. Fuck."

I look at the carpet, the ceiling, the floor, the dude bro that's still staring at me, his lips hooked in a smile as he watches me and not his girlfriend.

"Fuckety fuckety fuck," I say, and it's a complete sentence, dammit.

Although Jack and I need to have a talk about last night, I know I have what I need, which is just enough dirty laundry to hold over this guy's head if he tries to get in my way.

I look him in the eye, making sure he gets a nice, long look at my face. I want him to remember me and remember what I saw. Turns out after stalking him for a couple of weeks and with a good amount of dumb luck, things finally went my way.

Looking up, Layne!

Professor Pussy nearly falls out of her chair, screeching like she's a car and all her belts are loose, not that her boy-toy notices. No, he's too busy playing the stare-down game with yours truly. I don't look away, even when it goes on for way longer than it should, even though his face is literally still wet with this lady's cum. He smiles at me broadly, showing me his perfect dimples.

What god gave this guy dimples? It's like a slap to the pussy for women everywhere.

His smile widens, shock turning to laughter in his eyes, as I add another "Fuckety fuck."

Photographs don't do Golden Boy justice. He is heart-attack inducing gorgeous, and out of the cold nothingness that fills the center of me, there's a spark of something foreign, something I don't allow myself to feel. A strand of hot silk uncurls in my belly and spreads, sending tendrils of fire across my skin. My mother's voice skulks out of the nothingness to whisper in my ear.

You want him, don't you? she hisses.

No, I deny.

Don't lie to me, girl!

Please . . . don't.

You dirty fucking whore!

STOP!!!

My face flames, and my heart wallops, but I push her derision deep, deep down. Instead, I look at the Blakely heir with the same look that has saved my ass so many times over the years.

The one that says, *Game on, bitch. I don't give a shit about you.*

I'm *not* going to let this guy make me squirm, though I want to look away, so I don't have to see this lady's vajayjay anymore, so I don't have to see *him* anymore.

Awesome. In her scramble to right herself, she shows me her asshole.

I'm going to need to buy another handle after this shit, but at least this worked out. I really didn't want to have to buy drugs and plant them on this tool. His frat house with Phi Epsilon Alpha is always swarming with people, and I couldn't get in and out unnoticed.

I back out of the room, listening to the lady screeching for him to follow me, and I let a rare smile sweep across my lips as I head down the hallway, out of the building, and into the glorious afternoon sun.

I've already won, and Golden Boy doesn't even know it yet.

2

ARCHIE

*M*el has her feet propped up on her desk, her heels discarded on the floor. My left knee bitches at the thin carpet of her office, but I'm not about to let a little pain ruin a good time. I lean in and lave my tongue straight up the center of her pussy. She tastes like strawberries from the lube she knows I like, and she moans my name as I do it again. I flatten my tongue, running it over the slick, smooth flesh. Her manicured fingernails slice through my hair and sink into my scalp.

"Oh fuck," she breathes. Her plaid skirt is bunched up over her thighs, pooling in her tall leather chair and around her ass.

I'm pretty sure her toes curl against the top of her desk as I bury my face between her thighs and lick her pretty cunt again. She's hella gripping me. If I'm being honest, I wish she would lay off the Pilates. Holy shitstorm, she's strong, and it feels like she's trying to bust a watermelon between her thighs. Only my head is the watermelon.

Still, I'll give her what she needs, and in return, she'll blow me after or, better yet, let me bend her over her desk and take it in the ass like a good girl.

"Archie, oh, Archie," she starts chanting, and it's getting hot down here. She smells like the strawberry scented lube and sweat as I thrust my tongue in and out of her cunt. I reach up and around her thigh to pinch her swollen clit, and she starts shaking, vibrating against my face.

"Right there. God, yes, right there, baby," she croons as I lick her like I'm trying to enjoy my favorite lollipop. "Right there. Right there."

She's writhing and wiggling in her chair, her back arching up and off of the leather as I eat her out. Her thighs flatten against my ears like a pair of warm earmuffs, and it's sweltering now, though my cock likes the heat just fine. It's currently imprinting itself against my zipper and trying to bust through to the other side.

In and out, up and down, in and out, up and down, and over again. All the while, I rub her clit hard and fast, just like how I know she likes it.

Mel's the one exception to my *hit it and quit it* rule, which became sacred law after I learned my lesson freshman year. The reigning queen of the crazies keyed my Lotus Evora GT the day before spring break, scratching it up Freddy Kruger style like it belonged in a B-grade movie and not to me. She celebrated her new paint job by lodging a stiletto through my baby girl's sunroof. I thought my dad was going to shit a brick when I had to send him photos for the insurance adjuster, and it should be a recognized miracle that he avoided a full-blown cardiac event.

Queen Crazy was mad 'cause she walked in on me playing hide the sausage with her floor's hall monitor. She thought we were *exclusive*. Like bumping uglies for a week made her my girlfriend. *Pfft.* Whatever.

Everyone knows I don't stay and play.

Mel doesn't want shit from me though, no relationship status for her social, no engagement ring, no anything. In fact, I can thank my lucky stars that a relationship with me is completely off the table for her. Teachers aren't allowed to fuck students at Arlean University, or at least, that's what the official handbook says.

So licking her pussy like I'm savoring the last of my ice cream cone is illicit, dangerous, and nuclear fucking hot.

I thrust my tongue in and out of her hairless cunt faster as she grinds herself against my face. I look up, fingering her clit as her breasts heave against the pearlescent buttons of the white blouse she has on, her hair tumbling to her shoulders from her updo fastened with pointy things that look like chopsticks.

Damn, I love it when they look freshly fucked.

She glances down at me, her chest heaving, a sheen of sweat shining against her tan brow, and smiles, her eyes bleary. I bury my head between her legs again, swirling my tongue around her clit and sending her full-on bucking in the chair before light pours into her office from the hallway. It takes me a moment before there's enough blood flow to my brain to register that her office door has opened.

"Fuck! Fuckety fuck fuck fuck!" a sailor yelps behind me, followed by a torrent of expletives.

I turn and look over my shoulder at the door—because I have to see the shit storm headed straight for me—and I find a girl in the doorway. She's shorter than I normally like them, maybe 5' 5" and that's probably giving her too much credit. She's giving off a grossed-out vibe that makes me want to fuck the sanctimony out of her, despite wearing a pair of grody, *are-they-supposed-to-be-black?* Chuck Taylors from what appear to be the last century. I don't find myself staring at her shitty footwear, though. I don't stare at the raggedy denim overalls she's sporting either, the shorts ending mid-thigh and whitewashed so bright I wonder if she bleached them herself. I don't even stare at how her boobs stretch the faded denim straps like they are trying to pop the bronze buttons and bounce free.

No, it's her crazy red hair that has me drooling all over Mel's pussy. Her fire-red fucking hair.

Holy-freaking-hot-chick.

It's not orange or auburn or strawberry blonde, but something in between all three and entirely her own, like God or the universe or *whatever* forged her straight from the fire and turned her hair a brilliant red in the process. I'm certain it's natural, judging by the freckles that dapple the bridge of her nose and continue across her cheekbones.

Hell, I'd accept an invitation to check for myself, though.

Now I don't consider myself to be one of those weirdos afflicted by scarlet fever—who can't get off unless they are watching two gingers going at it like rabbits while a third watches—but I don't discriminate either. *Hot damn snap, crackle, and pop*, if this girl isn't about to single-handedly give me a permanent hard-on for redheads.

"Fuckety fuck," the girl continues, her button nose scrunching with the curse.

Such a dirty mouth for a pretty girl.

"Oh my God!" Mel says behind me, nearly toppling over the back of her office chair. She's only saved from the fall because I still have a hand on her thigh, so instead, she rears forward and nearly into me as she cartwheels to her feet and pulls down her skirt.

The girl looks between the space where Mel's ass had been and me, her eyes going bulbous. I'd laugh if Mel wouldn't slap me right now because the girl's got the poker face of a virgin. We lock gazes again, and goddamn if her eyes don't throw me for a rollercoaster ride because they aren't quite green or blue. No, it's like looking into the waters off the coast of Cayo Coco, Cuba, where my family vacayed last summer.

They are stunning. Gorgeous. Absolutely mesmerizing.

Aqua. She's got aqua eyes.

Jiminy Christmas, new kink unlocked, ladies and gents.

Her aqua eyes stay locked on me. Well, I'm giving myself a little too much credit, because it's more like she's playing paddle ball between me and Mel. Back and forth, back and forth, back and forth. Like she can't figure out which one of us is in charge here.

Oh, Red, there was never any question about that.

I lick the strawberry lube and Mel's cum from my lips and give the firecracker my best grin.

"Fuckety, fuck," the girl starts again, a pink blush blossoming across her delicious cheeks.

Where's her off switch? I don't mind the cursing, but I really want to know her name.

The girl backs away before she barrels out of the office, turning and gifting me a view of her perfect ass. Mel slaps my arm, attempting to knock some sense into me.

"Go get her!" she calls, on the verge of tears. "Go get her. Now!"

I climb to my feet, a little less graceful than I would've liked because my cock did not take Red's interruption as a hint to settle the hell down. In fact, it's having fantasies of threesomes and being sandwiched between Mel and her as one sucks my cock and the other licks my balls.

I follow the girl with a twinge of curiosity tainted by annoyance as I pull the crotch of my jeans away from my deflating dick.

I know what I have to do. I need to save Mel and make sure Red won't tell anyone. My dick, though, still wants to go back and finish what it started with Mel, instead of chasing this girl. I feel like I'm waddling like a pregnant chick before I finally manage to get my cock to behave.

Mel slides on her black silk thong as I scramble out of the door, closing it behind me as I go to find the cockblocking sailor. I look to my right and find the hallway empty. I turn to my left and find bootylicious already headed outside the building through the double glass doors to speed down the stairs. Jogging after her, I head out of the air-conditioned building and into pure sunshine and the perfect summer heat of northern California. I breathe it in as I continue after her.

Eyeing the back of her skull, I watch as she follows the curve of the sidewalk, nestled between two bright green patches of lawn. The sunlight makes her hair seem alive, like dancing strands of copper weaved with fire. She skitters down the sidewalk, her backpack resting on one shoulder as she does, and I call for her to stop.

"Hey, Red!" I say.

She doesn't look back, which is . . . unusual—normally, chicks don't run from me—but it's also kind of hot. My cock takes it as a challenge, and I jog a little faster. A minute later, I catch up with her. I look over and down at the top of her head. She's definitely on the short side of what I normally like—right at 5' 5"—but my dick doesn't give a fuck.

The shorter she is, the closer she is to your cock.

"Hey, Red," I say again, down to her fire hair. "Let's talk."

"No thanks," she quips, and she's still moving, not even bothering to spare me a glance as she mutters the words.

My tiny spark of irritation flares into annoyance, because since when do girls not talk to me? I brought home the NCAA Division I championship last year. I was named VIP for the past two seasons. I have done interviews with ESPN for fuck's sake.

Everyone wants to know if I will go pro. *No, unless I want my father to disown me.*

If I have a girlfriend. *Ha! Hell naw.*

If I'm as wild as the rumors. *Yes, but don't tell the parental figures that.*

Guys want to be me, and girls want to be beneath me. I don't ask anyone for attention. I am simply given it. And I certainly don't chase hot-as-fuck girls across campus to protect another girl's reputation. I guess it's for me too, though. If my dad finds out, he's going to be riding me hard enough to break me before next spring.

Or cut me out of the inheritance for being a never-ending embarrassment to him.

Well, fuck. That can't happen.

The girl is still not looking at me. And I really need this to be over with so I can stop stressing and get back to Mel, and let her return the favor. That is unless she's too skittish now . . . I sure as hell hope not.

I feel a frown start at the corners of my mouth, and I don't like it.

I don't frown. Ever.

I fuck when I'm happy. I fight when I'm angry. But I don't do sad.

The therapist my parents sent me to after their first divorce told me that it was okay to be sad, to break down, to cry. But she'd never cried in front of my father. I can still hear the asshole in my head.

Only babies cry, Blakely. Are you a baby?

Stop crying and grow the fuck up.

Be a man before I give you something to really cry about.

Red keeps walking and pulls me back to reality with her.

"I just want to make sure we're cool," I say down to Ms. Hot Tamale. "I don't want any trouble for Professor Givens."

Red keeps walking.

Like I haven't been talking.

Like I'm not two feet away from her.

Like I don't even exist.

She pulls her phone out of a pocket in her overalls and starts scrolling through Reddit.

Puppies. News. Bullshit. She keeps on scrolling.

What the hell?

"Red," I reach for her shoulder, turning her to look at me, "we cool?"

She stops walking, pins me with those unreal aqua eyes, and shoves me with both hands. The hit lands hard, smack dab on either side of my pectorals, and I rock back on my Jordans.

I release her.

Damn. Red's got balls bigger than most guys on campus.

"Don't ever touch me," she hisses, chewing up my personal space as she does. Her teeth are shiny and white, and I'm sort of afraid the ginger goddess is going to bite me. "We are not cool. You are fucking your teacher. And look at that," she swivels side to side, looking around us, "I don't care. But we will *never* be cool. Because we are nothing. And will never be anything at all."

Fried fucking potatoes. Where in the hell did Satan's bride come from, and can I get a second helping of giving-me-shit soup?

"Whoa, keep your voice down," I placate—because it's necessary—even though this is the most interested I've been in anyone since . . . well, ever, I think. "You could start some shit saying stuff like that."

Red rolls her eyes. "Then keep your hands away from me, Golden Boy." She looks down at them with disgust like she sees something invisible there that I can't. "God only knows where they have been anyway."

I slap a hand over my heart and give her a don't-be-mad-bae smile that works like ninety-five-ish percent of the time.

"Yo, not cool, ice queen," I tell her. "Didn't you hear? Slut shaming is last year."

"I don't think that applies when you're basically a hooker for GPA points."

"Whoa!" I whisper-yell, raising my hands in innocence like I can't still taste Mel's sweat and cum all over my tongue. "Keep your voice down. I am not fucking Mel for any reason other than I like it. And, for the record, I provide a *free* service to the community."

She raises a hand, clearly done with this . . . this non-conversation.

"Listen," I tell her, sounding annoyingly desperate, "I just want to make sure you won't mention this to anybody."

"Mention what?"

Good girl.

I nod. "Exactly."

"Ohhh . . . that's right, you mean you banging Professor What's-Her-Face, right?"

Goddamn! She is so loud!

"Stop. It!" I hiss, definitely desperate now. "What do you want, Red? Money? Popularity? What?"

Her nose scrunches, and she looks like she's about two seconds from upchucking all over my kicks. "I don't want shit from you, Golden Boy."

I wish she would stop calling me that!

"Then why are you acting like you drank too much haterade this morning?" I look over at her, biting my bottom lip as I consider her. She rolls her eyes to the sky again. "Is it like a jealousy thing? I mean I *guess* . . . we could go on a date or something."

Ugh. The d word. I hate the d word. It comes with an airplane of baggage and bullshit.

I don't date. I dick.

"What is wrong with you?" she blinks at me like I just sprouted a third eye. *Wait . . . what the fuck are we talking about? Oh yeah, her wanting a date.* "You know you aren't all that, right?"

"Pfft. I'm sorry," I say with a laugh. "I didn't realize you were blind."

She snorts and almost laughs too before she remembers I'm here.

"Tell you what," she says, eyeing me with a glint that gives me the heebie-jeebies, "stay out of my way, and I'll stay out of yours, m'kay?"

I fold my arms across my chest and regard her warily. "What does that mean?"

"It means," *God, she sounds especially bitchy right now*, "I won't file a complaint with the dean about you sticking your dick in a professor as long as you stay the fuck out of my life. Got it?"

"Deal," I agree instantly.

Red turns on her heel and starts away from me, and I want to say something, but what just happened?

The unnatural phenomenon raises her middle finger above her head as she continues away from me, sashaying with every step.

"Stop staring at my ass, pervert," she calls without turning back.

Does she have eyes in the back of her head? I was not . . . Okay, I was, but . . .

I snap a pic of her ass as her hair runs thick and red down her back, bright and bold against the white of her sleeveless shirt. The fabric of her whitewashed denim overalls perfectly cradles her thick ass. She's got big boobs, curves for days, and is the complete opposite of my type. Still, my dick doesn't get the memo.

I upload the pic to Insta with the caption, "Dat ass *chef's kiss emoji*"

The post gets ninety-seven likes in the span of ten seconds—not unusual when you have 90k followers—but I grin as I turn back for Mel's office.

Red's fine ass just might end up being one of my most popular posts ever.

3

ARCHIE

a text notification pops up across my phone screen as I scroll through some stats for the University of Eastern California, our first opponent of the season. The game's scheduled in just a few weeks. They've got a kickass QB, but their defense is shit, so I know I can break right through their d-line and straight to victory.

NCAA championships, here we go again!

I select the green bubble and open a group chat between me and my brothers. Ian Beckett, Everett Reynolds, and Chase motherfucking-rockstar Tallum, my boys since our playground days back in New York, my blood despite lineage and DNA, my best fucking friends.

I look down at it and see Everett has asked a question.

> **EVERETT**
>
> Mols wants to know if any of u twats r bringing a date.

I grin down at my phone. He's definitely asking about his recent engagement and upcoming wedding to Molly Bellamy, fellow Voclain Academy alumni and lifelong friend. I could answer him honestly—tell him I'll bring some lucky lady, I guess, when the wedding date arrives—but I'm not about that boring life.

Ah, time to stir the shit pot. It's my favorite pastime activity, after all. Well . . . that and fucking.

ME

Ur mom.

IAN

Chase checked into a detox retreat this morning.

ME

That what they're calling rockstar rehab now?

IAN

No, it's a no tech retreat. No cells, no TVs, no whatever.

EVERETT

Is he good?

IAN

MFer probs getting his dick sucked by a Swedish milk maid in the Alps while he sips alkaline water. He's fine.

Also, I'm bringing Harlow.

And stop making me look bad, E. Harlow's been going for forty-eight hrs straight about u popping the question to Molly on top of a lighthouse.

EVERETT

Just ask ur girl, u pussy.

IAN

After med school.

ME

I need to change my date. Ian's mom wants another turn on the Archie ride.

EVERETT

Are u gonna wait until she's a damn dr, Ian?

IAN

Yes.

Maybe.

Fuck off n fuck u, Blakely. Keep my mom out your filthy mouth.

Ah. I can feel his anger radiating from across the country. I grin down at my phone, thoroughly enjoying fucking with my friends, as I walk into the Physical Education Building, taking a shortcut to the stadium. My boys are a little sensitive about the *your mama* jokes after I let one of Chase's mom's country club friends blow me the summer before our junior year at Voclain Academy, our shared college preparatory school.

They got all pissy about it, even though I told them I wouldn't have let his actual *mom* go downtown. Well . . . not unless she asked politely.

Hell, I did enough cardio that day to meet my yearly goddamn quota. *And* I got banned from the Tallum family's summer beach house for life.

#worth it.

The PE building smells like rubber floor mats and the faint scent of BO, but I kind of like it. It reminds me of a good workout and the feeling of sore quads and actually accomplishing something. A girl in skintight black yoga pants and a neon pink sports bra walks down the hallway in the opposite direction, past the empty aerobics' classrooms, all prepped with stations of equipment —yoga mats, balance balls, and weights—for the afternoon classes. The girl calls my name like we're familiar. She's cute in a plastic sort of way that reminds me of an Instagram model I banged last Friday. But the way she's simpering at me makes me think we've probably already fucked, so I nod back at her and keep on walking.

Hit it and quit it is a bitch to keep up with.

I look back down at my phone after leaving Ian on read. I smirk as I type out my reply.

ME
K but Everett's mom is still fair game, right?

EVERETT
Fuck u, Blakely.

ME
kiss emoji

EVERETT
Bringing a date or not, Arch?

ME
u knock Mols up, bro? You shotgunning this party.

EVERETT
Keep my fiancée's name out ur mouth.

She's "planning." Says it has to be perfect.

ME
U r so pussy whipped.

IAN
Didn't know u were into CBT, Everett. Good 4 u.

EVERETT
Only when you're the one holding my balls, Beckett.

I laugh as I send the exit door swinging and walk across campus to the stadium. We're technically not supposed to cut through the other buildings, but just because I'm in shape doesn't mean I ain't lazy. Your boy needs to save his energy for his nightly—*and* daily —pursuits.

I reach the stadium and head to the side entrance. It's huge, made of giant steel pillars and sleek concrete work that stretches past the nosebleed section and then even higher still. Banners in the school's colors—forest green and grey—hang outside every entrance. Every fixture, metal entrance door, safety railing, and seat in the place matches the school's colors. On game day, people swarm the place, and you can't find a parking spot for miles.

I punch in the code to the door and use the service hallway to head downstairs to our locker room. I hit the heavy metal door with one hand and send it swinging back toward the concrete wall.

My teammates are in various stages of undress. Some in their tighty-whities. Others in their practice pants and cleats, fishing around for a jersey.

"Blakely!" Mendez shouts, banging on the locker before he shirt-whips my ass.

"The one and only," I say with a grin as some of the guys start a chant, "Bring it home, Blakely! Bring it home!"

I wink at my grumpy defensive lineman, who mutters my name like someone told him he couldn't have cookies for the rest of his life. Miles doesn't spoil my good mood, though. The dude is quiet, reserved, and an absolute beast on the field. Hell, that was a friendly hello for him.

I saddle up to my locker, my name placarded on it in white letters, and yank it open to grab my practice gear. I pull off my shirt and stop changing to add a GIF of a guffawing gorilla to the group chat. Gotta keep the boys on their toes, after all.

ME

E, tell the future Mrs. to put me down for plus 2 because I bring all the ladies to the yard.

EVERETT

U know a wedding date is like a serious thing, right? Like a commitment.

ME

Wut? Nah, bro.

My parents are on their billionth divorce. Weddings happen all the time around here. Like bringing a girl to a birthday party. Nothing 2 it, gents.

EVERETT

Wtf is wrong with u?

IAN

Don't ask questions u don't want the answer 2, Everett.

Also, put him down for 0.

He'll definitely run out of the female population by then.

ME

@ pracky prack. Make that 3 dates, E. *waving emoji*

CHASE

Mfer stop calling practice pracky prack. You sound like a pussy.

EVERETT

HE LIVES! How's being #1 on the Billboard 100 feel?

CHASE

Hate the label. Hate staying clean. Hate all of the bullshit.

Like the fans . . . I guess.

ME

Ah, a true troubled musician. Don't do the hard stuff, my man. Bye bye for now, bro babes!

IAN

Told ya, Blakely, if u call us bro babes 1 more time, I'm gonna fly to California on the nearest flight just to kick ur ass.

CHASE

Book the ticket. Make it stop.

ME

Gotta catch me first.

Smirking, I take one long look at my phone before I grab my practice uniform from inside my locker and drop my phone in its place. Coach will rip off my balls and wear them as his own personal jockstrap if he catches me on my cell one more time. We aren't supposed to have them at practice, and although the water guy has gotten really good at catching my throws—saved my screen more than once—I'd like to keep my family jewels, thank you very much. I might need them later.

Much. Much. *Much.* Later.

Like when I'm eighty and marry a Playboy bunny and decide it's time for an heir.

I put on my gear and chuck my clothes on top of my phone before I head out of the locker room and toward the field, grabbing my helmet off the wall on the way out.

I follow my teammates through the tunnel and out into blissful California sunshine. I miss New York—where I spent my toddler years at the best boarding schools in the country—but damn if the west coast hasn't been blessed by the weather gods.

"Let's go, Tigers!" the cheerleaders shout as I walk further out onto the field. Their coach calls for them to wrap up as a tide of football players arrives.

They never practice when we do. They're rarely even here on our training days. Coach doesn't like us all to be on the field at the same time. He says the cheerleading squad is too distracting.

Pfft. Don't get me wrong, they're pretty and all, but why not let us practice ignoring them? They're going to be present on game day anyway.

"My man," Brentley, my fellow Phi Epsilon Alpha brother, says before he slaps me on the shoulder and brings me in for a hug.

Shit, he's high.

Bro always gets touchy-feely when he's high. Plus, I can smell the reefer on him. Shit, I'm getting a little lightheaded just being near him. Still, though, I nestle into the hug because dude's built like a walking Paddington bear. And everyone wants to cuddle with Paddington.

"How you holding up?" he says as we break away, a look of concern on his glassy-eyed face.

"I'm good, man," I reply, an anvil landing in the pit of my stomach and telling me where this is going.

Whatever. Don't care. I got a hug from Paddington.

"Well," he looks at me—his watery eyes damn near twinkling with his unspent laughter—as his face reddens, then reddens even more, then turns tomato red. "I'm just sorry I won't get to be your new daddy, bro, but your mom let me down easy and told me it was over."

I laugh because it's funny and I'm used to it. The entire team knows my parents' sordid history. Shit, the entire world knows it too. The gossip sites post every time one of my parental figures files for divorce. I think my parents must hold a world record for post-divorce reconciliation because this is like their sixth . . .

No, seventh—*maybe?*—divorce.

My mom said she was over Dad for good this round, and that they were never getting back together.

Bitch, please.

Same shit, different day of the week.

It's like a crappy annual holiday tradition at this point. Santa and stockings and shit-talking between the people who raised me. Mom's currently holed up in an all-inclusive resort in Barbados, where she's been for the past nine months since the most recent round of family law court began.

Last night, she was photographed going out with some local businessman and those photographs made the outlets early this morning, so I should have expected Brentley to fuck with me about it. Heck, I had notifications from the social media tags staring at me when I woke up.

The divorces and the reconciliations, the fact that my parents are gossip fodder as eccentric egomaniacs, none of it bothers me. It doesn't matter because they always get back together, as if the cosmos draws them close like an open flame to dry kindling.

The most recent separation is starting to get to me though

because it has definitely been the longest my parents have gone without reconciling.

I may secretly despise my father and pity my mother, but they are toeing the line with eccentric and crossing into becoming a statistic.

Their last separation was five months. The one before that was seven.

This one's up to nine and speeding toward a year. In fairness, Mom was really *pissed* this time after she walked in on dad getting a blowie from a pair of strippers. Of course, she's ignoring the fact that two rounds ago, I walked in on her riding the pool boy, though my father was seated in a chair in the corner of the room, his face emotionless, like he was reading his morning paper. Honestly, I have no idea what to make of that life moment.

I am going to need therapy to dig that shit out of my brain.

Or a shovel.

And I don't know which one would be more painful.

"Hurry your asses!" Coach calls from the sidelines as some of the stragglers walk out of the tunnel that feeds into the arena and out onto the gridiron.

Dude needs a chill pill and a hug. He's always in a bad mood, looks like he smelled a fart, and never smiles. Even when we won the championship last year, he just sort of glared at the camera without showing any of his teeth. But he's got plays that make the NFL long-timers look like amateurs, and he brings home the big trophies for the university.

So he stays . . . grumpy, grouchy, and incapable of joy.

We've already got this season in the bag, though. It's senior year, and I can do whatever the fuck I want, when I want, to whomever I want, well except fuck Mel, apparently. She put a hiatus on our hook-ups after yesterday's interruption. I don't blame her. She's worked her ass off to become the university's youngest ever tenured professor. But I'm going to have blue balls the size of Montana by the end of the week if she doesn't come around.

Fucking Mel is easy, convenient.

No expectations. No conversations. No we-have-to-talks.

Most importantly, no stilettos through my sunroof.

The sun is right at fuck-me position on the horizon, and it says hello like a football to the face as I walk farther out onto the field. Coach tosses Slaten, our quarterback, the ball. He's got an arm like, well, like Ian, my brother from another mother. The difference? Slaten wants to make it pro, and Ian doesn't give a fuck about that. He just wants to do his own thing, probably with music if I had to guess, though he's been tightlipped about his plans for after graduation. Chase and Ian are the ones all attuned to their feelings and stuff, though I'm not really sure either one of them would admit that.

I called them pretty boy emos one time, and I thought they were going to explode. Like full-on guts-fountain explode.

Molly, Everett's fiancée, and Harlow, Ian's longtime girlfriend, thought it was funny. Thankfully, their presence saved me from immediate castration.

"Offense, line up!" Coach calls, and then he makes my day even better by saying, "Run Blue eighty-nine."

This is a new play that he came up with over what had to be a fever dream during summer break, and it is goddamned genius.

It's a triple fake-out with three passes, ending with me wide open and running point.

I've got a bird's-eye view of a fellow team member's ass when Slaten calls, "Blue eighty-nine! Blue eighty-nine! Hut, hut, hut, hike!"

In the blink of an eye, Danvers hikes the ball back to our QB. Our QB passes it to his left to Smith, one of our wide receivers. Smith passes it to the opposite side of the field, to Pince, another wide receiver. Pince throws long to our halfback who's running up the left-hand side. In turn, our halfback, looks across the field to me, finds me wide open, and throws the ball. My cleats meet the cushion of the field instantly. The fucker overshot a little, probably on purpose. I'm guessing he's still angry after I accidentally railed his girl last season. But, I mean, how was I supposed to know she was *that* Briana?

I push harder, the hot air bursting from my lungs on a quick exhale as I jump and snatch the ball from the air, the pebbled leather hitting my fingers. My feet meet the lawn again, and I run for the end zone.

Coach could tell me to stop. He would if it was anybody else, but he knows how much I like to run.

Ain't nobody keeping Bring It Home, Blakely! on a leash.

Vaster, our tight end, goes down to my left and then Giuliani farther up on the field, though it's more like flag football than a real tackle. As my teammates battle it out, I sprint, breathing in the hint of fog still hanging over the gridiron and the scent of fresh-cut grass. My heart hammers in the hollow of my chest as I push out my breath between my teeth and run toward a touchdown.

Ten yards left.

Five yards.

One.

My toes inch past the finish line, and I hear phantom applause as I raise my hands and roar. Nothing can compete with the high of the game, and nothing can ruin it for me either.

Not coach having an aversion to smiles.

Not the *yo mama* jokes from my teammates.

Not the red firecracker who cockblocked me yesterday.

Football season has arrived, and it's time to bring home another championship title.

4

ARCHIE

I walk out of track, which has got to be the easiest class ever. It's even easier than the music appreciation class I took last semester, and all we did in that one was listen to rock gospel and *feel the rhythm* as the professor called it.

In track, I get an easy A for doing nothing except gaining my daily dose of fresh air and dopamine. All I have to do is run. Well, that's not entirely true. All *I* have to do is show up, and Coach looks at me like I am the North Star guiding his precious lost soul home. But whatever, I run anyway. I don't mind running as long as it's not as hot as Satan's asshole and my balls aren't sticking to my leg like a top-shelf clinger.

I cross the sidewalk, and my stomach grumbles at a decibel only dogs can hear. I could go for a slice, or an entire pie as they call it out east, but I have a mandatory meet-and-greet this evening with my mom's baby daddy. Though he's more sperm donor than parental figure. He for sure didn't ace the father-of-the-year exam.

So . . . no yum yums for this tum tums. Not until I see dear old dad, at least.

My stomach objects loudly, and I sling my backpack around to the front as I walk to the frat house. I unzip the front pocket and find surprise candy—a forgotten stash of Sour Skittles. I nearly tent my basketball shorts as I tear open the bag and toss a generous handful into my mouth.

Thank the fucking candy gods. This is awesome.

I almost moan as the gates open to sour, sugary heaven, and my eyes roll back in my skull.

"Blakely," someone croons nearby. Reluctantly, I open my eyes and follow the sound of the voice to find the captain of the cheer-leading squad preening for me, wishing she could captain my dick. Her tan boobs are spilling out the top of her purple pushup bra, her thin white tank top showing the purple lace underneath. "You going to the party tonight?"

"Maybe," I answer with a toothy grin before I go in for another handful of Skittles. *Fuck, yes, green all the way, baby!* I give her a wink that's sure to make her panties drip . . . if she's even wearing any. She wasn't the night she rode me reverse cowgirl after the last game of the season sophomore year. "Only if you are, beautiful."

She smiles brilliantly, and maybe I shouldn't have given her false hope 'cause there's zero chance she's getting back into my pants.

Though I could put *hit it and quit it* on an annual basis . . .

Damn, Mel's pussy embargo is already getting to me.

"Meet you at nine?" Bianca suggests.

"Let's not put a time on it." I tell her, killing off the rest of my candy.

She pouts and thrusts her boobs out even further, which I didn't know was possible.

"See you tonight, football star," she croons.

"Later," I call.

Damn, I eye the empty bag and toss it into a trashcan as I keep on walking. All out of Skittles, and I'm still hungry. I wish I had a cookie or a chocolate bar or, better yet, some of those jerk chicken nachos from the food truck that parks outside the stadium on game days. Hell, I'd even take a pound of raw broccoli and a quart of ranch dressing right now, and that's saying something.

One of these days, my shitty food habits are going to bite me in the ass, or at least that's what my friends, my teammates, Coach, and the nutritionist Coach sent me to said. But until then, I'm going to enjoy every fat, sugary, calorie-laden tasty treat I can get my hands on. Plus, I do *actually* eat fruit and vegetables and lean protein and drink enough water each week to drown a horse, despite what they might think.

I pop in my AirPods and open my playlist as I continue to my frat house. Outkast starts through the speakers, and I turn it up a notch, dipping my head in time to the beat. I don't even care that it's the first day of senior year or that I have to see the father figure or that I'm still starving. Life is good, and I've got nothing to worry about.

Today was easy. And so will the next day and the day after and every day after that because I signed up for the equivalent of Walking 101 for all of my classes. Well, except for one, but I can't get out of that. Trust me, I tried. It's a goddamn prerequisite to graduate that I put off for the past three years. Like if I waited long enough, the Board of Trustees would change their minds and make it voluntary. I had hoped they would at least, but alas, they failed me in my time of need.

So tomorrow, I gotta spend three hours of my day in the boringscape of Statistics, wanting to gouge my eyes out with a pencil, but—you know—*whatever*.

That's tomorrow Archie's problem, not mine. And I'll tell tomorrow's Archie to be a man, suck it up, and cool his roll. Tomorrow Archie can be a little bitch.

I continue to my house, and I'm like four songs into the album when I finally arrive, swiping my key card across the access pad next to the front door. We had to get keycards last year after somebody's crazy ex-girlfriend broke into the place with a copied key and carved her ire into every mattress on the second floor before she got caught.

The new keycards must be a pain in the ass for guys with girlfriends, I guess, but I couldn't care less about the required card access. I don't let anyone into my dorm room, and I certainly don't invite any girls back here. This is my sacred spot, my space where I can go and relax and just be. If I fuck here, we use the pool house out back or the gaming room in the walk-in attic. No girls in my room. *Ever.*

I head up the wooden stairs to the second floor and continue past the landing and toward the third. My feet barely greet the top floor in the house before my ears confirm that one of my brothers has a screamer. Kaden, a fellow senior, passes me in the hallway and heads down the stairs, smiling to himself as the girl someone is railing lets out an ear-piecing shriek that sounds painful.

At least she came, I guess. Good for her. My blue balls want to join in on the fun. Do balls actually turn blue? If they do, your boy's gonna be looking like a Smurf down south.

I make it halfway down the hall, my stomach screaming for seared meat and fat and glorious sustenance when I pass the door of the screamer that's shacked up with Mitchell. I quicken my steps a little as I do, not because I need to go rub one out after her performance, though I'm going to have to get reacquainted with my hand if Mel keeps this up. No, I speed up because I try not to let the girls who come here know where I live. They might find out during parties if they stumble into the wrong room, but I don't advertise my space. I don't want anyone to get too comfortable, and I can tell you from firsthand experience that it's hella awkward when one of them goes to look for my room after they're done bumping uglies with one of my boys.

The screamer doesn't need to see me walk into my room 'cause I'm not adding fuel to that potential shit fire.

She still must be snuggled up with Mitchell, though, because I slide undetected into my room and close the door behind me with one hand. I toss my backpack and keys on my bed before heading to my closet. I could hop in the shower, but I'm not even remotely sweaty from track. The first day was mostly a bunch of bullshit paperwork and introductions anyway, so I skip the shower. Instead, I pull out a pair of chinos as boring as my father off the top shelf—where all my father-approved clothes go. I put them on, following them up with a pair of brown leather loafers—just as boring as the chinos—and a polo, popping the collar a little as I do. The paternal figure has a dress code, and I abide by his bullshit because, well, he pays for everything and he also holds the not-so-metaphorical key to my future, a cushy job at his company, Axium, Inc., where I will be able to do whatever the fuck I want as long as I keep my nose relatively clean and free of the white stuff.

Everyone I know from my preparatory school days seems hell-bent on getting away from their familial ties and forging their own path. But me, I don't want to forge anything. Instead, I choose a nice paycheck I don't have to work for and an easy life. Is it an asshole move to say that? Yes, but I'm only an asshole because I'm getting what everybody in the world wants. Wealth and power without the work.

I check the time on my phone.

Fuck, I have to go. If there's one thing my father won't tolerate, it's tardiness, especially when I'm the one who's late. I spot my keys on my bed. I could drive the G-Wagon. It would definitely make not-parent-of-the-year happy if I did. Pops acted like he was giving me the moon when he forked over the keys at my birthday in June, but then again, if I get one more ticket, he'll definitely repo my ride.

I'm already dreading going to this family dinner, which is Blakely code for my dad wants to talk about personal shit and needs to do it in public, so I don't go off the tracks and embarrass him. I don't need to take the chance of reaching for my phone and getting another hands-free driving ticket.

For me, the lure is bad enough on a good day, but today, when I'm not really digging eating dinner with the old man? Fuck, I might as well turn myself in. I don't give a flying fuck if the government follows my every tweet and crawls out of my phone screen like the girl from The Ring and eats my face. Satan give me a second helping please.

But . . . No. More. Tickets. Or I can wave bye-bye to my promised cushy life.

I open an Uber request and check myself in the mirror before the driver arrives six minutes later. I bound down the stairs and slide into the silver Prius the guy is sporting.

"You Archie?" the guy asks as I climb inside before the dude does a double take.

"Holy shit, you're Bring it Home, Blakely," he says like I don't already know.

"The one and only," I say, gifting him a smile.

"Man," he says, looking back out the windshield as he pulls away from the house, "this season's gonna be lit."

I doubt the dude knows much about the game. If he did, he'd be spouting off game-loss percentages like it's his second job, but I appreciate the sentiment. Bro may not care about football, but he cares about the team and what we mean to the university. That's enough to turn me sappy.

"You headed downtown?" he asks after a long moment.

Called it. Zip, zilch, and zero about the game.

"Yeah, man," I answer, checking my Insta before I toss him an escape ladder for this conversation. "Dinner with the old man."

He makes a face and eyes me via the rearview mirror.

"Sorry, man," he says. "That sucks. Your dad a prick?"

"He can be," I admit.

We fall into a comfortable silence, and he turns up an audiobook he's listening to, after I decline the radio. If I could hookup my phone and play Spotify, it'd be turned up in here, but commercial breaks? Hard pass. I'm all about instant gratification, and nothing about listening to an ad about a car wash is gratifying.

We take the interstate and make good time despite the heavy traffic headed into the city for the night, though it's not unusual. We live in a college town where the students like to party, even when it hasn't been a full twenty-four hours since the semester started again.

Dude takes a shortcut behind a taco place that promises 2-for-1 margaritas and smells like freshly fried tortilla chips. My stomach pinches again, and I rub a hand over my belly as we pass the tasty taco place and the food trucks that line the road beside it, promising glorious fried goodies and hand-churned milkshakes. We arrive in front of an old people's bar-slash-restaurant my father thinks is hip. The truth is that only out-of-towners and middle-aged men come here. Well, college girls on the prowl for a sugar daddy too. I'd tell the bastard, but I don't think he'd care. Hell, with his history, he's probably on the prowl for young meat.

I tip the driver and rate him five stars as he lets me out in front of the restaurant. He wishes me good luck with the upcoming season, yelling out the passenger-side window as I stride up to the glass double doors. They are invisible except for an alien-looking handle on each one, and I nearly walked straight into them the first time he made me join him here for dinner.

The doorman eyes my attire, frowns, but then decides it's not worth another argument about wearing a dinner jacket. We've had this conversation before. Apparently, it's *preferred* but not *required* for the comfort of their guests.

Like I give one jacket-wearing fuck about the comfort of a bunch of middle-aged farts. Even my father doesn't wear a jacket in this place, which is probably some weird power move I don't understand, but fuck it, if he doesn't, neither will I.

I give the crochety doorman a three-fingered salute as the guy frowns and opens the door for me. I enter the place, walking beneath an avant-garde silver chandelier that resembles a medieval torture device and up to the maître d'. A smile that hides all of her teeth slowly stretches across her lips when she spots me.

She's like a robot covered in human flesh.

Ever polite.

Ever smiling.

Never accepts my offer for drinks.

I'd say my reputation precedes me, but normally that means women invite me for a drink, not vice versa, because word on the street—and the gospel truth—is I never leave a lady unsatisfied.

The maître d' glues her smile on as I approach, and when she speaks, I swear hand-to-Bible I hear her circuits warming up.

"Mr. Blakely," she says like she isn't my age or even younger, perhaps, "your party is waiting for you. Follow me."

Wait? My party?

This chick has said the same line to me every time I've been here for the past two years, or whenever she started working at this joint. *Mr. Blakely, your dinner guest is waiting for you.*

She says it every. Single. Time.

Without fail.

And it never ceases to crack me up because my father has never been called a dinner guest in his life.

Friend, maybe. Family, I guess. Partner, sure. *Devil*, absolutely.

But never a dinner guest. You don't invite my father anywhere. He decides to grace you with his presence and you have exactly zero say in the matter. My father is always the one pointed out in a crowd and thanked for his attendance. He's no one's reserved seating.

I follow the maître d' through the restaurant, passing the stocked bar filled with men old enough to be my father on barstools and women teetering next to them, no older than the one walking in front of me.

Oh, look at that. Sugar babies spotted in the wild.

The restaurant has a clinical feel and a cleanliness my father expects, but the place scratches at my brain every time I visit, like it's trying to dig in and find the civilized Archibald Orson Blakely hiding beneath my popped collar and Chinos.

Yeah, right. Like that's gonna happen.

I may have a pretty face, but there's nothing civilized about me.

We cross the dining hall, passing between the tables of stuck-up businessmen and their wives, who probably only change out of their athleisure for this place. Then we continue deeper into the heart of the restaurant, past the kitchen with chefs bustling behind glass windowpanes and to the reserved seating area at the rear of the dining hall, where my father always sits, like he's too good to be near the commoners seated at the front, like he owns the place, probably because he does. There's the pop and sizzle of grease in the air, and *mhmm*, I could go for a steak. Images of seared sirloin, medium rare, pop into my brain as I fantasize about stealing a plate from a passing table and running away.

My father is sitting at his semi-secluded table at the back of the room. A white linen cloth covers the round table in front of him, and a glass of honey-colored liquid, probably bourbon, sits nestled between his fingers. He's wearing his suit sans jacket, like he always does in this restaurant, but my feet falter when I see he's seated across from someone.

My father doesn't even bring my mother here, not pre- or -post any of their divorces. This is his spot, his place to grill me about my grades and make sure I am on the Eli-approved track for success. He doesn't bring people here. Ever.

A cannonball takes shape in my belly and hits the floor, weighing down my feet. I can't quite make out who his guest is because their top half is hidden by a dividing wall of polished gray stone that separates the table from the rest of the room. My gaze locks on the lower half of a bare leg peeking around the wall and the owner's shiny candle-apple red stiletto.

My heart lurches up into my throat. He brought a woman. A woman who's wearing fuck-me shoes. And it's definitely not my mother. My mother hates red. I've never seen her wear the color, not once in my entire twenty-two years of existence. So who the hell is this chick? And why is she so important that she is here at *our* family dinner?

I move around the maître d' and up to the table.

"Father," I say, greeting him first, even though it feels like it's going to kill me, but he would settle for nothing less.

"Son," my father says in reply.

"Your table," the maître d' announces before she realizes no one is paying attention to her and scurries away back toward the front.

I look down at the owner of the fuck-me stilettos and porcelain leg.

Her gaze barrels through me like a runaway train, and I feel the impact rattle my bones.

Red.

She smiles at me, pretty, *polite*, and pretending like she didn't bust in on me tongue-fucking a professor last week, only to tell me to *stay out of her way.*

What is this firecracker planning?

I frown. I just know my day's about to combust so hard that the argyle carpet is going to smolder beneath my feet.

My father releases his crystal glass and reaches across the expanse of the tablecloth to grab the cockblocker's hand.

I feel dizzy.

I'm going to be sick.

I can hear my dreams of an easy life circling the drain as my eyes zero in on the massive rock sitting atop *that* finger.

What. The. Fuck!

"Archie," my father says, smiling across the table at Red, "thank you for joining us tonight. Let me introduce you to my fiancée, Layne Steele."

I barely even register his words because I'm busy gawking at Red.

Two questions smash through my thick skull at once.

First, why is my father engaged to someone who's not my mother? That's not how this story is supposed to go.

And second, why is his fiancée staring back at me with a cunning smile on her lips like she's not at all surprised to see me?

It's my turn to think the words she threw at me the first time we met.

Fuckety fuck fuck fuck.

5

LAYNE

*A*s the Blakely heir looks down at me from his position lording over the table, I can't help but think how nice it is that everything worked out this way. Because this is so much more enjoyable than just knifing his beloved daddy in a parking lot. This is pure, lovely ruin, and I can taste the singe of his ire reigning down on top of me and hear the far-off rumble of a dynasty's downfall.

Not that I want the younger Blakely to pay.

Not that I don't.

I am . . . ambivalent about him.

But the way my fiancé is about to crack a molar glaring at his dumbfounded son, both milliseconds away from losing it, it's just . . . perfection.

Their family will suffer, just like mine did, just like *I* did for the past twenty-one goddamn years, and I have a front-row ticket to the show.

It's perfect.

Still, I steel my expression. They can't know I'm enjoying this, though the younger one, with his nostrils flaring like a dragon about to shoot fire, definitely suspects it. I guess that's to be expected, though. I did intentionally insert myself into a *very* private moment between him and the university's professor of the year just to black-mail him.

Well, and because I enjoyed it, getting one over on the campus king.

But mostly, I did it because I can't devote my attention to cutting his father's empire into tiny little bits if I have a 6'4" blond Greek god breathing down my neck every chance he gets. I know, though, what I'm holding over Golden Boy's head isn't enough to stop him, not forever at least. Maybe it'll slow him down just a little, and that's all I need. Well, *that* and a little bit of luck, so I can broil the Blakelys and smile as they crumble to ash.

"What the fuck?" the college football star spews, his lips retracting over his perfect, pretty boy teeth. The three tables closest to us all turn and look.

Holy fuck, this is glorious! Somewhere, the revenge angels are looking down and singing hallelujah.

I blink up at him, doe-eyed and feigning hurt, and turn toward my fiancé, gripping his cold, dead hand tighter across the table. I pout, my painted bottom lip trembling as I do. I couldn't be bothered to care what this entitled princess thinks of me, even if my life depended on it, but I sure will put on a good show for my soon-to-be husband.

Survive the wedding.

Destroy the man.

And if I can't have it all, then blow the entire thing to smithereens . . . literally.

Focus, Layne!

"Archibald! You will not talk to my fiancée that way," Eli snarls and stands, and I can see the resemblance as they stare daggers inches away from each other.

Both tall. Lean. Built.

Both with piercing blue eyes that look like the universe created winter-freaking-wonderland in their skulls.

While Eli's gaze is . . . colder, more calculated, and downright malevolent at times, his son . . . well, Golden Boy looks like he'd toy with the idea of committing murder but pussy out. It's a shame too because he sure would look sexy as sin covered in someone else's blood.

Eli and me, though, we're cleaved from the same cutthroat cloth. I am the way I am because he destroyed my life. Who knows what fucked-up monster made him into a walking anathema, though? Or maybe he arrived in the world this way, a psychopath with no real feelings.

He's svelte and charming when it suits him, like the night he found me at the club, yet cunning and ruthless when he's pissed off. He doesn't frighten me, though I'd never let him in on that secret. I spent my childhood listening to my mother's ramblings about the man I now call my fiancé, and every time I got my greasy little hands on a phone or a spare computer, I'd search his name, reading everything I could find on him, devouring the tiniest morsels of information.

Learning.

Absorbing.

Metamorphosing.

I'm a butterfly, designed and tailored specifically for Eli Blakely's *very* particular tastes. I wear contacts because the CEO doesn't like his women in glasses—a snippet I gleaned from an interview the former Mrs. Blakely gave to *Cosmopolitan* back in 2017. I endured a Brazilian because three years ago, Eli was recorded guffawing with a fellow billionaire about a lady's hairy nether regions at the country club pool. I kept my V-card while all my friends were out fucking every chance that they got because I read the stories online, the rumors that he collects popped cherries like his son collects one-night stands.

I don't have tattoos—though I'd kill for one—because I knew from a 2019 interview with *Corporate America Weekly* that he wouldn't approve. I even changed my identity, dropping my given name— Layla, not that I ever liked or used it—and choosing the surname of Steele, a common enough last name in North America. I had the records sealed too, all so he'd never find out about the target locked straight between his eyes. Luckily for him, he likes redheads and big boobs, so I didn't have to dye my hair or go on a diet cleanse. I like my hair and I like carbs, and I'd straight up commit murder if I had to give up either one.

At first, my goal was to get close enough to draw blood. I never imagined that he'd let me in instead. And this is *so much better* than I could have ever dreamed.

I watch as the table shakes and the silverware and glasses clatter as the younger Blakely flops into a seat, pouting. I nearly giggle before I can stop myself and cover it with a cough that they both ignore. Serendipity must be friends with karma because it looks like she also hates Eli Blakely's rotten, black guts.

Eli returns to his seat only after his son sits, slithering back into the cloth-covered chair as a waiter watches us from across the room, standing to the side of the swinging doors that lead into the kitchen. His glass-rimmed gaze goes wide before he listens to his survival instinct and decides to give us another minute.

"Does Mom know?" Archie asks his father before plucking a silver knife from the tablecloth and putting it on end, digging the blade into the table.

"Of course," Eli replies, side-eyeing him before he reaches for his bourbon and takes a sip. He offers me his hand again, which I accept, though I hate touching the bastard. He may be pretty to look at, even for someone over twice my age, but damn, if I can't feel the frigid bite of evil on him. It seeps out of his pores and slithers across his tan hands, leaving them cool and clammy, like he's absorbed the ghosts of all the lives he's fucked up.

I squeeze his hand, and his son's gaze lands on the massive engagement ring.

Three carats.

Platinum band.

Worth an upper middle-class home, maybe more.

I plan to pawn it the moment this charade is over, but for now, it sure looks pretty on my finger.

"Isn't she a little young?" Golden Boy asks, but he's not looking at his father as he says the words.

He's got those big baby blues pinned on me, and I am glued to my seat, his stare sending fire dancing across my skin. Blond stubble shadows the lower half of his face below cheekbones carved from granite, and he's close enough now that I catch a whiff of his scent, aged vanilla and something entirely hedonistic, char and smoke like the burning embers of a dying fire. I am hot all over, but I stare right back at the king of Arlean University, refusing to break first.

Finally, he looks away, his gaze cutting to Eli, who sips his bourbon and scowls down into the glass.

"And aren't you a little old for another walk down the aisle?"

"Watch your mouth, boy," Eli warns, his tone cold as death.

"Are you fucking kidding me?" Eli's son whines, and *ah, there's the spoiled princess I am learning to hate.* "She's obviously a gold digger after the money, the company, the . . ."

"Quiet!" Eli bellows, and this time, the entire restaurant goes silent *and* still, the world suspended beneath his rage. It's like even the air itself is afraid of moving and drawing his wrath.

"I don't give a shit if you approve, son," Eli snarls. "You will not insult Layne or me by saying another goddamn word."

Golden Boy chews on the inside of his cheek, hard enough to draw blood by the looks of it. Pain shuts him up. Point noted.

"At least tell me you're getting a prenup," he says, the words barreling past his pretty-boy pout as his cheeks color crimson. "Keep her! I don't give a shit." *Oh yay. I'm a possession.* "But don't marry her. You didn't marry what's her face . . . Angelina . . . Ashley . . . whatever her name was." For the record, he's talking about *Angelica*, Eli's ex-mistress who graced the front pages of the tabloids for weeks on the heels of Eli's fourth filing for divorce. "You didn't marry the one before her, either—or any of the others."

Eli's phone buzzes on the table, and he looks over at it, his frown deepening as he does. Whomever it is just saved his son from getting his ass kicked.

"I have to take this," he says, standing with a sneer. He pins his son with a glare. "Behave." He heads for the direction of the cigar room at the back as the waiter finally arrives.

"Tonight, we have . . ." the man begins, his Adam's apple and man-bun bobbing in time with every word, before Golden Boy interrupts him.

"I want a whiskey, neat. You know what? Why don't I save you the trouble? Just bring me the bottle." He gestures to me with three fingers. "She'll take anything old, decrepit, and expensive."

The waiter looks at me, wide-eyed, and backs away from the table. I can't blame him. He definitely doesn't get paid enough to deal with Blakely's temper tantrum.

I hold up two fingers to the guy to signal I want a drink too. Dutifully, less than two minutes later, Golden Boy and I are sitting in silence, sipping—well, in his case, gulping—our drinks.

"Shouldn't you be drinking something," he scoffs at me, "girlier?"

"Shouldn't you be nice to the future wife of the guy who pays for all of your," I take a long, meaningful look at his choir-boy attire, "shit?"

"Please. This polo is Armani, and you'd know that if you belonged anywhere in our world." He shakes his head and scoffs before he downs the rest of his glass and pours another. "My father know you have such a dirty mouth?"

"Your father know you're fucking your way to graduation?"

Ice crystallizes in his gaze. "If you tell him, I will ruin you."

"Why?" I blink at him. "Worried how he'll react? That he'll cut you out of the will? That he won't let you inherit the family business?" I stick out my bottom lip and give him puppy dog eyes. "Are you one fuck-up away from being taken off your daddy's tit?"

His glare tells me that's exactly what he's afraid of. It's not a surprise, though. Eli lives up to his moniker, the mercurial man, a title given to him by the Wall Street advisors decades ago, thanks to his proclivity for changing moods and violent outbursts.

Eli's son snickers as he leans across the table, planting his palms against the table and directing his hot breath, smelling of whiskey and mint, into my face. "I don't know what your game is, Red, but I've been doing this a long fucking time, and you aren't about to hitch and ditch with my fucking inheritance. *I* earned that right, not you, and I paid for it with blood, sweat, and tears every day for the past twenty-two years."

"First of all," I lift one finger, "don't call me Red. Second of all, who says I want his money and not his big dick? And third, like I said before, Golden Boy, stay out of my way and I'll stay out of yours. Got it?"

He sneers at me. "Aww, Red. You're not his pre-wife. You're his midlife crisis." He looks me up and down, his gaze lingering on the swell of my breasts where they push against the svelte fabric of the silk bandage dress clinging to my curves. "He should have just bought a Harley and been done with it. It would have been less pathetic than marrying someone young enough to be my . . . my *sister*."

I cock my head at his never-ending tantrum. "Why would he do that when I can ride him instead?"

Golden Boy looks like he's half a second from detonating the moment before the curtain falls, and the only remaining hint of his anger is the pink flush blossoming across the bridge of his nose.

He leans in farther, sending another whisper of vanilla and burning embers across my skin.

"Is that what you want, Red?" he says, his words a caress.

"I said don't call me that."

"You want to ride his dick? Let those juicy tits of yours bounce while you fuck him hard? Want him to flip you over and fill your pussy so good you blackout when you come?"

I clench my thighs together beneath the table as my breath plasters against the back of my throat. My mother's voice slithers out of the back of my brain.

You like him, don't you? You dirty, cock-sucking whore.

He leans even more, swallowing the distance between us and close enough he could kiss me if he wanted to—if *I* let him.

Slut.

He smells like sin delivered in a devastating blond package.

Slut!

"Let me give you a piece of advice, Red," he murmurs, his arctic eyes holding me captive. "If you wanted that, you chose the wrong Blakely."

SLUT!!!

I finally let out the breath I've been holding, my heart thumping furiously against my ribs, and he falls back into his seat, a knowing smile perched on his delicious lips.

Moments later, Eli arrives back at the table, texting furiously on his phone.

"Everything good?" he asks, casting us each a quick glance before he takes his seat.

"Just peachy, Pops," Archie mutters with an eyeroll.

I open my arms and welcome the cold of the nothingness, pushing everything I threaten to feel away.

"Of course, babe," I say, reaching over the table to grab his hand and squeeze it tight. His son scoffs, looking between us like he's seconds away from upchucking his guts.

But *Bring It Home, Blakely!* isn't the only one who knows how to fight dirty at this table.

I'm just getting started.

Keep your gloves on, Golden Boy, and watch the grownups have some real fun.

6

ARCHIE

I shuffle across the quad, exhausted. I slept *maybe* a total of twenty minutes last night, dreams—*plans*—of murdering a certain ginger goddess playing in my head. My parents were supposed to get married for the thousandth fucking time again, and I was supposed to be set for the easy life. The old man wasn't supposed to get engaged to some chick who doesn't even use social —I looked—and put the entire family fortune on the line just so he can get his dick wet.

Did he learn nothing from the ones before her? A quarter of a million dollars there. A hundred thousand here. Hush money squirreled down the drain to hide my father's kinks, the ones the public relations companies never quite managed to erase from the Internet. Shit, I heard the rumors in elementary school before I even knew the meanings of the words.

Busty.

Red-headed.

Young.

Virgins.

Like those even exist anymore. Finding a cherry to pop is like winning the sex lottery these days. I don't even know why the freak has such a hard-on for it anyway. I don't do virgins. Virgins come with expectations, and I don't want our one time together to be taking her V-card and breaking her heart.

Why would he even put a ring on it anyway? It's not like girls like Red wear a promise ring. The girl has a mouth like a drill sergeant and an attitude to match. No way she's still untouched.

You wish you could touch her.

Fuck.

Surely, the dumbass will get a prenup. I keep telling myself he'll definitely get a prenup, but apparently, he's going senile in his old age, so I don't know what he'll do anymore.

Marry some girl he could have fathered? Apparently.

Risk everything he's built for a rando? Definitely.

Cut his only heir out of the will and give it all to a crazy red-headed bitch that is only marrying him so she can hoard his wealth like a motherfucking dragon? Probably.

Aw, hell to the no.

I can spot the warning signs flashing from miles away. Red's going to get knocked up. Probably before the wedding if she can trick him. Then, even if he does get a prenup, she'll lock him into child support and alimony, and when he finally dives six feet under, she'll inherit it all.

The money.

The company.

Every-damn-thing.

Fuck!

All my plans—the shit I have put up with from the rotten bastard for the past twenty-two years for nothing. My reparations stolen by the aqua-eyed she-devil.

She puts everything at risk.

No cushy job.

No easy life.

No inheritance.

FUCK!

I snatch an ibuprofen that may not be an ibuprofen from the bottom of my backpack as I head to class. Some girl in my Global

Economics class last semester gave it to me one morning after a particularly hard night before. She'd stood in front of my desk and blinked at me—her eyes enormous behind thick, bottle-eyed glasses —and smiled, showing zero teeth. Back then, I was like ninety percent sure she was going to roofie me, and I did *not* want to add that shit to my already raging hangover, so I pretended to swallow it dry before I tossed it in my bag.

Win for me, I guess.

I didn't get taken advantage of by the weird girl who spent every class alternating between staring at me and chewing on her hair, only stopping to click her nails together in a nonexistent rhythm that drove me nuts.

Tick. Tick. Tttttiiccckkk.

The nightmare down memory lane gives me a shudder as I pop the probably-not-ibuprofen into my mouth and keep on walking, not giving a fuck.

I can see the headline now.

Archibald Orson Blakely, III, son of wildly successful entrepreneur Eli Blakely, dead at twenty-two. A stark reminder to never take a pill from the weird girl.

I keep walking, headed to my first class, ignoring when someone calls my name. I don't even look in their direction. I just keep going, following the sidewalk and pretending I don't hear them.

If I have to play nice today, I'm going to bite a bitch. And *not* in the fun way.

Because in a never-happened-before turn of events, I have zero desire to get kinky with anyone right now, unless it involves Red and tying her up and making her beg for mercy while I mark every inch of her freckled skin with my cum before sending my father the video.

My dick stirs to life at the thought. I know the way she looked at me across the table last night—like she wanted me to finger her with the butter knife before fucking her on top of the table in front of the entire restaurant. Red wants me, whether she likes it or not, and it brings the hope of a smile to my lips as I trod up the concrete steps of the building and head to my Statistics class. It's the perfect way to continue my already shitty morning—attending the class I've been dreading since freshman year, an all-time favorite contender for the most boring class ever.

My phone buzzes in my pocket, and I pull it out and look to see my mom returning my call. Five minutes isn't long enough for everything I need to tell her, so I decline the call and shoot her a quick text, telling her that I'll call her after class. I follow a group of students down the hall and into the seminar room. It's big and round-ish and full of a bunch of people who all look about as thrilled as I am to be here.

Already hating every second I am in this class, something red catches my eye, and—like a spotlight shined onto a stage—I find her on the other side of the room, headed to look for a seat. It would be hard not to spot her with her hellfire hair.

The world pauses the moment before I zero in on her, everything and everyone else fading away. I can't help myself. It's like I don't have control of my limbs. I barrel straight for Red, pulling her out of line with an *oomph* and toward the exit door on the opposite side of the room. I have no idea where it goes, and I don't care, but I'm not about to have this—whatever the fuck *this* is—in front of a classroom of students.

That's how people get convicted of murder.

"You," I seethe as we both stumble through the exit door and into an empty hallway on the opposite side.

Red yanks her arm out of my grasp and glares at me, the seas in her eyes churning.

"Don't you ever fucking touch me," she snarls, taking a step toward me, like I should be the one who's afraid.

Ha! Of her? Of this pipsqueak? No thanks. I still have my big manly balls, thank you very much.

"You're going to stop whatever game you're playing," I hiss, stepping toward her, crowding her, but she doesn't back down, even when the tips of her suede boots kiss the toes of my kicks. "I don't give a shit what you tell my father, but call it off, Red, or it won't end well for you."

"Fuck you," she bares her pretty white teeth at me, drawing my attention down to her blood-red painted lips—a fitting color for a cold, dead vampire.

"Does your resting bitch face affect your hearing?" I snap. "Let me make it real clear for you, Red. You don't get to fuck up my life."

"I don't give a shit about your life," she claps back, her cheeks flushing with her hate as the air sparks between us, a thousand living wires needling and licking at my skin.

We stand there, her fists curled at her sides and my fingernails biting into my palms.

Neither of us moves.

Neither of us blinks.

No one backs down.

Her nostrils flare, more proof she's a dragon, the second before her scent slaps me in the dick.

Chocolate and cinnamon.

Sweet and fiery.

And I want to lick her skin to know if it tastes as good as she smells.

Something changes between us. I feel it more than I see it. It's in the way her chest heaves beneath that tiny white crop-top she's wearing and how her lips fall open on an exhale.

"No games," I tell her.

She blinks up at me, her painted lips curling at the corners.

"No games, Blakely," she murmurs back, "just my undying love for your father."

The way she says it—her conniving smile, the spark that brightens her eyes, the lilt in her voice like she's an angel and not the devil—it's too much. I am going to splinter apart, torn to shreds with my guts pooling on the hallway floor.

That or I'm going to kill her.

I catch her elbow and haul her against me, erasing the distance between us. She lets out another *oomph* as we collide, expelled from her nostrils because her mouth is firmly shut.

I can now attest that the devil radiates heat. Soft, laving heat from her breasts flattened against my chest, her knees pressing against mine, and her belly sealed to my dick.

"Let go of me," she hisses, the words cutting across her teeth before they land like knives across my face. "I told you, Golden Boy, don't you ever touch me."

"Make me," I snarl back, my lips hovering over hers as she goes ramrod straight in my arms.

"Let go of me or I will make sure your daddy and everyone else on this campus knows you fuck for your grades."

I steel my expression. "Why should I care? You're a nobody. Everyone loves me."

She lifts one shoulder. "Sure, maybe the school will side with you, and fire your fuck buddy, but do you think Eli will forgive you? We both know he has quite the temper."

Her words land like his belt used to—fast, hard, and scornful— and I wonder if he hits her before I suffocate the thought.

Fuck if I care about her.

Red leans in, and I don't see her say the words as much as I feel the heat of them warm my skin. They carry with the smell of chocolate and cinnamon again, her scent.

"You think the board will let you have a seat if your entire college career is put into question?" she hisses. "Every time they see you, Blakely, the other board members will wonder if you had to fuck your way to graduation. They'll talk behind your back. They'll plot against you and use your fuckup any chance they get. They'll say shit that isn't true just to get in your head. Then they'll break you, your father's weakest link, and take him down with you. Eli knows it too. He won't risk his company to save your ass."

The words sting with truth, and I hate that they do. This little brat already has me figured out.

Goddammit!!!

"Fuck with my family," I tell her, "and I will fuck with yours."

"I don't have a family, Blakely. And I'll save you the trouble. There's not a damn thing in this entire world I care about. You will never find anything on me. So, just stay out of my way, and I'll stay out of yours, m'kay?"

My lips curl with my sneer. "I don't believe a word out of your pretty mouth, Red. And if you want me to stay out of your way, fine. End things with my father, and we never have to see each other again."

She presses a kiss to the side of my mouth and breaks away from me abruptly, a snide laugh following her.

"Why would I do that, Blakely? We're just getting started."

My mouth tingles at the almost touch of our lips, but I don't give her the satisfaction of letting her know that. I'm not about to continue this infuriating fight either, especially when the smirk on her face tells me that she's enjoying it.

I can't physically force the red-headed wrecking ball to deny my father and end the engagement.

And I don't have anything to hold over her, not yet anyway.

Time to switch tactics and open up a can of Blakely charm.

7

LAYNE

I'm three seconds from putting the pretty princess of the football team in his place when suddenly, his anger just . . . evaporates . . . into thin air, out of existence, like God snapped his fingers and made it cease to be.

What the hell?

Not this again, just like at the restaurant last night. Only the hint of a pink flush lingering on his cheeks betrays his recent mood swings, and all appears forgotten, which is . . . well, weird—really fucking weird—and I don't like it one bit.

Does Golden Boy have short-term memory loss? Like *really* short, short-term memory loss.

Is this the eye of his own personal hurricane?

What the hell is going on?

I blink at him, waiting for an explanation, but he doesn't even look at me. He just cocks his head and looks around me. Straight at my ass.

Come on! Dickalicious isn't even paying attention anymore.

"What are you doing?" I demand, snapping my fingers in front of his perfectly chiseled face.

God, it must be nice to be born filthy rich and pretty.

The campus king's gaze slides lazily back to me, and he gives me a lopsided grin that shows his pearly whites. I ignore the flop of my slut-tastic heart.

"Sorry," he says, "I was looking for the stick up your ass, but this must be your naturally sunny disposition."

I laugh, despite the fact that not even ten seconds ago, I wanted to kick him in the balls, watch him fall to his knees, and rid him of his family jewels.

His grin stretches even wider when I laugh, and he's looking downright proud as the moment falls, screaming and dying to the hollow air between us in the throes of its last breath.

"Whatever this is, won't work on me, Golden Boy," I tell him.

He raises a lonely eyebrow. "What's not going to work, Red?"

"Don't call me that," I warn.

"Don't call me Golden Boy," he quips.

Touché.

"Fine," I acquiesce.

He raises that eyebrow again. "You going to stop?"

"No," I admit.

"Good, me either."

I frown at him and run a hand in the air beside him, trailing the length of his tall frame. "This really isn't going to work on me. I'm not one of your cheerleaders, Blakely."

"No," he tips his chin and looks down his nose at me as he steps forward. Everything in me wants to step back, but I'll be damned if I do that. "You're much more interesting than any of them."

I swallow my laugh this time as the clock on the wall above our heads nears the hour mark with another *tick*.

"I have to get to class," I tell him.

"Save me a seat?"

"Fuck no."

He nods, a grin splitting across his face until he's downright beaming at me like a crazy person in the hallway, and it's making me . . . uncomfortable. He was already supposed to be down for the count, but instead, he's acting like we are suddenly best buds about to hold hands while we walk into class together.

"You know," he inches forward, and I swear on everything holy, it's like he glides across the tile because I don't see his feet move at all, "we could always skip class and go back to my place."

I scrunch my nose at him. "That's the best you got, Golden Boy?"

His jaw ticks at the name. "I don't invite people over to my room, Red. *Ever*. It's a once-in-a-lifetime invitation."

I snort. "Yeah, right. I totally believe that."

This prick must think I'm a moron to fall for the *you're special!* trick.

"It's the truth," he says, grabbing hold of my forearm as I try to scoot by him and to the door.

"Then do us both a favor," I tell him, eyeing his arm on me, "and keep it that way."

He releases me, something that looks like hurt flashing across his unreal blue eyes. I feel a twinge of guilt that he has been dragged into this war I've waged with his father, but I tell myself if he had just stayed in his lane, then he wouldn't have been. He doesn't have to be a casualty. He is choosing to be.

I slide past him and swing open the door to the classroom. I climb the stairs to halfway to top and find a seat up in the middle. He follows a moment later and takes a lone seat in the nosebleed section off to my right. From the furtive glances of the girls beside him, his arrival makes them very happy.

I grab my notebook out of my backpack and start to take notes as the professor begins, but I'm barely paying attention. All my thoughts are on tonight and how I better not fuck it up, not before I've had a chance to inflict real, lasting damage on the man who ruined everything.

FOUR CLASSES LATER AND WITH MY FIANCÉ'S TALL AF SPAWN IN two of them, I am finally done for the day. I've got an unreal amount of homework that makes me want to hide under my desk and a burgeoning headache, but I don't give myself the luxury of stopping for a minute. I don't give myself many luxuries at all. Maybe when this is all over and justice has been served, I'll take a moment to just sit and breathe, but until then, I have to be on top of my game at all times.

I take the bus to my apartment off-campus, the one space that is mine. It annoys the ever-loving fuck out of Eli that I am slumming it in a mid-town condo, but I wouldn't let it go, not even when he proposed our arrangement a couple of weeks ago, surprising us both. Unfortunately, the rich people clothes he buys me take up nearly all my closet space and a corner of my very small living room, but that can't be helped.

I couldn't stomach the idea of having him any closer to me than absolutely necessary, and I'm certain if we lived together, I'd shank him in his sleep within a week, which, although satisfying, wouldn't be good.

Not for my otherwise spotless criminal record, but especially not for all that glorious blood money Eli tosses around like its pocket change.

I drop my stuff on the bar in my kitchen and head to the shower, basket-balling my clothes in the hamper as I do. It feels like I need to wash this entire fucked-up day away, but no amount of scrubbing is ever going to make me feel clean again. I lost that luxury years ago.

Don't go there, Layne.

After I've toasted myself for at least half an hour and probably driven my landlord's water bill up an entire decimal point, I finally exit the warm cocoon, grabbing a thick terry towel off the hook on the wall and wrapping it around myself. I prop open the door to my bedroom in hopes of defogging my bathroom mirror and get to work.

I dry and style my hair down, just like Eli likes it. I put on makeup—bold lips and black eyeliner, like he prefers—and zip on a lace dress that hugs each of my curves before I slide on a pair of matching pumps, courtesy of my fiancé. My stomach somersaults inside my belly, and with each passing second, the feeling grows. I like the chaos—I am at home in it—but not the calm, not the waiting period with a thousand *what ifs* and worries.

I sit down on my bed and text Eli to send the car. As usual, he doesn't reply to me, but the driver calls me ten minutes later when he pulls up outside my apartment. I climb into the shiny Cadillac, and he gives me a smile in the rearview mirror before he drives me downtown to one of the fancy restaurants in Eli's rotary dial of expensive places to take women.

I hate this one, with its nuevo American cuisine that tries too hard and always leaves me hungry no matter how much I order. Not that I ever have much of an appetite here anyway. This is the place Eli took me on our first date, and every time I'm here, I'm reminded of the first time he kissed me, the sharp bite of an evening of smoked cigars lingering on his breath.

Yet, here I am, dressed up like a Barbie doll, wearing the engagement ring he paid for and the outfit he chose, my makeup bolder than I'd prefer but my poise demure, just as he likes. The maître d' spots me before I even enter the building and calls my name as I open a heavy glass door and walk inside.

"Follow me, Ms. Steele," he says, and I oblige, my heart racing and my mind whirling, adrenaline surging through my veins as I lock eyes with the psychopath I'm engaged to.

Eli looks up from his position at the table, his brow furrowed beneath his head of graying hair, and when I arrive, he doesn't stand. The maître d' leaves without a word.

Great, I can tell he's already in a bad mood, and I hate it when he's in a bad mood because the urge to stab him through the heart with the nearest utensil is almost unbearable. I sit down in a chair, and Eli looks me over, his gaze lingering on my breasts.

"You look lovely, Layne," he remarks, the words devoid of human emotion, just like him.

"Thank you."

"I took the liberty of ordering for you," he tells me, his blue-eyed gaze impassive. "I hope you don't mind."

"Of course not," I say, though he always orders the steak tartar here, which he knows—or at least suspects—I don't like, given I always eat very little of it. I'm starting to think he might be trying to starve me to death before the big day.

"How were your classes?" he asks, sipping his wine.

"Fine," I say as the waiter arrives and fills my glass. "How was your day?"

"Slow," he shrugs, the move calculated, practiced even. "Frustrating. I wish you'd come see me some time."

His hand slides atop my knee beneath the table and grips my leg tight, rubbing hot circles over the fabric of my dress.

"One day," I tell him.

"As you keep saying," he grumbles, removing his hand as he acts like the blue balls I've been giving him for the past five months are too much to bear.

"You should quit," he tells me. "Come work for me. I'll pay you better, and you won't need a degree for what I have planned for you."

Ew! I grab my glass and take a long sip, trying to wash down the rising tide of vomit climbing up my throat.

"What?" I say. Not this again. I cut my eyes at him. "No."

Not my classes and not my job. Classes are my release, and my job is how I get my run-the-fuck-away money if this all goes sideways.

"You should," he says like the matter is decided. "There will be no need for either once we are married. Hell," he chuckles, "there's no need now."

"Eli," I purr through a smile, though I want to stab the fucktard in his eye with my salad fork, "you promised me I'd get to enjoy myself."

"Yes, and don't I know it," he says bitterly as the waiter delivers our food. I take a long, disgusted look at the lump of raw meat he's ordered for me, and I stab some of the garnish off the side with my fork and chew on it like I'm a rabbit.

"I've made you an appointment," he says. "Next Wednesday at 9:00 a.m."

"An appointment?" I ask, reaching for my wine again because if I'm not going to get to eat, I might as well drink. "For what?"

He cuts into his cooked steak, rare and bloody, and takes a dripping bite.

"To check your hymen."

I nearly spit my wine across the goddamn table.

"My what?!" I wheeze.

That slimy piece of shit!

"We have a deal, darling, but if you'd rather, I can check it myself tonight or," he leans across the table, a challenge solidifying in his cold gaze, "if you prefer, I could always do it right now. Spread those sexy legs of yours wide open on the table and fuck that tight little cunt of yours like a real man."

I'm going to vomit. Bile clambers up my throat, and it's carrying the taste of rancid wine with it. I swallow it back down. Eli settles back into his chair and starts stabbing his steak again.

"If I'm buying it, baby," he tells me without looking up, "then I want to know what it's worth."

The deal.

The one he proposed four weeks ago after months of trying—and failing—at getting into my pants.

I'd accepted instantly.

I could scarcely believe it when the words left his mouth. His hand in marriage just to fuck me. Everything I had wanted, the entire Blakely legacy, now within reach all because of my fiancé's fetishes.

"The lawyers have drafted the prenup." He stabs an asparagus spear and lifts it to his lips to bite the head off of it. "I'll have them send it over."

I look at him indignantly, not because I actually am indignant. I just want him to believe that like any good gold digger, all I want is his money.

I want more than that, though. So. Much. More.

"I'm not signing that, Eli," I tell him.

He frowns across the table at me.

"Do not test my patience, Layne," he warns. "I may want your cunt, but I'll take it if you insist on continuing to test me."

I choke on air at the ease with which he threatens rape but

swallow my shock quickly. Instead, I acquiesce and eat another bite of garnish because having a prenup isn't a deal breaker.

It never was and never will be.

That little piece of paper won't mean shit when I kill the bastard on our honeymoon night.

PART II

MIDDAY

— **Gil (Years Prior)** —

I rifle through my desk drawer, pushing aside pens and paper clips until I'm rewarded with an open bottle of acetaminophen. I try to check the expiration date, but the label has peeled off the plastic. It doesn't matter anyway. I'll take what I can get, anything to ward off the impending migraine needling its way up my shoulders and sinking into my neck. Not that it will stop it, but it might at least slow down the approach.

I screw the lid off the bottle and shake three small orange pills into my palm. I return the cap, drop the bottle back into the messy drawer, and snatch a pack of Alka-Seltzer tablets in its place, closing the drawer when I'm done. I always thought antacids were for old crochety men who ate too much steak and drank too much hard liquor, well, until three months ago, that is, when my stomach started trying to peck its way out of my gut. I thought I was too young for an ulcer, too healthy, but apparently not.

I drop the tablets into a glass of water next to my empty coffee mug and watch as they sink to the bottom and begin to fizz, sizzling and popping thousands of tiny white bottles inside the glass.

We shouldn't have invested all our liquidity in that electric battery product out of China. I shouldn't have allowed Eli to talk me into it, but the man could sell ice to an Eskimo. When he arrived in my office at the beginning of the year, yapping about a deal that would pave our way in gold, he made it sound like our salvation, our winning lottery ticket. But three months later, the manufacturer experienced quality control problems at its Shanghai facility, temporarily pausing production. By the time they were up and running again, we were a quarter of a million in the hole. Then the new export restrictions from Chile on lithium freight halted production again. Now our business is going the way of their product: dusty, useless, and all but forgotten beneath an avalanche of fresh competition with new money and deep pockets.

I swipe the bubbling glass of water from my desk and chug it in one go, letting the fizzy concoction settle over the ache in my stomach. It tastes like nothing, but I grit my teeth as I finish the last swallow from the glass, the chalky grit at the bottom of the glass slowly sliding down my throat. As I do, I look over at the framed photograph atop my desk of my family—my wife and child smiling at me—before I resume combing through the balance sheets again, determined to fix this for them.

8

ARCHIE

I barely survive the misery that is Statistics. I'm on the other side of the room, separated by dozens of students, yet all I can think about is the human-fucking-cannon ball that just declared war when she rocketed into my life.

That half-smile she gave me when she refused to end the engagement. That fucking *smile*—smug like she had already won— prickled at my brain, digging a little deeper with each passing second. I swear I could hear the fucking thing chipping away at my sanity bit-by-bit until all I could think about was launching myself from my row at the top of the classroom and soaring through the air like a flying fucking squirrel to land on top of her self-assured ass.

My knee bobs beneath the fold-out desk as I glare down at the back of her head. It's going so hard now, it's vibrating my desk with a *tap, tap, tap* that the students next to me can hear. The girl beside me keeps looking over like she's waiting for me to bust through the desk like I'm Dr. Banner becoming the Hulk.

Mind yo'self, chica.

I don't give a fuck if her MacBook rattles like it just laid off the hard stuff after a week-long bender. It's either bob my knee or go Norman Bates on Red in this bitch.

Tap, tap, tap.

It's not like they're getting married for love either. Anyone with half of a brain knows that. He's old enough to be her father, and let's face it, even if Red has daddy issues, my father isn't exactly warm and cuddly, so it's not like he's the one to fucking solve them. Eli Blakely is cold, conniving, and treats every moment of his life as though the whole thing is one big business deal.

What people can do for him.

What he can do for them.

How he'll always come out ahead.

Tap, tap, t-t-t-tap.

Professor Puts-Everyone-to-Sleep finally wraps up his lesson at the front of the room, pointing behind him to something written on the whiteboard. I have no idea what he's covered or what I'm supposed to do before the next class, but I really don't give a shit either. I'm still thinking about all the ways Red is trying to fuck up my life and how I have to get her to stop before it's too late and daddy dearest gives away his estate to his up-and-coming trophy wife.

T-t-t-t-t-a-p-p-p-p.

I mean mug the back of Red's head as teach finally calls time of death. She stands from her seat like she was waiting for the exact moment, packed and ready to go. She walks down the stairs and toward the exit, the first out of the room. I want to follow her and figure out what makes her tick so I can use it against her and put an end to all this shit, but I have more important things to do right now.

Like skip classes, go to my father's office, and surprise him with an impromptu pussy intervention, *pussy-vention,* if you will. Which is sure to piss him off, but I can't stomach staying on campus one second longer.

I'll get a note from the campus clinic later for the missed hours. The nurse fucking loves me . . . and loves fucking me too.

I barrel down the steps and out of the room, sliding past dicks taking their sweet time, and head out of the building and to the campus garage, walking like a wildfire is on my heels. I resist the urge to run, but just barely. It takes nine minutes for me to reach the parking garage, and I chase the stairs all the way to the top level, finding my white Mercedes G-Wagon waiting right where I left her.

Hot damn, she's pretty.

A ray of sunshine peeks through the shitty skies of my morning. My girl's shiny and polished and a damn honor to drive. I hit the right button on the key fob so that she purrs to life before I even reach the driver's side door.

I press the unlock button next, open the door, and slide across the leather seat into my car. Cold air-conditioning automatically blows into the space as I pull out of the parking spot and head down the ramp to leave the garage. I don't even check my phone as I do—not for tags or tweets or even an e-mail from Coach attaching plays he wants us to memorize before next practice. I don't give a shit what any of it says right now. All I can think about is Red pirating everything my family has worked for and curb-stomping my promised easy life in the process.

The conniving little vixen.

And she dares to use Mel against me too.

Fuck her!

No one tries to screw with my life and gets away with it. I'll be damned if I sit back and do nothing while some . . . some *girl* . . . threatens everything. I'll find Mel a new job. I'll empty my trust fund and pay her so much money she never has to work again. I'll do whatever it takes to not fuck-up everything she's worked for, but I can't just roll over and take it like a good boy.

If Red wants to bury me, she better take a deep breath, because I'm pulling her down into the grave with me.

I don't even turn on the radio as I drive, though my Spotify playlist connects automatically. I smack the mute button so hard that I'm surprised it doesn't fly off and hit me in the eye, but I don't want music right now. I can't fucking handle music right now. Not unless that music prophesies Red's demise and my ascension to the Blakely throne. But I doubt Kid Cudi has a song dedicated to *that.*

My father moved the business to California nine or so years ago, after his fourth separation from my mom, uprooting the entire company from the east coast and saying hello to the land of sun and supermodels. Now, from what I understand, the business is *technically* tax-sheltered in the Virgin Islands, but my father's office is only an hour to the north of campus, nestled in a city he built from the ground up, pouring the fortune of ten lifetimes into it. When my parents eventually got back together, he traveled back and forth across the country, one office in New York City and the other here. Mom always acted like it annoyed the shit out of her, that the distance caused her to look elsewhere to satisfy her needs, but I don't think that's true. My parents cheated regardless of if they were sleeping in the same bed at night or not. The only difference was he got California pussy out here.

I take the interstate because it's faster, and my Mercedes glides across the asphalt, the ride smooth on my custom-ordered, platinum-engraved twenty-two-inch rims. I might even enjoy the drive, except I'm too pissed to enjoy anything at the moment. I've been steaming since last night, set to broil and left in the oven until your boy burnt *extra* crispy. Red is like a smoke alarm going off at three in the morning, blaring through my good dreams, pissing me off, and impossible to ignore.

I take the exit when I hit the commercial district. This place used to just be his business, a giant office building in the middle of nowhere, but now it sprawls across the landscape, bringing cookie-cutter houses, other commercial buildings, and money to the area. I'm almost proud of him, though I'd *never* tell him that, for bringing prosperity to an area that had never seen it before, but he definitely didn't do any of it for altruism. If anything, he did it to feed his huge ego and so he could piss off my mother.

My father and his massive superiority complex had to keep the tallest building for himself. By the time I pull up to it, I'm gripping the steering wheel hard enough to leave permanent indentions in the black leather. It repeats in my head, like a visual stutter I can't shake off my back—Red staring at me, her eyes sparking with amusement before she grinned. She knew what she was doing. She knew the game she was playing, and she was enjoying it.

Ruining my life for shits and giggles.

I pull my black keycard for the parking garage out from beneath my visor, and I swipe it to enter the concrete building. I park in one of the spots reserved for executives at my father's company when they visit from the south American, central Asian, or northern European divisions. I snatch the keys from the ignition and am out of the vehicle half a second before I race across the concrete. I arrive at the elevators and press the up button. And I wait.

And wait.

And wait some fucking more, until my patience gasps its last breath.

I jog to the stairwell on the opposite side, against the far corner of the garage, and start running the stairs. Up and up, around and around, until I'm dizzy and hot in this miserable concrete coffin that no one uses. There's a reason they call these things emergency exits, and it has to be because only people in emergencies want to use them. Still, I don't slow down. I'm committed, even if it means inhaling the scent of stale farts and piss and running up nineteen flights at full freaking tilt.

Inhale.

Exhale.

Out and in.

I go up and up until I finally reach the top floor. I hit the panic bar on the door and send it careening into the wall on the opposite side. I'm somewhere I've never been before, in a hallway, offices on either side of me. Those that can see me through the glass walls facing the hall stare at me, sweating and out of breath as I start through the building. At least one of them has probably called security because I'm sure I look like I'm going to murder someone.

My father, people. Calm down. It's just my father.

On second thought, I hope you don't mind being an eye-witness for the prosecution.

I speed down the hallway, rounding corners and a small kitchenette, abandoned except for a coffee maker and a small wooden table with no chairs, until I spot my father's receptionist at her desk in front of his office. The door is closed behind her. This lady's new with platinum blonde hair that my father has certainly gripped between his fingers from behind and big boobs that barely squeeze into the white button-down she's wearing. Normally, I'd at least throw her a smile—she has to put up with my old man, after all—but I have more important business today.

"How can I help—?" she begins cheerily before her smile vaporizes beneath my impact. I leave her mouth-open and gaping as I beeline past her and toward my father's office. She hits a button on her headset and drops the call on whomever she's been chatting with. She probably thinks I'm a murderer who has come to kill her boss, and by the looks of it, she can't decide if the paycheck is good enough to let him live.

Hint, sweetheart, it's not.

Unceremoniously, I swing the door open. My father looks up from the papers strewn on the glass desk in front of him, not even remotely surprised. It annoys me more than it should that he already knew I was here, no doubt having already told security not to tase my dumbass self halfway up the stairwell. He *let* me storm in here like I was going to catch him off guard.

But that will never happen. And shit, I hate him for it.

"Father," I say.

"Son," he says in the exact same tone. He eyes me over his papers and returns to his work. "How can I help you?"

"Call off the engagement." I step forward, continuing until my legs press against the desk and the large expanse of glass tabletop is the only thing separating us. "Don't marry her."

My father tips back in his leather chair and frowns at me, adjusting the limited-edition Rolex clasped around his wrist. The thing reflects the light filtering in through the south-facing windows along one wall, casting prisms of color across the gray hardwood floor. My father sits there in his chair and stares at me for one excruciating moment, not blinking, not reacting, not even breathing from what I can tell.

What a vampire.

"No," he says, dismissing me with one word.

"No?" I scoff. "Surely, you can't be in love with her!"

He actually laughs at that, a rare, wide grin splitting across his face. It's disconcerting and sends a shiver spider-walking up my spine. "No, of course not."

"Then why marry her?" I lean forward and slam my fist onto his desk, rattling the glass, and honestly, it's a testament to whomever built the thing that it doesn't shatter under the force. "Just tell me why."

Fuck. I sound weak, threatened even, probably because I am.

My father's gaze scrolls lazily to the spot on his desk where my fist hit. He looks mildly surprised that it didn't break as well. His jaw tics once with his rising irritation.

"Son," he placates a moment later, which is rare for him, though he's definitely choosing the method he thinks will work the quickest to make me leave—that's all he ever does with me, *dismiss* me, *send* me away. "Layne fetches a high price, and she wants a wedding. I'm giving her what she requires."

A high price?

What she requires?

What the fuck does that mean?

Oh my god. That little vixen is cockblocking him until he puts a ring on her gold-digging hand.

"Find someone else then!" I nearly yell. "You don't have to marry her and put everything in jeopardy."

His gaze shutters. Cold, rigid death stares back at me. Placating Eli is gone. My real father sits in his place.

"I'm marrying Layne because I want to marry her, and I get what I want, son. Have you learned absolutely nothing from me?" He steeples his fingers together in front of his thin lips before he brings them down to the desk in front of himself. "You stomp in here like a child and act like marrying the girl is the end of the world. What are you so concerned about? That you'll lose your place in line?"

When I don't answer immediately, he warns, "Answer me."

"Yes," I admit. *And . . . no.*

"We're getting a prenup," my father says matter-of-factly before returning to his papers like he's already done with this conversation.

He's dismissing me . . . again.

"Prenups don't stop her from popping out a kid," I say, "and . . ."

My father holds up a hand to stop me.

"I'm marrying her, Archibald. End of discussion."

"But you could find someone like her anywhere," I nearly shout over the voice at the back of my brain that whispers the words are a lie, that tells me she's different, one of a kind.

She says no to you, it tells me, *and you can't let it go.*

"There are other women," I continue, "other red-headed women—others of your . . . your *type*—other . . ."

"No."

"Anyone else," I plead, the grinning face of my father's fiancée blinking at the back of my brain, haunting me. "What about Mom? You've always gotten back together. After everything you've been through, all the memories and shit."

Memories of affairs and arguments and acrimony.

"Stop!" my father commands, and I do because his tone is enough to freeze my blood solid. "Your mother and I are over, son. We will never reconcile. Your mother understands I have needs she cannot meet."

Yeah, thanks to your freaky ginger fetish and wanting to keep them as young as legally allowable.

"Anyone but her," I say, the words quiet, defeated.

"This matter is settled." My father waves his hand, dismissing me. "Get out of my office."

Fuck.

With a sigh, I turn to leave. "Oh, and Archie?"

"Yeah?" I look over my shoulder at him.

"That was your one and only pass, boy. Don't ever storm into my office again, or I will have a baby with my future wife so I can get a proper fucking son."

The words singe when they land, leaving my flesh burning hot, but I nod my understanding before I stride out of his office, even angrier than when I walked into it.

9

LAYNE

uin.
Rot.

Death.

I'm choking, drowning beneath the cold, heavy weight of the dark.

I scream, but no sound leaves my mouth.

I try to move, but my limbs don't obey. The blackness has captured me in its whirlpool and dragged me down into its crushing depths.

I try to swallow, but my trachea is collapsing, little by little, more and more, until every breath is a battle. I gag in the suffocating silence, but no sound comes out. I'm suspended, mouth open and unmoving, held captive by the enormous weight of nothingness.

I blink out into the dark, unable to stir as the weight compresses, squeezing me until my every heartbeat is a tap against the anvil sitting atop me, the blanket of black that grows heavier with each passing second.

I can't see.

I can't move.

I can't breathe.

Breathe, goddammit!
Breathe!
BREATHE!!!!!

I awake abruptly with a desperate gasp that's louder than the cars driving outside and the white noise machine humming steadily in the corner that never manages to completely cover up the traffic.

Tha-thum, tha-thum, tha-thum sounds my heart as it hammers in my ears, ricocheting around in my brain, my pulse bouncing against my skull.

I sit upright in bed, my back straight, and look against the barren white wall opposite me. The light from the streetlamp outside passes in through the space between my curtains and marks a bright light diagonally across the center of the wall.

Like a target drawn to get my attention.

Tha-thum. Tha-thum.

I suck in a breath that sends cool air between my teeth and reach a hand to wipe my hair out of my face, unsticking it from my sweaty brow. I'm going to need a shower. I can feel the cold stickiness everywhere, gluing me to my comforter.

Tha-thum.

Another nightmare.

It's always a nightmare.

The shit the campus doc prescribed me doesn't keep them away. If anything, all those pills do is knock me out and leave me unconscious for the monsters to carry me away into the dark every night. At least I could wake up this time. Sometimes, I can't. Sometimes, I'm stuck in the space between asleep and awake, floating and silently screaming into the blackness.

It's not enough that my life haunts my waking hours, it has to haunt my only respite too.

I tip my head back, closing my eyes at the ceiling. The stars from my nightlight circle above me, peeking through my eyelids with a kaleidoscope of soft pinks and reds. I breathe in from my nose and out through my mouth, trying to calm myself and my pounding heart.

Tha . . . thump. Tha . . . thump.

When I feel like I can finally breathe again, I climb out of bed and walk the short distance to my kitchen. I open the fridge and dig a Red Bull out of the near-empty box at the back, popping the top and taking a sip.

Not going back to sleep now.

I never do after a nightmare.

One brings more, and then I'm trapped beneath them, unable to wake, unable to move, scared out of my mind, like the demon of dreams has come to personally torment me.

I switch on my lamp and walk over to my loveseat, which is basically a glorified, over-sized chair, because the space won't fit anything larger than that. I sit down and curl up, drawing my legs beneath me and sip my drink.

I should get up and do something.

Homework, maybe.

A shower, too.

Mop the floor, perhaps.

Something.

But I don't. I never do because the monster that haunts my dreams pulls everything out of me and takes it all for himself.

I eye the stack of mail on the end table beside me, the open letter from the Town of Chester sitting on top of it. Written on pretty pressed paper with the town's official seal at the top of the cover page.

Notice of the tax sale of the property located at 1694 Monroe East.

My mother's home.

My father's home too, at one time, at least.

But not mine, not for the last eighteen years, when he left me with *her*.

I could pawn the oversized lump of coal Eli put on my hand and cover the balance, and then some.

I don't want the house, though.

I don't want any part of the filth.

The city can keep the house, bulldoze it, and build a sewage treatment plant on the property for all I care. Because I don't care. Not one bit.

My blood beats icy and indifferent.

Because I am cold inside.

Cold and dead and empty.

I feel absolutely nothing as I look over at the fancy paper setting a date for the sale at auction. Deep down, buried beneath the cold, I ache to feel again, but the avalanche of ice extinguished everything but the white-hot hate years ago. I'm a husk of a person now, a pretty doll. I have memories—the rancid fetor of dried dog shit from the mutt my mother hated even more than me, the sight of newspapers crumbling brittle and yellow and stacked everywhere, the crunch and crackle of trash beneath my feet. I remember all of it, every last tortuous memory, but I feel nothing.

The worst part is the memories, the ones where you recall smiling or laughing or being content, but you can't recreate the emotion. It's like you're watching a movie of your own life, but you can't connect with the characters. It's a nice picture, but it's not yours. You are separate and apart, and those memories seem like a dream, not your past.

I remember being able to see the golden oak boards on the floor of the dining room and playing on the bare carpet in my bedroom. I have glimpses of happy times: our Christmas tree decorated with candy canes and strings of popped popcorn and then my birthday cake, white icing with pink flowers and three lit candles on top. Our home was never tidy but always clean, where you could take a step without roaches scattering for cover and breathe without choking on the dust and mouse shit polluting the air.

I think we might have even been happy before Eli Blakely ruined everything, before my mother changed. She was no longer the loving parent and devoted wife, but a meat suit choking on her cigarettes and beer and bitter hate. It took months, maybe even a year, before the hoarding sunk its claws into her back. Then she stopped leaving the house.

She stopped showering.

She stopped caring.

I'm not sure exactly when it all went downhill, but I know the slide was slow initially, then fast, like she gained speed the more she tunneled forward. First, she stopped going to work. A few weeks later, she stopped taking me to school, and I walked alone to the bus stop every morning. Sometime after that, she stopped going to the grocery store or checking the mail or even leaving the confines of her front porch. She paid the neighbor twenty bucks to deliver groceries when she was hungry, but her diet mainly consisted of beer and the occasional cigarette, while I was left to pilfer through what I could find at school or steal from the grocery mart a block over. If her presence was required for anything for me—a mandatory parent-teacher conference or school sign-ups, for example—then she paid the same neighbor another twenty to pretend to be my dad and take me. When she needed cash, I took her debit card to the gas station two blocks north and used the ATM on the sidewalk.

But none of it ever made her happy.

The beer bottles piled up in the beginning, the bags so heavy I couldn't drag them out of the house. Then the food containers came next. She refused to let me throw away the plastic ones, stacking them one atop another on the countertops, in the cabinets, on the top of the fridge, and across the floor. At first, she cleaned them up, but eventually, she stopped doing that too. Next, it was the newspapers, glimpses of the outside world, that she hoarded. It was amazing she never set the house on fire with as many as she collected, but that's probably because she rarely actually lit up. No, she'd dangle the cigarette between her lips and chew on the end like it was a lollipop until the tobacco started to spill out, and she'd throw it on the floor and start on another.

I used to wish she would actually smoke one, so the ash could fall and catch the papers on fire and the firemen would come and rescue me. I dreamt of it, lying in bed at night, wondering if one of the firemen who came to save me would bring a teddy bear or a chocolate bar, if he would smile and hold my hand or if he would let me play in the front seat of the firetruck. Maybe, he'd even take me home with him to a nice family with a mom who baked cookies and played pretend.

I prayed every night that someone would save me. Until one day, I just stopped praying because if there was a God, he wouldn't have left me to rot with her.

I learned to save myself.

I'd lay on my lumpy bed at night, before my mother's hoard took over my room as well, trying to breathe through my mouth, and wishing sleep would come and wash away the stench that permeated through the walls. There was no cleaning her treasures. I was a *spoiled, ungrateful brat* if I tried.

She surrounded herself with a throne of shit, the towers of newspapers scraping the ceiling and so tall I wished they would fall over and crush her to death. It would have been merciful for us both.

On a chilly night in the summer before sixth grade, I lay in my bed, the stench prickling my eyes and scalding the inside of my nose. I couldn't see the floor anymore. Her garbage blanketed everything by then. I tossed and turned, tossed and turned, waiting for morning to come so I could move everything out of the tub and get a shower. I had to shower before I left for school because if I didn't, I smelled, and the other kids made fun of me.

I tossed and turned, rolling and unrolling myself in the comforter until I couldn't take it anymore. I grabbed the backpack I'd snatched from the neighbor's front yard, discarded on the lawn, books and all, by the kid who lived there. I stuffed it full of everything I could reach, what I thought I might need, like clothes and pillows, and I tiptoed out of my room, down the hall, and over the cracks and crinkles of trash breaking beneath my feet. My mother sat passed out in her fraying, checkered recliner, probably drunk, as I snuck out of the house and to my father's small shop out back.

It was the only place she'd left untouched. Even in the beginning before the madness set in, she couldn't stomach setting foot in there. She had always said it was off-limits, but I didn't care. I couldn't take living with her anymore. I picked up a rock and threw it at his shop, breaking a window. I used my backpack to clear away the glass and hoisted myself up and through the window frame, tearing my sleeve on a loose shard of glass. It was dusty, but it smelled better than inside the house with my mother. I found an old cot among some camping gear and managed to make a bed for myself in the center of the room between the dust-covered tool benches on either side of me and beneath the hanging light. I slept like a baby that night, not dreaming of falling victim to the hoard. Every night from there on out, I snuck away to the shop to sleep, waiting until my mother finally passed out before I did.

It was my refuge, my safe space, and I made it my own, cleaning it up as best I could and using water from the faucet outside to wash away the years of dust. I didn't let anyone in there for years. I never told anyone, not until *him*, the boy with black hair and a toothy grin who sat in front of me in English class in eighth grade. Corey wasn't much better off than I was, living in a tiny house five blocks north with his six brothers and sisters, his father, and his *shitty stepmom*, as he called her. The first time he saw the shop, he smiled and told me it was cool that I had my own space.

He was my friend. Or so I thought, anyway. And for a couple of years, I guess he was the closest thing I had to one before he tried to take my virginity two summers later in the shop. I clocked him in the nose and told him to stop messing around, and when his gaze snapped from the floor to me, he wasn't the boy I thought I knew.

"Cock-teasing whore!" he spit, his nose a geyser of blood dripping down onto the front of his dirty white shirt. The words stung when they landed. I cried after he stomped out, leaving through the door I always left unlocked because I had never found a key. I cried for hours, holding my pillow against my face, sobbing until the sun came up the next morning.

Something inside me broke because of him until all I felt was the cold wet of the tear-soaked pillow against my cheek and the shame and anger burning through me.

I grabbed hold of that anger and cinched it tight. Anger was better than feeling nothing at all.

Anger on a good day. Dead the rest of the time. There's no

happiness for me, only misery. Just as it was back then, just as it is now.

My fingers find the inside of my right thigh reflexively and the little scars of white that pepper the skin there as far up as they can go, hidden from the world.

They are *control.*

Power.

Mine.

I follow the lines, jagged and ugly, like someone took a razor blade to the pale flesh over and over again for years. Because that's exactly what I did. To scare away the nothingness. To see if I could feel. To bring me back to life.

Some scars are new. Some are faded, and I have to hide them at work as best I can beneath layers of make-up because the men don't like girls with ugly parts.

I know I shouldn't do it even as my fingers snake between the cushion and the arm of the chair. Still, I pull the box cutter from the space next to the cushion just the same, hitting the button on the side to free the blade.

So much danger in one little thing.

I could slit Eli's throat with it.

I could slit my own.

I could cut off Golden Boy's dick and destroy his life.

I won't though, well not now anyway. I don't hate him enough for that. I don't feel anything for him. Maybe if I could feel, I'd feel pity for the poor little rich boy because, like me, he didn't ask to be brought into this world. His mother is vain and narcissistic—anyone can see that from the words she spews all over the internet in every interview and blog she can sink her self-absorbed claws into. Even in the good times, when she and Eli had reconciled, the former Mrs. Blakely never said *we.* It was always *me* or *I*, like no one in the world existed besides her, not even her son. His father is worse, a murdering psychopath that hides his crimes behind multimillion-dollar altruism. I don't pity the Blakely son, though, because then I would have to feel something besides the cold disassociation and searing anger, and I don't. Not ever.

I bring the blade to my skin and watch as the tapered end skims across the old marks. Light reflects off the silver blade, and I press deeper, indenting my skin. A spark pops inside my chest at the pain. I press further, and it's like a firecracker ignites in my chest, scaring away the cold.

I tilt the blade, letting the corner slide into my flesh. Blood oozes from the cut, clinging to the blade. It burns and stings and makes me feel alive as I watch it, mesmerized. Slowly, I draw the blade further, watching as it splits open my skin, separating it with the ease of a hot knife through butter. The burn stretches down my leg, and the thing inside me pops and crackles, burning away the cold. I lift the blade away and draw a finger to the cut that spills blood across my flesh. I drag my thumb across the fat drops where it clots together and spread it, mesmerized as it paints the inside of my thigh red. I let the pad of my thumb catch on the open skin and spread it wider, fire burrowing deep as I do.

For a moment, for one glorious second, the warmth scorches away the ice, unfreezing me. But as I withdraw my hand, the tips of my fingers painted red, the warmth recedes, and I'm cold again, dead and rotting on the inside.

Just like my mother.

Just like her house.

The tax man can have the place, but before he does, I'll go back to snatch one thing still laying there and yellowing on the dirty mantle, as it has been for as long as I can remember.

Then the government can raze the bitch to the ground, and I'll feel nothing as they do.

10

LAYNE

*F*uck wedding planners.

Better yet, fuck weddings.

If I have to look at one more swatch of fabric or at nearly identical floral arrangements, I'm going to shank this bitch in front of me. She's nice enough, but everything else about her is so fake that she makes my upcoming union to Eli look real.

Lip fillers.

A spray-on tan that someone declined to tell her is a little too orange.

Enough foundation to coat my entire wedding cake.

At her recommendation, we've been meeting every Saturday for three weeks now to get the wedding scheduled, especially since Eli insisted it happen as soon as possible. The freak just wants to pop my cherry. Too bad for him, the closest he's going to get to taking my virginity is by having his friend, a physician who owns a network of emergency clinics across the country, confirm it was there last week.

I might kill that gross fucker too before this is all said and done.

"What about this one?" the planner asks, pushing a sample of a shade of lilac across the table at me. I swear it's the same as the one that came before it, but she says her question so sweetly that I almost feel bad for imagining slapping her across the face with one of her sample books.

Almost.

"Looks great," I say, matching her sugary sweet tone.

I learned at our first meeting twenty-one days ago that I can't say *fine* or *okay* or *all right* or even *good*. She accepts nothing less than perfection. Eli must be paying her well, though in fairness, I'm only here because isn't this what sugar babies are supposed to want? To be showered with gifts and adoration and expensive things? She's the top wedding planner on the East Coast of the United States, according to her website. She's literally planned weddings for movie stars, and the fiancée of Eli Blakely should *absolutely adore* her presence. The real me, though, wants to hurl.

The planner starts yapping about floral arrangements again, and I tune her out. I can't help it. Someone would have to zap me with an electric cattle prod at this point to get me to pay attention anymore. My mind drifts away from the conference room in Eli's office, which we commandeered for our meeting today.

And I think of *him*, the golden pain-my-ass, the one person I should not be thinking about right now as I plan my wedding to the elder Blakely.

The blond footballer is probably shacked up somewhere with a sorority pledge this late on a Saturday morning. Not that I care, not that I give a fuck who he sleeps with. Yet . . . I feel a tiny twinge of something—guilt, maybe—at the thought of dragging him into this, but it's not like Eli would care if the situation was reversed.

Plus, I told Golden Boy to get out of my way, but he's so fucking stubborn, the command apparently can't penetrate his thick skull. But then again, maybe it was because he hasn't so much as looked in my direction since his outburst on the second day of classes at the start of the semester. Well, except for one time last week, when I caught him glaring at me like he was trying to practice his telepathy and tell me to dig a hole to Hell and say hi to his father on the way down. Other than that, he's been remarkably well-behaved for how poorly he took the news of our engagement.

Maybe that's why I'm developing an unexpected regard for his feelings. Yes, it must be because I haven't had to deal with his asshole-ness for a while. He's so much more tolerable when he doesn't open his sinful mouth.

Or it's because you want to fuck him, you nasty, filthy whore!

I nearly flinch at the unwelcome commentary from my dead mother. *Nearly.*

"How does that sound?" the planner asks me with a cheerful grin.

Fuck. What did she say?

"Great!" I answer, matching her tone again and giving her a toothy smile. "Is there anything else you need me for?"

Please, on all the saints, say no.

"Mmm," she looks down at her iPad and starts scrolling with her index finger before nodding. "Yes, just one more for today. We put in the change order for the red velvet with pomegranate ganache filling, like you asked, but the baker cautioned me to advise you against it. Are you sure about the change?" she eyes me warily, a frown on her pretty, plastic face. "He said it's going to look rather red when it's cut into, almost like blood."

She grimaces with the image, but I barely notice.

All I can think is I did *not* put in a change order.

And I certainly wouldn't have put it in for damn pomegranate anything, not unless I wanted to die of anaphylaxis before I had a chance to dethrone my new husband.

"Change it back," I tell her. "You've convinced me. And you know what? Tell the chefs to make sure no pomegranates are used in the food preparation either . . . *please.*"

"Oh . . ." she blinks at me, her big green eyes going wide. "Okay! Wonderful. I'll just type that out now."

She hits a couple of buttons on her iPad and reaches into her bag to pull out a wireless keypad. The thing's blindingly white with shiny silver keys, and it immediately gives me a headache. She powers it on and starts typing furiously before announcing, less than a minute later, "All done!"

"Terrific," I lie between my teeth before I tune her out again.

How did he find out?

I haven't told anyone about my unusual allergy, but I know it—I feel it in my bones—that somehow the Blakely spawn is behind this. Any iota of guilt I'm harboring for the football star evaporates. I don't know how he found out, but this is too far. Without an epi pen, he could've killed me.

Golden Boy fucked up.

I stand abruptly, and the party planner's gaze snaps to me.

"I have an appointment," I tell her. "You can see yourself out, right?"

"Um, sure, yes," she scurries to gather her papers and samples and tucks them back into her large canvas bag, "of course."

"And Tasha," I say, "why don't you call me in the future to confirm any change requests, okay?"

"Absolutely," she replies with a nod. "No problem."

I leave the conference room, and although I want to barrel straight back to campus, find Archibald Blakely, and punish him for not heeding my warning, I don't. Instead, I take a right and walk past the empty desk of the secretary I'm pretty sure Eli's fucking. Not that I mind, I don't. She deserves a raise and a corner office as far as I'm concerned for letting him stick his dick in her.

"Layne," Eli says as I enter his office, eyeing me from behind his desk, "done so soon? What a wonderful surprise."

"Eli," I murmur, closing the door behind me, and fuck, I guess if I had a thing for older men, he might do it for me. I look at him, seated behind his giant glass desk, Californian sunlight spilling over him from the exterior windows that run floor-to-ceiling on the opposite side of his office and casting him in gold. His salt-and-pepper hair looks almost blond again, his tan face flushed with warmth from the sunshine. He's almost . . . pretty. Too bad for him, I know the monster that lurks behind that handsome face and working on weekends is the most likable thing about his personality.

"Why don't you come over here?" he asks, leaning back in his chair and cocking his head at me. A command, not a request. "Let me take a good look at my wife-to-be, hmm?"

I stride forward, my footfalls soft on the gray carpet. I stall to play with the trinkets sitting on the end of his desk before I round it to stand in front of him.

"Better?" I ask, raising an eyebrow at him.

"Mmm," he says as he runs a hand over the curve of my hip and up over the white sundress I'm wearing. "You are so fucking beautiful."

He abruptly pulls me forward and yanks me on top of him, so that my thighs straddle the outside of his legs, pinched between the armrests of his chair, tight enough to cut off circulation.

"That's better," he purrs as he digs his cock into me, rubbing it against my panties.

My heartbeat flounders. I start to sweat.

He runs his lips across the column of my throat, his breath carrying the scent of black coffee, and growls, his chest vibrating beneath my palms pressed flat against him. His fingers knead my ass, and he rolls his hips again, digging his cock against the thin piece of fabric between us. I'm dizzy and lightheaded and feel a little sick, but I do what I do best.

I disassociate. I shut everything down.

No disgust.

No fear.

Nothing at all.

"You drive me nuts," he confesses, laying wet, sloppy kisses across my throat, brushing my hair out of the way and behind my shoulders. "I knew the moment I saw you that I had to have you."

I shut my eyes, disappearing into the unknown and away from here.

"God," he says, his breath like fire against the coolness of my skin, "I'm going to fuck you so hard, baby, you won't be able to get up from the bed. Then when you beg me to stop, I'm going to keep on fucking you until you're a filthy, crying mess. Know why?"

"Why?" I whisper, the word cold and dead.

"Because, baby, I bet you look gorgeous when you cry." He thrusts up one more time, rubbing his dick against the most intimate part of me again, and I can't help it, I gasp, though not for the reason he thinks, and he shoves me off him. I fall to my knees, landing with an *oomph*.

"Suck my cock, pretty girl. Show Daddy how much you want it."

Uck. I extinguish the urge to vomit.

It's not the first time he's required this, and I know I should be thankful he's not pushed me down to the carpet and face-fucking me already, slamming his balls against my chin and making me choke on his dick. He unfastens his belt and drags his pants down his ass, taking his black silk briefs with them.

There it is, Eli's cock, thick and wide with a blunt tip. I open my mouth obligingly, and he grins down at me as he curls a hand around the back of my skull and brings me down to his crotch. The first time we did this, I couldn't feel the lower half of my face for a week. Since then, I've learned to relax. I tell myself it'll be worth it when I not only ruin him, but everything he's worked for as well.

He'll hurt.

He'll suffer.

He'll *bleed*.

The head of his cock hits the back of my throat, and I hollow out my cheeks, making the sounds of appreciation I know he expects as he sets the rhythm, up and down, faster and faster, until it hurts and there's snot clogging my nose and I can barely breathe.

His hand cinches in my hair, and my scalp stings as he continues to rock into me.

"That's it, baby girl," he says with a moan. "Take my cock like the good bitch you are."

He thrusts up out of the chair, humping my face in time to his pulling me down. I can't breathe at all now, and his wiry pubic hair is stabbing my flesh as I close my eyes and wish it would end. A knife burrows into the side of my jaw as he humps my face faster, bringing both of his hands to my head and pulling me down on top of his dick.

"Oh yeah. Fuck, right there. Yeah! Yeah! Yeah!"

He comes, spilling his salty seed down my throat, and I swallow obediently as he empties. One swallow, two, three, the taste of snot and mucus and his cum poisoning my tongue.

"Fuck," he says with a groan as he readjusts in the chair and throws his head back with a sigh. "You almost make waiting worth it, baby."

"Thank you," I reply because he expects it and I stand, straightening my dress as I do.

"See you for dinner?"

"I can't tonight," I tell him. "I have work."

"Quit," he says. It's not a request.

I blink at him. We've had this fight before. Work is the only thing besides school I wouldn't give up instantly. We agreed that I'd quit after the wedding. After that argument, I had to lay down and let him furiously face-fuck me just to calm him down.

"Fine," he pouts when he knows I'm not going to acquiesce. "Remember, I'm out of town on business, starting tomorrow."

"For a week," I say. "I remember."

"Good," he reaches around me to smack my ass. "Now get out of here, fiancée, before I decide to fuck your pussy and watch you bleed all over my desk."

The thought sends my stomach nose-diving to my feet, and it takes everything in me not to wretch right then and there on his office floor. He doesn't have to tell me twice. I skitter out of his office, and he laughs as I go.

11

ARCHIE

I tear into my club sandwich, praising the givers of cafeteria grub for delicious ham, turkey, and bacon on this fine Monday afternoon. Smother the meat with honey mustard between two hot slices of ciabatta and screw-me-sideways, I'm in ecstasy. My eyes roll back in my head as two of my fellow Phi Epsilon Alpha brothers and Mila Riebertsen, aka the girl who can't take a hint, walk up to my table. Mila sets her plate beside me, and I side-eye her rabbit food as I take another chunk out of my sammy.

She's got carrots, cucumbers, and not much else on her plate. I feel bad for her before my club carries me away to food heaven.

I nearly moan with the bite. I've been starving since morning, after I found out that the cafe I normally order breakfast from unexpectedly closed due to a water leak. I'm going to have to find another morning spot asap because my low blood sugar almost made Mila look hot-as-fuck.

Okay, she *is* actually hot-as-fuck with brown eyes so big she resembles a freaking anime character and hair halfway down to her hips that wraps like silk around your hand when you're sticking it up her ass while you finger her pussy. But fucking Mila again is a bad idea and violates numero uno.

Hit it and quit it, boy!

Still, she sits next to me nearly every time she spots me in the cafeteria like somebody forgot to tell her about my rep. Or maybe she considers getting a second notch on my bedpost a challenge. Whatever. I will not sleep with her again.

But does it count if you fuck her normie-style instead this time?

Yup, gotta be the low blood sugar, I think, as I chew through another bite. Onyx Madison and Carter Culver, fellow seniors and pledges with me since freshman year, claim a couple of seats across the table from me.

"Blakely, you hear the news, man?" Onyx asks, grinning at Carter, whose ears are turning red and about to catch fire.

"Nah, what?" I manage before devouring another bite.

Onyx knocks a shoulder into Carter, sending him swaying, which is no easy feat since Carter's my height and has at least fifty pounds of lean muscle on the cross-country runner currently giving him shit.

Onyx starts laughing before he even gets the words out but manages to quiet as Carter tears into a ketchup packet, squeezes it out on his tray, and angrily stabs the ketchup with a fry.

"My man over here," Onyx says, throwing a hand on Carter's shoulder, "got *fucked up* at the Delta party last night and tried to dick down Ellie's sister. Ellie is *pissssseeeeddd.*"

"Oh shit," I say, eyeing Culver, whose entire face is the color of Santa's red jacket.

Damn, bro looks like he's about to cry.

"You okay, man?" I say, sipping my soda as Onyx obliviously guffaws in between words I can't make out, though I catch *twins* and *fucked up.*

"Man," Culver chomps down on a fry, "Ellie won't talk to me." He groans and hangs his head. "They look the same from behind."

Onyx chokes on the chicken tender he's chewing and coughs before he rights himself.

"Ellie'll understand," I say. "Give her some time, bro."

"I don't know." Carter shakes his head down at his tray. "I never seen her that mad."

He says something else, but I don't catch it because my attention snags on a girl blazing across the cafeteria. *Red.* Her gaze locks on mine and tunnels deep, like she's trying to peel me back layer by layer until she finds what makes me tick.

I want to meet her halfway, scoop her into my arms, and kiss the glare she's giving me away.

What the fuck is wrong with you? Get it together, Blakely!

I shift in my seat as I watch her arrival. Mila says something, but it's background noise as her fingers land on my forearm, my skin exposed where I've rolled up the sleeve of my shirt.

"Where have you been?" the vixen spits when she lands at our table.

"What?" I ask.

"Where. Have. You. Been?"

"Were you looking for me?" *Interesting.* I give her a grin that's sure to melt her panties. "Red, sweetheart, if you want to take a ride on the Archie train, all you have to do is ask."

Onyx snorts as Layne leans in and sneers at me, pressing her fingertips against the table, blanching them white. The smell of her smites my hopes of avoiding a hard-on. No doubt Mila will notice and take the credit.

Milk chocolate and Snickerdoodle cookies. I want to fucking *bite* her.

I do my best to ignore her, reaching down between us and taking a good-sized chunk out of my sandwich. Her upper lip twists in disgust as she glares at me like she's trying to set me ablaze with her eyes.

"What?" I say eventually as she keeps glowering at me. "I'm a carbivore, okay? You worried I'm going to develop my moobs early or something?"

Carter chokes on his spit while Onyx and Mila snicker.

Layne blinks, throwing hate straight for me, before she reaches over one-handed and grabs Carter's tray of ketchup, fries, and a hamburger and dumps the bitch right on top of my head.

Cold ketchup sticks to my left cheek. The hamburger bun slaps me on the shoulder, and a bunch of fries land direct deposit on my lap.

DAMMIT, Red!

A growl vibrates past my clenched teeth, and I glare at her before something hot and wet flattens itself to my cheek.

What the . . . Mila.

Jesus, she needs to learn boundaries. Still, I let her lick me and watch Layne as her glare splits wide, and she gawks at us, a flush bridging her cheeks. With some effort, I hit the off button on my impending tantrum and reward her with a toothy grin to cover my simmering anger.

"Cleaning me up, baby?" I ask Mila, though my gaze is still locked on Red.

"Mhmm," Mila murmurs obediently as she licks my face clean and gets to work on my shoulder.

Red goes completely still, her feet cemented to the gray cafeteria floor the moment before she presses the nuclear button.

"How did you know?" she snarls, her hand landing heavy on the table, clattering the trays and cups with it. She crowds my space even further, and Mila abandons the clean-up aisle. She must sense what I do as Red's fiery hair settles against her bare, freckled shoulders like it's kindling beneath the pyre she's setting for my funeral.

Scalding, explosive anger.

The calm before the hurricane.

Incoming Red alert.

I don't flinch.

I don't stand.

I don't even breathe.

"How did I know what?" I murmur, my gaze hooded as I zero in on her glossy, wet lower lip.

Beautiful. Kissable. *Mine.*

"How did you know I was allergic?" she shoots back.

Fuck me. She smells like cinnamon and cocoa.

"What?" My gaze lands on the tropical waters of her irises again.

"How," she inches closer, "did," and closer, "you," closer, "know?"

A quarter of an inch, and I could kiss her and end this torment.

Does she feel it too? I back away, just a little, enough to give her the look—*that look*, which gets me what I want, when I want, from whomever I want. It's a half-smile beneath long lashes that all the chicks around here seem obsessed with and a straight stare that asks *wanna fuck?* Red's fought off that look twice, but hell, maybe the third time's a charm, especially when we are already so close.

I hear the stutter of her breath as her mouth parts—*oh yeah, she wants it too*—before she hits the executioner's switch and fries my hopes of hate sex to extra crispy.

"How did you know I was allergic, Golden Boy?" she demands.

I blink at her. *Allergic? Allergic to what?*

"Pomegranates? Really?! You could have killed me, you arrogant prick," she snaps, reaching behind her before slamming something on the table between us. My gaze lowers to the table, and I stare at a yellow-and-orange Epi Pen on the white tabletop. "I told you to stay away from me, Blakely. I warned you."

She's allergic to pomegranate? Oh . . . Ohhhhhhhh, fuck.

I had forgotten about contacting Tasha—the wedding planner for all my parents' nuptials—from a catfished e-mail account and hedging my bets. One of a thousand ways I intend on fucking up the big day.

"You're not a golden boy at all, are you?" she asks, her gaze narrowed. "You're just another conniving, money-hungry asshole with a dead fucking heart."

She snatches the Epi Pen, turns on her heel, and storms off. The gazes of everyone at the table—hell, probably the cafeteria if I cared to look—follow her.

She was allergic. I could have killed her. I didn't know.

I just wanted the cake to be red, like her hair.

I was trying to fuck with her, that was it. The shit with the cake was an afterthought in bigger plans. I wasn't trying to murder her.

Shit!!!

I stand, spilling Carter's fries to the floor as I do. Mila blurts something, but I ignore her. My pulse gallops after Red, and I follow along with it.

"Layne!" I call, but she's already near the double doors, hitting both of them at the same time, and sending them swinging in the opposite direction. I'm at the doors five seconds later, but by the time I get to the main hall that leads outside, she's already at the entrance to the building, her crazy hair catching the glint of the afternoon sun.

"Layne!" I shout again as I push through a gaggle of prima donnas preening for a picture and out the door.

My heart plays paddle ball with my ribcage as I watch her ignore me, not even throwing a glance back in my direction.

Goddammit!

I pick up the pace until I am at her side.

"Layne," I say down to her, frowning both because she's already frowning and because I'm not digging the ease with which her name keeps rolling off my tongue, "come on. Stop and talk to me."

She keeps walking, chin held high, scorning me.

"Where are you headed? We can talk there if you want."

"Shove it up your ass, Blakely."

"I'd rather shove it up yours," I mutter under my breath, and she raises an eyebrow at me, though her steps don't falter. I take it as a win that she doesn't slap me.

"I'm sorry, Red," I say. "I didn't know you were allergic, okay? I was just trying to fuck with you."

We round the corner of the building, walking the path between tall cedar trees.

"Hey," I grab her by the wrist and tug her toward me, "I'm sorry, okay, but you aren't exactly blameless here either, beautiful. You fucked up my good thing with Mel. You threatened me. You've actively tried to fuck up my life."

"You don't get it, do you?" she snaps, yanking her hand free from my grip and pushing me away from her so hard I rock back on my heels. "I don't want your apologies, Golden Boy. I want you out of my way. I've told you. Stay the fuck out of my life, and I'll stay out of yours."

"What if I want to be in your life?" I blurt.

Fuck.

I can't believe I said it. I don't even want to *think* it, but there it is, between us, hanging in the air while her mouth parts and she blinks up at me. Surely, she feels it. She has to feel it. God knows, it's *all. I. feel.* The bond that binds us together is sharp and tenuous and painful. I want to curl it around me and hold on tight. Then I want to scream and try to pull away.

It's terrifying, consuming, *crazy*.

I want her to admit the thing between us and then deny it in one breath. This isn't me. This isn't the guy known for one night stands. This isn't how my life's supposed to go.

She haunts my waking moments. She pervades my dreams. She's always there, and she's been there for *weeks*, since the Friday before the semester began.

Her snarky comments.

Her take-no-shit attitude.

Her defiance.

Fuck!

"You don't know what you want," she finally answers in a whisper.

I shake my head at her, refusing to back down, even if it scares both of us. God knows it terrifies me. My heart leaps into my throat as she goes rigid, barely even breathing. Vulnerability doesn't come easy to me or her. We are two sides of the same fucked-up coin.

"Don't discount what I feel, Red," I tell her.

"That's rich coming from a pretty football player known for fucking, not feelings."

"Just because I fuck 'em, Red, doesn't mean I don't feel. I don't want to be enemies with you." I run a hand through my hair, desperate to get the words out, even though it feels like they will end me if I do. "I want you."

She rolls her eyes. "You just want what you can't have, Golden Boy."

Fair—probably true—but her saying it irritates me all the same.

"No," I growl. "What did I tell you about discounting my feelings? I don't give a fuck that you're my father's. I want *you*. I want to find out if I fuck you hard enough if you'll undergo an attitude adjustment. I want your smartass attitude and the way you come at me when you're pissed off. I want your gorgeous red hair between my fingers and to kiss every freckle that dots your cheeks. I want all of you, Red." She sucks in a breath, her enormous eyes locked on me. "We don't have to be enemies."

"We can never be friends."

"Then let's be something else entirely."

My lips crash onto hers as I flatten her to me. She tastes just like she smells, and holy hell, cinnamon and sugar and salt explode across my tongue as I reach around to knead her juicy ass and pull her even closer, flattening her tits against my chest. I taste her and touch her, feeling every inch of her skin I can reach and digging my cock against her stomach. She tenses, but when I do it again, she mewls, her body purring in my arms.

Soft.

Warm.

Heaven.

"I want to *own* you, Red." I murmur, leaving her lips to scrape my teeth across her cheek, down her jawline, and to her throat. "I want to hear you scream my name and memorize the look on your face when you shatter for me."

"Oh fuck," she says with a moan, and I almost come in my pants at the sound.

"Let me show you how a man your own age fucks," I tell her, licking and laving across her skin. Her fingernails cinch into my white t-shirt and tug me against her. I feel her heartbeat pattering in her chest, echoing the fast beat of my own. I catch one of her hands and tug it down between us until she's holding my dick.

She .gasps. They normally do, but I like it much more coming out of her luscious mouth.

I slide a hand beneath the waistband of her jeans with one hand as she wraps her fingers around me through my jeans and strokes with me.

Fuck.

We're not even flesh-to-flesh yet, and I'm about to spill. I squeeze my asscheeks together to stop from coming in my pants. I slide a finger further down, beneath her soft panties and over her pussy.

This is crazy, wrong, and just what I need.

Hot damn, she's dripping. My breath stutters as I run a finger over her clit and she shakes in my arms, choke-holding my dick. It may be a balmy seventy degrees, but right now, in the space between us, it's hot and humid from our shared breath. I kiss her mouth, sucking the air out of hers and sliding my finger through her wetness.

"I'll make you come so hard you see the stars," I promise her.

I hook a finger inside her. Goddamn, she's so tight.

"Oh god, yes," she mewls, and I smile against her skin.

"Not quite, pretty girl, but I fuck like one."

A second finger joins my first, and I thrust up roughly inside her, her needy pussy clenching around me. She arches against me, rubbing her pelvis against mine, her head thrown back.

She bites her bottom lip, her eyes flutter shut, and I kiss her again, sucking her bottom lip between my teeth as I finger-fuck her. She's already shaking, quivering and bucking against me, and I've barely touched her. I sweep my tongue inside her mouth, claiming.

Sugar.

Salt.

Bliss.

Her hand rubs me over my jeans, and fuck, I'm going to explode. I push inside her, a third finger joining my other two, and she sighs, breathy and soft.

Abruptly, something rings, sharp and grating to the over-the-jeans hand job I'm currently receiving, and she startles away from me, pushing me as she does and sending me stumbling back, my fingers still wet with her juices.

"Fuck!" she says, her lips swollen, and her face flushed. "I can't do this. *We* can't do this."

She shakes her head violently.

"It's okay, Red," I say as her phone call goes to voicemail. "He doesn't have to know."

She side-eyes me. "I'm engaged to your *father*."

"So?"

She sneers, disgusted. *Hey, you kissed me back, Red.*

Her eyes widen, then narrow on me. "He'll kill us both if he finds out."

"I'm not going to tell him." It's the truth too. He'd kill *her* at least, and I'm starting to enjoy her company too much to see the shade of her blood.

She starts away from me, looking the most frazzled and least unlike-Red I've ever seen her.

"Hey Layne," I call to her as she abandons me and my blue balls. "This isn't over, beautiful."

"Yes, it is, Blakely," she snaps back.

"I think you'd actually like me if we fucked."

She doesn't give me the satisfaction of a reply. Probably because she knows I'm right.

"You know," I cross my arms at her receding back, "you're not a black-hearted bitch like you pretend to be."

She stops in her tracks and turns to stare at me. In the pinched furrow of her gaze, I spot vulnerability, a crack in the armor she always wears before she steels her expression a second later.

"You don't know anything about me," she says, "except what I choose to show you."

I shake my head at her. "There's a softie in there," I cock a challenging eyebrow, "I just know it."

She shakes her head again. "I'm not black-hearted, Golden Boy. I'm brutal. I will destroy your life and everything you care about and not give a fuck."

"I don't believe you." I shrug, her words not scaring me away. "Even brutal hearts bleed."

"Not mine," she murmurs, her aqua irises latching onto mine with her next words. "To bleed, I would have to have one."

Then she continues away from me, leaving me half-cocked, frustrated, and with the taste of snickerdoodle cookies and hot chocolate on my tongue.

12

ARCHIE

Six points down.
        Fourth quarter.
Two minutes left on the clock.

Fuck. We screwed up defense really good this time. We underestimated our opponent. We thought we had it in the bag. Hell, Slaten, our QB, practically said so before we left the locker room. The stats and sports commentary supported his statement. This game is set to be the biggest upset of the season, and it's the first one for our team.

We need the win. I need the win, something—*anything*—to erase last week's kiss with Red from my memory, if only for a moment.

Pull it the fuck together, Tigers!

"Blue eighty-nine," I suggest in the huddle.

"No," Coach says, shaking his head, his bald spot shining beneath the stadium lights.

"Blue eighty-nine will win the game," I argue.

He stares at me—well, glares actually, because he hates being second-guessed—but I watch as he considers it. Whether Coach wants to admit it or not, the strength of the Commanders' offensive line surprised him—shit, surprised all of us—tonight. It's going to take something outside his normal playbook to come back from this.

I look around the circle at my fellow teammates, silently daring them to speak up. Coach can bust my balls after we bring home the W.

"Blue eighty-nine," Jones says with a nod before popping his mouthguard in his mouth.

"You sure, Blakely?" Slaten asks.

"Just get me the ball," I tell him with a grin, "and I'll bring it home."

"Shit," Coach murmurs, stroking his beard like it's a kitty cat. "What the hell. Blue eighty-nine, it is."

He hits the roll of paper with his scribbled notes and red-inked plays against his clipboard with a *smack*.

"Get your asses out there!" he booms. "And get that win."

I jog beside my brothers out onto the gridiron, sweat prickling in my eyes. I flex my fingers inside my gloves and adjust the wrist straps, cinching them tight.

We get into formation, and this is the best part of the game for me. Not the touchdowns or the wins or the football groupies who throw themselves at me after the game.

It's the moment when we line up, and the roar of the stadium dulls to a hum and the flashes from thousands of cameras fade into the background. When I stare at the other team's defensive lineman, and he stares back at me.

There's the stench of sweat and dirt in the air, and the slight itch of the polyester jersey across my biceps. A bead of sweat rolls down my spine, slow and steady and the defensive lineman in front of me pussies out and throws a nervous glance at our QB. His fingers twitch, and I'm going to laugh if this motherfucker false starts.

Everyone wants to be the one to bring down the guy known for bringing it home, but this stocky twat needs a newsflash. No one's brought me down my entire collegiate career, and it ain't about to happen today to a dude built like a tank with beady little pigeon eyes too small for his head. Well, *technically*, I got tackled once during the last game of sophomore season. I landed on the field like a brick house when the fucker hit me, but it was worth it to watch the ref bite into that boy's ass like he'd just found some OG Big League Chew and was going to town. The asshat who tackled me got benched, the opposing team lost yardage, and I winked at him as he did the walk of shame off the field. A false start doesn't count against my record for no tackles, and I'm not about to let Thomas the Tank Pigeon take me down today.

I flex my fingers, already fantasizing about the hit of pebbled leather into the palm of my hand.

"Blue eighty-nine!" QB calls, and I smile. *Game on, bitches.* "Blue eighty-nine! Hut! Hut! HIKE!"

It happens fast as I sidestep the barrel of the tank and smirk as a lineman takes him to the field.

Danvers hikes the ball to Slaten. Slaten catches it in his white-gloved hands, taking two steps back as Danvers takes a hit for him, and passes it to his left to Smith, a wide receiver, who catches it and starts a fake run before he turns on his heel and throws long to Pince, a wide receiver up ahead of me.

I run up the field, my cleats cradled by the turf as Pince throws to our halfback, who catches the ball in white-gloved fingers and brings it in tight, searching the field for me as another one of our teammates slams into a defensive lineman a couple of yards away and takes him down with a roar.

Reigns looks at me, his jaw set, his green-and-white helmet glorious under the stadium lighting and throws long. It's a perfect throw as two of the Commanders on the opposite side of the field from me, those still standing, watch the spiral and make a run for it. My breath whooshes out from between my teeth as I dig the sole of my foot into the ground and push forward, my heart hammering inside my chest, adrenaline surging through my veins.

The ball falls in a beautiful arch, and I'm running and looking at it, watching as the Commanders zero in. Not that they'll ever catch me. Not that I'll let them.

The ball hits my outstretched gloved hand, and I bring it in tight as I run. My cleats pound the field, and I breathe in through my nose and out through my mouth. In and out, in and out, fast but steady. I don't turn back, though I could. There's no way they can catch me down. There's a reason the track team tried to recruit me freshman year.

I'm fast. Five-minute-mile, the-field-smoldering-beneath-my-feet fast, and none of these boys are going to keep up with me now. The roar of the stadium crescendos as I pass the fifteen-yard line, then the ten, then the five.

Three.

Two.

One.

TOUCHDOWN!

I slam the ball into the ground and roar at the crowd, raising my hands as they scream and shout along with me. My heart still hammers against my ribs as Coach claps on the sidelines. Is that a smile I see from him? It's gone as quickly as I spot it, like a trick of the light.

The stadium speakers broadcast the jingle for touchdowns followed by the radio announcer, "Blakely Brings. It. Hoooomm-mmmeeee!"

My brothers jog over to me, congratulating me as the Commanders sulk and look at me like they hate my pretty guts. In fairness, if I were them, I'd hate me too.

I blow the nearest one a kiss that makes him wince as Slaten throws his arm over my shoulder.

"You fast little fucker," he says with a laugh. "I can't believe you pulled it off."

"We pulled it off," I correct.

"Damn right," he says with a grin. "We pulled it off." Then he starts a chant, his fist punching into the air, and we all join in, chanting through the handshakes with the opposing team and the celebratory dunking of Coach beneath the Gatorade cooler and into the tunnel back into the locker room.

The locker room buzzes with energy, the team psyched about the win. Coach comes in to congratulate us and shake my hand as Danvers snaps a rolled-up towel across my ass. It lands with a sting and a *smack*, and I look around at him, my gear on the bench behind me.

"Mmm," I tell him with a grin, "*harder*, big boy."

Slaten howls with laugher while the rest of the team guffaws. Danvers throws me a kiss, and I can't keep my shit together. I crack, laughing with the rest of the team as Jones gawks at us, shirtless and smiling from down the row of green-painted lockers.

Then he turns bright red and starts laughing too, shaking his head and murmuring to himself. I howl even harder, grabbing onto my locker for support. I strip, shower, and change into my post-game party attire. Some of the boys like to wear their jerseys all night, but not me. I don't have a mysophilia kink, and I'm not about that stank.

"Party at DST," one of our new teammates—a freshman who joined this season—calls on my way out, but it isn't a surprise. Delta Sigma always throws us a party after a win. I'll stop by, enjoy myself, and get a certain Red-headed torpedo out of my head. I pull my jeans away from my crotch as I head further down the tunnel and into the lower level of the stadium.

I always fuck after a game, burning through all the unspent adrenaline. Normally, I'd find Mel and go at it like an animal. She always liked it rough. She said the best sex was when I was riding the high of a win and trying to pound my pent-up energy into her. And I have a lot of pent-up energy tonight. I feel like I could punch a hole through a wall with my dick at the moment, but the game can't take all the credit.

Red.

The spitfire left me ready to blow last week, and unsurprisingly, I'm not getting over it anytime soon. I bared my soul to her, and she threw a bucket of ice water over my head.

She. Chose. Him.

I can't lie, it hurt.

She won't even give us a chance, choosing a loveless marriage over a shot at something more, something with me. I'm not used to getting told no, yet she's developed a talent for it.

No, she won't end the engagement.

No, she won't fuck me.

No, she won't choose me.

Can you blame her, though? The thought sours the high I'm riding from the game.

She's right. I am known for fucking, not feelings, and if the situation was reversed, as much as I don't want to admit it, I'd doubt her sincerity too, but something has . . . *switched*. Maybe before our kiss, but certainly after I learned that she was allergic to pomegranate.

She's allergic.

One bite, and I could have killed her.

She could've fucking died.

It's so much more final than a bullshit piece of paper with my pops. She wouldn't be there to stick her hands on her hips and glare up at me. She wouldn't have the chance to glower at me and stand her ground, not giving an inch. She wouldn't be . . . with *me*.

Fuck, maybe this is all part of her master plan, to buy 2-for-1 Blakelys and steal the entire empire, but the more I think about it, the more I find I don't care. A terrifying thought. Everything I've given up my own life for—my independence and autonomy free from my father's control—washed down the drain like dirty dishwater.

She has her reasons for the union, and my father has his, but whatever they share is nothing more than an extended business deal. It isn't real. We could be real.

I must be losing my damn mind.

She wants nothing to do with me. She told me to get out of her way, and she'd stay out of mine. She's wearing an engagement ring put there by my old man. Yet, she's all I can think about, all I've been able to think about since she stormed into Mel's office weeks ago and cursed enough to make a sailor proud. When she turned on her heel and skittered away, and I wondered what it would feel like to let her straight, fiery hair slide between my fingers and knead her juicy ass.

She's the first girl I've ever wanted to tell me no and actually mean it, not in the coquettish, hard-to-get way either. She wasn't setting up a challenge. She was slamming the door in my face and locking the deadbolt.

Then the way she looked at me when my father introduced her as his fiancée, when she called my bluff and told me to keep my hands to myself. God, it was hot-as-fuck.

I don't want her to marry my father and not just because I'm worried about her fucking up my plan for an easy life. I don't want her to marry him because I want her for myself. It's hard to admit. It hurts, and I don't like it. Maybe wanting her just means fucking these confusing feelings away and spilling them into her with my cum, or maybe it means something more, something *different*.

Jesus Christ, the blue balls must have given me blue brain as well.

I need her out of my head. She's going to drive me nuts before this is all over. My phone vibrates in my jean pocket, and I pull it out and spot a text from Mel. I swipe it open.

> MEL
>
> Congratulations on the win. Meet me at my place?

All my plans to go to the party obliterate. I'm back in business! If Red won't accept my offer, I'll find someone who will. I send a quick reply to Mel.

> ME
>
> See you in 20.

It's the longest twenty minutes of my existence, my dick like a hound dog that's caught a scent, before I pull up at her condo. I knock on the door, and she opens it quickly, dressed in nothing but a black lace thong. I barely have time to enjoy the view before she yanks me inside, shutting the door behind me.

Then she's on me, kissing me and rubbing her sweet tits against my chest.

"I missed your cock," she murmurs against my lips, purring when she finds my dick hard in my jeans. If we were in a real relationship, we'd probably talk about feelings and shit, but all I feel right now is the desire to fuck Red out of my system. We stumble through her foyer and into her living room. I'll take her upstairs later, but first, I need to be inside her.

I break away from her, lowering my mouth over a dusty rose nipple, and she arches against me with a moan before she claws across my abdominals, hitting every ridge.

She pushes me backward hard, and I let myself fall to her leather couch. She unhooks my belt and pulls my pants and boxers to my ankles, freeing my dick. Smiling, she sinks to her knees and looks up at me, her pupils huge, coloring her mocha eyes almost completely black. Then she lowers her mouth to my dick and sucks me like I'm her favorite lollipop.

Fuck yes!

I groan, pushing my hands into her hair and let her take control, bobbing and slurping and sucking me like a porn star.

"Goddamn, Mel," I murmur as she reaches between my legs to tickle my balls. I'm too big to fit in her mouth, but she takes me as far as she can, and I almost come on the spot.

She hollows her cheeks and speeds up, bobbing and looking up at me, her mouth full of my cock. My eyes roll back in my head, and my head lolls back against the couch.

Down, up. Down, up. She squeezes my balls. *Down, up.* She wraps a hand around the base and rubs in time with her mouth. I buck up against her. *Down, up. Down, up.*

Saliva and spit wet my crotch and spill across my thighs, but I don't care. If anything, it adds to how fucking hot this is.

Down, up. Down, up.

"I'm about to come," I grunt, and she hoovers me even faster, sucking and mewling. I'm going to fuck her so hard after this that her pussy will feel the bruises for weeks. It's probably what she's counting on.

I feel my balls tightening, and I'm so close, soft heat pools low between my legs, the pressure building.

"Oh," I say, delirious, my eyes shut as she sucks. "Oh fuck, Layne. Right there, baby."

Hold up.

A second later, I come, and she swallows, my eyes popping over as I spurt into her mouth. She's not looking at me when she sits back on her heels, her nipples hard. She lifts her thumb to the corner of her mouth.

"Who's Layne?" she asks.

Oh fuck! I did actually say that.

"No one," I say, feeling like a colossal dick.

She eyes me as I stuff my spent cock back into my pants.

"You've never done that before," she remarks.

What do I say? *I'm sorry? I fucked up? See, there's this girl, and she's put a curse on me, I think, and . . .*

Fuck!

"I think you should leave," she says, standing gracefully despite the tall black pumps she's wearing.

"Mel," I plead. "She's nothing. I'm . . . I'm sorry, all right?"

Goddammit!

She walks over to her chaise and picks up a silk robe, throwing it over her shoulders.

"It's fine," she says, offering me a smile. "It's just sex. I never expected monogamy." I know because you were *perfect.* "I'm just tired."

I call bullshit, but I don't fight her on it. I already feel like the world's biggest prick.

"Sorry," I murmur as I walk to the door and see myself out because I don't know what else to say.

I've caught a sickness, and her name is Layne Steele. I feel her in the nervous sweat on my brow and the feverish ache that dances across my skin. She's going to be the death of me before this is over.

I just know it.

13

ARCHIE

The weekend passes in a blur of self-pity and shots. I feel like a fuckboy for what I did to Mel, and it's a feeling I'm not familiar with. I'm the guy who makes women laugh, who never takes himself too seriously, and is always there when they want a good time. I'm not the one who leaves them unsatisfied and irritated with the taste of cum still on their tongue. But that's exactly what I did to her.

Luckily, Mondays are a Red-free day, but Tuesdays, I stall having to see her, stopping by the campus post office on the way to class and checking my P.O. box. I don't check it often enough, and when I do, it normally involves me tossing a pound of coupon inserts and advertisements in the shred bin. Sometimes, I get a card from Mom —normally a postcard from whatever country she's currently visiting—or a letter from my grandma. Occasionally, my friends back east send me glitter bombs, the remnants of which still sparkle on the post office floor. Apparently, it was Ian's idea after I sent him a bag of gummy bear dicks freshman year.

Because, ya know, he's a dick.

Fucker's glitter-bombed me *three* times in retaliation. Then Chase and Everett got together and sent me a card that played Footloose nonstop for seven hours straight with no option to turn it off. Joke's on them, though. I liked that one.

I pop my key into the gold lock of my box and turn it to the right. I pull out a massive stack of bullshit as expected and set it on a nearby table to sort through it.

Advertisements.

Coupons.

More advertisements.

More coupons.

A handwritten invitation to come back to a local church for sex addiction counseling. *Ha! Someone's got jokes!*

Even more ads.

Until I get to a small white envelope addressed to me and printed on paper embossed in gold.

Oh no. Surely not yet at least.

I thought planning the wedding would take at least a few months, but when your parents go all out every time they reconcile and invite half the freaking continent to their impending nuptials, you learn what a save-the-date card looks like.

You've got to be kidding me.

I tear into the envelope, nearly ripping it in two. Exactly as I suspected, a save-the-date card stares back at me.

Save the date
to celebrate the union of
Elijah Lee Blakely
&
Layne Anne Steele . . .

I skim the card. Two months. The girl who let me finger her in broad daylight behind a building on campus is marrying my father in two fucking months. This has got to be a goddamn joke. I can still feel the vise grip of her pussy on my fingers, and she's setting a fucking wedding date. I can't even fuck her out of my system without her ghost popping up in my brain and ruining the moment.

But she's getting married in *two months?!*

TWO. MONTHS!

Oh fuck this. Over my dead body is my father going to have her. If I can't have her, then he sure as fuck can't either. I don't give a shit if I have to chain her to my bed for the next eight weeks and gag her. I'll commit numerous felonies at this point because those two getting married is just . . .

Wrong?

Disgusting?

Irritating?

Drives you insane because why would she choose *him*?

Ding, ding, ding! All of the above!

I shove all the shit into the shred basket beneath the table and start toward class. She doesn't get to do this, not give us a chance and wed him. She doesn't love him. He doesn't love her. And we could be something, goddammit!

Jealousy scalds my insides as I jog through the quad. I don't know what I'm going to do, but I know it doesn't involve sitting in boring-as-fuck Statistics and watching her self-assured ass take notes. I'll fail both of us if I have to, even if it does piss the old man off. If she was going to tell him about Mel, she would have done so already, and he'd already be riding my ass about *jeopardizing my future*. Ha! What future when he's giving it all to a sugar baby so she'll ride his dick?

I bound up the steps into the building and down the hall, spotting the back of her head like a beacon as she walks toward the classroom. I barrel toward her, and she doesn't see me coming. She's in the doorjamb, inches from entering the classroom, when I catch the back of her backpack and yank her back, one hand still on the loop of her bag, the other at her back, shoving her down the hall. The suede boots she's wearing screech and scuff against the floor, but I don't give her the chance to fight me. I shove her into an unlocked classroom and shut the door.

"What the fuck?!" she snaps the moment before the motion sensor lights turn on, and I find her eyes latched on me. The tropical waters that normally reside in her irises aren't calm now. If anything, I swear I see them churning.

"End it," I snarl, my nails cutting into my palms, sending bolts of pain hammering through my hands.

She takes a step forward, eating away at the space between us and gets in my face, leaning up on her toes to do so. The words slash across her white teeth and land with her hot breath on my face.

"Fuck. You."

Everything holding me together splinters at once. She hasn't even raised a hand, yet it feels like she's cleaved me open and put my insides on display for the world.

"You wish," I snarl, searching her eyes for a sign, a reason there's an unraveling in my middle, spinning faster and faster with every step she takes toward my father.

"I *wish* you would leave me alone."

"I'll leave you alone when you admit it."

"Admit what?" she scoffs with a scornful laugh.

"That you feel it too."

She tips her chin in defiance. "I feel nothing for you, Golden Boy, that a vibrator can't fix."

I stab my finger at her chest, above her breasts, but the touch still shoots a bolt down to my dick just the same.

"You." *Poke.* "Want." *Poke.* "Me." *Poke.*

"I want to marry your father."

No one on this planet buys what she's selling.

"Marry me instead," I challenge, my finger still pressed against her pale skin, atop the constellation of freckles below her collarbone.

Her eyes go wide. "What?"

Yeah, fucking WHAT?!

"If you want the Blakely fortune so bad, then marry me, Red."

She shakes her head, laughing. "You've lost your goddamn mind."

Maybe.

Probably.

Most fucking definitely.

"No, I think I'm finally using it, *Layne*." I snarl, stepping forward and pushing her back until she's against the whiteboard, and there's nowhere else for her to go. I lean in, inhaling her sugar and cinnamon. I trap her legs between mine, flattening us together below the belt, then I let my words kiss the side of her face.

"I fucking want you so bad I can't stand it. I can't eat. I can't sleep. I can't have fun. I don't even recognize myself." She stops breathing, and I grin against her flesh as I brush my nose across her cheek. "You know what happens when I let another woman suck my cock? I say *your* goddamn name, like you're always here." I stab a finger above my temple. "Always in my brain, driving me crazy."

"My presence seems to do that to people," she remarks, breathless.

"Then marry me," I challenge. *Holy fuck. Am I actually being serious? I think I might be.* "It doesn't have to be this way for the next few years or until whenever he gets tired of you."

"You don't know what you're talking about."

I pull back and pin her with a stare. "I know I want you."

"That's not a reason to get married."

"Seems good enough to me," I remark with a cock of my eyebrow.

She laughs bitterly, and I can taste the spearmint of her toothpaste in the air.

"You don't want to marry me, Golden Boy. You want to fuck me."

Yes. No! Maybe.

"Hmm," I say, relishing the quiver of her flesh as I run a hand up and over her side and across her stomach. "If I marry you, I get to fuck you, right? So, what's the difference?"

"You don't marry someone just to fuck them," she snarls.

"Isn't that exactly what you're doing?" I challenge.

She gapes at me. That's right, Red. He didn't have to say the words to tell me what's up.

"You don't know what you're talking about."

I really wish she would stop saying that.

"Enlighten me then." I tell her, lowering my hand between her legs, beneath the waistband of the leggings she's wearing today. She sucks in a breath but doesn't stop me. It's all the permission I need.

I thrust two fingers through her slick folds and deep inside her, and she rocks against me.

"Always so wet for me, Red," I murmur.

She doesn't deny it, doesn't say anything, probably because I'm too busy finger-fucking her in this classroom.

"I *will* have you, Layne," I tell her, slowly thrusting in and out, dragging the pad of my fingers along with her walls. "Even if I have to wait years until he finds someone else. I'll be waiting, pretty girl, and I'll fuck the memory of him right out of you."

"S . . . stop," she says, her walls spasming around my fingers.

I *tsk*. "Say it like you mean it, Red, and maybe I'll listen."

She says nothing, but throws her head back against the board. I thrum her clit with my thumb, and she comes, calling out my name as her orgasm soaks my fingers. She looks at me, dazed, floating down from the clouds.

"You're really good at that."

"Let me show what else I'm good at," I murmur before I crush my lips to hers and sweep my tongue inside her mouth, licking, laving, biting, and sucking. She groans as I free my hands and wrap them around her ass, lifting her. She wraps her legs around me, and I carry her over to the desk at the front of the room. I don't give a fuck if anyone walks in at this moment because I'll do anything to have her.

I sit her ass on the edge as she kisses me back, her hands running over my stomach and around to my back, moaning and dry humping my dick. I yank her leggings down to her knees, and she wrestles with my belt and frees my cock. She stares at it and bites her lip. I want to take a photo and frame it forever before she gingerly reaches over and grabs my cock. I hiss as she starts to stroke, and I swear to God, she's going to be the death of me.

"Let me feel you, baby," I breathe as something shifts, and it scares the shit out of me. I have to have her, but I know as soon as I get a taste, it's never going to be enough.

I grab a condom from my wallet and slide it on. Then I scoot her ass to the edge and line us up, her pussy weeping across my dick.

We both stare as the thick head of my cock brushes against her, and I feel her stop breathing as I push inside, just a fraction of an inch, before she goes completely still, and I look up to see her crying.

What the fuck?

"Red," I say, unsure. This isn't a normal reaction for me. "Talk to me," but she has her eyes shut, and she's shaking against me, the cords in her throat jutting out with her clenched jaw.

What. The. Actual. Fuck?

"You're scaring me, beautiful," I tell her. "What's wrong?"

"I can't do this," she sobs, pushing me away from her. In one move, she pulls up her leggings and jumps down to the floor between us. Then she picks up her backpack and runs out of the room.

I scramble to put my dick away and start after her.

14

LAYNE

*W*hat have I done? What have I done?!
FUCK!

I almost gave it to him, the only thing Eli wants from me, and I almost gave it to his son and sole heir. I spread my legs and almost let him fuck me in a classroom on a teacher's desk in the middle of the day.

Like a whore, my mother would have said.

Slut.

Skank.

Cum dumpster.

The barbs she would have thrown at me hit head on and slice deep, drawing blood. You can't see it, but I can feel it, the gaping wounds oozing as something inside me—something akin to actually feeling awakes from its slumber—and it hurts. Make it stop!

Make it stop!

Please fucking stop!

I choke on a sob, the wetness between my legs unfamiliar. Golden Boy is addicting. I see why everyone loves him now. I was stupid not to see it before.

He points those big baby blues at you, gives you a wicked grin that shows his dimples, and shoots you a look—*that* look—and it's all over. It's his superpower apparently, conning women out of their panties. And bringing the dead back to life, too.

Cold and hate gives way inside me to warmth and yearning when he's near.

He scares the nothingness away. He thaws my frozen veins.

He's compulsion and obsession in a hard, powerful body.

I want him. I *need* him. I can't fucking take it!

You filthy, nasty whore!

The slap of my mother's hand burns across my cheek, just like it did years prior, when she could still leap like a feral animal and catch me off guard. Before the booze took away what was left of her mind and made her forget everything, her husband, herself, her only child. She wasn't any nicer though, even at the end when her mind started to go, and I prayed to God she would die. Pray for her death and then pray for forgiveness, the cycle never stopped, not for me, not until she finally ceased to exist.

The coroner, an old man with kind eyes, told me she threw a blood clot, likely caused by a recent fall that bruised her left femur, a fall that occurred among the stacks of shit she loved more than me. He had said her brain was riddled with damage, and it was likely she was suffering from alcohol-induced, early onset dementia, which would have progressed had she not died. The coroner said she had maybe six months left, and at least she gave me that I guess, six months of not having to deal with her hand-crafted version of hell.

The world trips and falls, and I go along with it. I'm in the hall, losing my mind. The students are staring at me, as someone far off in the distance asks if I am all right.

Like it matters.

Like anything matters when the only way to feel something is to cut and scar my flesh unless . . . unless you're with him.

The center of my heart splits apart and sends the liquid heat spurting into my chest cavity. I'm warm in the middle, a bright sun erupting inside me and burning me alive. Shame, regret, disgust, and my mother's sneer before her slap, it hits all at once.

You fucking cum slut! Spreading your legs for every boy you see!

I suffocate on another sob as I scramble to stand, the evidence of my arousal slick between my thighs. I don't get wet, not for Eli, not for another, not for anyone, not *ever*.

Except for him.

A guy with kind eyes and brown hair tries to help me stand, but I jerk away from him, stumbling until I'm headed down the hallway like a baby giraffe on its first day on earth. Bile scalds my throat as the slickness rubs between my thighs and soaks my panties.

One touch, and I was wet.

One look, and I opened my legs.

One kiss, and I was his.

Maybe my mother was right. Maybe I am a dirty fucking whore.

I scramble outside into the fresh air and then around the building, not even considering attending my other classes today. I have to get out of here. I have to get far, far away, where he won't torment me, where he won't break through the nothingness and the cold to make me feel alive.

It hurts!

I stumble across the lawn and around a service entrance until I reach the visitor's parking lot. I hop in my car and start the engine. The Camry fires to life on the first try, and I don't even have my seatbelt on before I shift her into reverse, back out of the spot, and hit the gas pedal. Tears cloud my vision, but I don't know why I'm still crying. Everything inside me is cold and dead again, and I have been erased from existence along with it.

I can still see and taste and hear and touch, though.

Traffic. Pennies. Buzz. Cold.

But it doesn't feel like I'm really here. Why would I be?

Your greedy cunts wants him? I'll show you what it's like when he rips you apart!

FFFFFFUUUUUCCCCCKKKKKK!

I sob into the car, the only sound apart from the buzz of the air conditioning, and depress the gas pedal, pulling out on the highway. I know where I'm going, where I should have gone weeks ago when I first received the notice of the tax sale. A good fiancée would call her husband-to-be and tell him she's going out of town, but I'm not good. Plus, he might call me, but I doubt it. He's on an airplane traveling across the world right now to seal an important business deal in Luxembourg.

I think he told me to impress me. He even offered for me to join, but the idea of riding on a private jet with him over miles and miles of ocean had me imagining jumping ship and drowning in the sea.

I drive until the tears stop and then dry, until the morning runs into afternoon and then evening, and I finally arrive.

Conway, California.

The place where I was raised.

Hell on earth.

By the time I arrive, I'm happy to feel nothing. Because this place was a living, breathing nightmare. My mother and father moved here after I was born for the job opportunities. The town's dried up now, though, abandoned and decaying as people move elsewhere for higher paying jobs, better schools, and less crime. Every year for as long as I can remember, the city has gotten worse, rotting from the inside out until the plaster began to crack and fall off the faces of city buildings and the graffiti artists couldn't even cover the worst of it.

I exit the highway and roll down Main Street, the lights in my car automatically turning on as dusk blankets the horizon. The city looks exactly how I remembered, a town on its last breath, desperately hoping something will show up and save it. Most of the businesses and restaurants are shuttered now, littering the sides of the roads with windows boarded up with plywood and for-sale-by-owner signs. I reach the corner mart I used to walk to when my mother needed beer or cigarettes, where she had me pay the homeless man who slept outside to get them for me. It's now closed too, shuttered by the recession that has gripped this town for nearly two decades.

I turn at the abandoned store and take the first right and then the first left, and there it is, the windows dark and a red notice stapled to the front door. I turn the car into the empty driveway, tall weeds growing in between the concrete cracks and reaching for the sky.

1694 Monroe East.

I park in the driveway, leaving my headlights fixed on the broken garage door that never quite shut evenly, like someone had hung it slightly diagonal. The truth, though, is behind that door and peeking out from the three inches exposed on the bottom of the left-hand side. You can see the corner of a cardboard box with hundreds of others stuffed along with it. All are filled with my mother's treasures, the only things that mattered to her after the loss of her husband.

Mouse shit and old newspapers meant more to her than me.

I sit there for a moment in my car and just look at it. The paint peels from the siding and loose shingles lay on the roof. The house looks worse than before I left, when I took the money I had begged, borrowed, and stolen and applied to Arlean University.

I climb out of the car in the fading hours of daylight because there's no way in fuck I'm going in there at night. I've had many nightmares about suffocating to death beneath the hoard, and although some of it was cleared when the EMTs arrived, declared my mother dead, and took her body, it's only a small path. The rest of it rots where it sits. I dig my house key out of the center console and walk to the front door, little bits of gravel crunching beneath my feet. I thrust the key into the doorknob and jiggle it until I feel it unlatch. Then I open the door.

The smell hits me first, the stench of death and decay, mold and something far more sinister. Roaches scatter, and they really must be able to survive the apocalypse because God knows what they found in here to live off of. I try the light switch, but I'm not surprised when the light overhead doesn't turn on. The power company probably killed the electricity months ago.

I turn on the flashlight on my phone and step inside, my eyes stinging and my throat closing at the stench. It's worse than I remember, but it's not surprising. The home has been vacant and unconditioned, stewing through the Californian spring and summer. I step over the carcass of a dead mouse and descend further into the darkness, the light from the door doing little to permeate the walls of rotting trash surrounding me. My mother's recliner is still in the space cleared by the EMTs, rotting in the living room. There's a dark stain there, marring the plaid fabric where she pissed and soiled herself at the end, dying in her own filth. It's getting hard to breathe, and I can taste the garbage decomposing around me. My light illuminates the stacks of trash with every tremble of my hand.

Stained food boxes and dust-covered magazines.

Dirty clothes thrown on top of piles of yellowed newspapers, chewed in the corners by mice and mottled with their droppings.

The ceiling bulges above me from all the trash my mother stuffed into the attic when she couldn't find any more room downstairs, bowing it in the middle of the room, like at any moment, it's going to split apart and send the entire attic down on top of my head. My heart rate kicks up a notch as I spot the black water marks and mold there. I scoot between two tall stacks of decaying cardboard and yellowed newspapers, so tall they almost touch the ceiling. I suck in a breath and close my eyes as I pass them, careful not to knock either one over. The house of cards could fall at any moment. It was unsafe before the EMTs arrived, and then they moved pieces, and like a 3-D puzzle, things started to fall.

Finally, I stand in front of the fireplace, shining the light of my phone across it, over the brick work peeking out from behind the piles of books my mother had stacked on the wooden mantle. I comb over the photographs there and the knickknacks until I find the one thing I came back for, the only thing I wanted to keep: a picture of my father when he was younger on the day of his college graduation, smiling at the camera, his brownish-blonde hair scooping down over his eyes. He laughed at something the photographer had said, smiling in pure joy I couldn't hope to feel.

This was my father before I knew him, before it all went bad, and my mother stopped caring, drowning in the booze until she changed into something unrecognizable, mean, vile, and downright despicable. This is the guy that knew a different person, and in the photograph, when he smiled, it looked like he would own the world some day.

PART III

DUSK

— Gil (Years Prior) —

Smoke murmurs through the black of nothingness before my eyes pop open, my forehead still flat against my desk. An alarm blares in the building, and all my senses are slapped awake at once.

Slivers of smoke.

Pops and crackles of a nearby fire.

The bite of ash in the air, needling my eyes and stinging my nostrils.

Fuck.

Rumbling sounds in the distance, low beneath the shrieking fire alarm. I jump to my feet, throwing my chair back into the bookcases behind my desk as I do. I grab my keys out of the top drawer of my desk and dart out of my office into the wide-open room, the cubicles, chairs, and computers long sold to pay the creditors. Smoke seeps beneath the doors on the opposite side, pushing plumes of gray and white into the air.

It doesn't smell like a campfire. It reeks of chemicals and

charred plastic and shit that shouldn't be burned. I cough as I cover my mouth and stare at the haze that's clouding the room.

Shit. Shit. Shit!

I dart toward the emergency exit, the stairwell twenty feet or so away from me. My loafers pad against the thin, commercial carpet. My heart thrashes in my chest, and I cough again into my hand as my mouth dries, my tongue thick and heavy. I reach the heavy metal door and hit both palms against the panic bar, swinging it open into the concrete wall behind it with a dull *thunk*.

The lights in the stairwell are still on, and my feet hit the smooth concrete of the first stair a moment later.

Tap, tap, tap sounds as I race down the steps, running for my life.

15

LAYNE

I stand in the living room of my mother's house, staring down at the photograph, the walls of filth fading to night with the setting sun. I inch backward, away from the fireplace and the mantle above it, between the towers of trash. There's no room to turn around, and my fingers skim the rotting stacks as my feet slowly find my way. Something squelches loud and wet beneath my shoe, and hackles of disgust skitter up my spine.

Don't look down, Layne. Don't. Look. Down.

The stench of mildew and decay poisons the air as my bare forearms scrape against folded newspapers, the brittle paper crumbling against my skin. I keep inching back, holding the photograph of my father in one hand, until I'm finally at my mother's favorite chair, the rotting recliner she pasted herself onto during her final days.

My gaze drifts in the final breaths of the dying light down to my mother's recliner, the green-and-gray plaid fabric covered in dirt. Putrid black seeps through the middle and onto the precious patch of carpet in front of it, and there's a carton of cigarettes where she left them on the end table next to the chair. Bits of trash litter the space, left by mice that have chewed through her knickknacks and treasures. Beer bottles and loose caps sit discarded on the end table too, next to a jade ashtray overfilled with chewed-up cigarettes. I don't know why she never smoked them. Like it fucking mattered that she didn't when she drank herself to death instead. A box of matches lays there too, among the filth, unopened and yellowing beneath the plastic wrapper.

I pluck it from the table and keep shuffling backward. The box is sticky and small in my palm as I pass the recliner until I'm finally able to turn around. I leave the rest of it—the photographs, the loose change, all my mother's precious treasures, the shit she loved more than me. I stare at the sunlight filtering in through the open doorjamb as I run my thumb over the top of the box, the plastic wrapping crinkling as I do.

I step outside into the last rays of sunlight, finally able to breathe again without my lungs roasting from the stench. A dog barks off in the distance, and an engine revs a few blocks over, but everything else is quiet and still, utterly blank and lifeless around me.

I turn around in the doorjamb, looking back at the hoard. I easily tear away the plastic around the box of matches, and it flutters to join the trash and dirt imprinted onto the stained carpet. I open the box and pluck a single match out, rolling the sliver of wood between my thumb and forefinger.

Back and forth, back and forth, feeling the thin sides of the wood.

I look down at the matchbox and light the match. I watch as the tiny flame, orange with tips of blue, dances against the dark.

I shouldn't do it.

I could get arrested.

I could go to jail.

I don't care.

I feel the frigid chill of my nonexistence as I throw the match onto the trash, watching as it lands on the newspapers stacked alongside my mother's chair. It takes a moment, a second or maybe two, before the paper catches light and the flames grab hold. Smoke blankets the stench of rot and mold as the fire spreads onto another pile, stretching up and chewing at the yellow-stained ceiling above. From one pile to another, across my mother's shit-stained chair, until the entire living room glows orange and yellow and burns hot against my face, smoke fogging the air and scalding my lungs.

I cough, but I stay.

I choke, but I don't move.

I stand there, watching it burn, until it's hard to breathe, until sweat pops up on my face, and the heat licks at my skin. Only when I can't stand it anymore do I finally step back outside, the flames following me, warming my back as smoke billows through the front door.

I walk to my car, the house crackling and popping behind me as I fulfill my childhood dream. Only it's over a decade late, and I don't want a firefighter to save me now. I don't need rescuing. I need fucking retribution.

Something thunders inside the house, shattering windows with the force, and I look back to find the roof has caved in above the living room, shingles falling into a giant hole cratered into the middle of the home. Four walls and a roof reduced to one big tinder box of my mother's creation.

Good. Let it all burn.

I open my car door and step inside, starting the engine and backing down the driveway. I'd hoped to feel something as I watched the place of my nightmares fall victim to the fire. I'd thought, in the moment at least, that I might even feel . . . happy.

But I'm as dead and cold as ever. I can't even be bothered to *want* to feel anymore.

I am numb.

Detached.

Frozen.

Utterly ambivalent.

Ice in my middle spider-crawls through my veins and whittles away at my fingers and toes.

I'm dead on the inside, where it counts.

I drive three blocks north and stop at an overgrown park I used to visit as a child. At least back then, the place was somewhat inviting. Now it looks more like an outdoor meth den than a playground for children. Homeless people have set up camp on the outskirts of it, rows of sun-faded tents and pieces of plywood making their tiny homes. I turn off the engine, pocket my keys, and step outside into the cool air. I can smell the burn of the house even here, and it prickles at my eyes and my nostrils as the blare of fire engines draws closer.

Wee-ooo. Wee-ooo. Wee.

The sounds fade to nothing as I take a seat on a park bench, the cracked wood hard and unforgiving against my ass. I fiddle with my keys and unlatch the hidden blade on a keychain I bought off a guy at my high school years ago. It's definitely illegal, or if it's not, it should be, but I don't plan on using it on anyone else.

It's enough to hurt myself.

Well, until I can hurt Eli, at least.

I bring up a knee and sit half crisscross on the park bench. I take the blade to the inside of my thigh and cut through my leggings, splitting them open, until I see the scars, still pink and raised from my last round.

It's going to be a bitch to cover them up for work.

Not that I care.

I finger the sharp slice of the blade before I take it to one of the old marks, thin and white, faded by time. I watch, mesmerized, as I follow the line of the scar, splitting it open once more. The pain knocks against the numb and recedes. The smoke carries thicker in the air, cloudy as the wind pushes it my way, like even after its death, the fucking place still tries to haunt me.

I go again, pressing the blade deeper this time, and watch as my blood falls onto the silver wood of the bench, staining it a ruddy brown. A hiss slices past my teeth as my flesh opens, unzipping beneath the blade. More blood falls, and I'm mesmerized, staring at the shiny sanguine drops as they pool on my thigh and fall to the wood, oozing between the boards and spilling over, dripping down to the dry, hard earth. It smells like copper pennies, the scent so thick I can almost taste it on my tongue.

Drip.

Drrrrüüpppp.

The ground doesn't accept my sacrifice. My blood sits,

suspended on the surface, staining the tawny weeds. I drop the blade and dig my thumb into the wound. Shards of pain slice through my leg and radiate outward as I press even harder, going deeper, forcing the cut to open, coating the end of my thumb in red.

The numb evaporates.

Scalding pain takes over.

The sirens continue to scream, but the sound is distant, far away. I watch as my thumb rolls across the cut, captivated by the gleam of my blood. A man, his beard long and matted, his clothes dirty and torn, peeks his head out of his tent and eyes me warily before disappearing back inside. I barely see him as he does.

Another drop of my blood falls to the ground and stains the earth. Night curtains the world as I sit there until the smoke in the air dissipates and the sirens silence, until one lone dog barks and the man rustles inside his tent.

I sit there until the cut finally clots, and my blood dries and cracks like flaking rust across my skin. I sit until the pain recedes to a dull ache, and an owl hoots in the distance.

My phone vibrates on the bench beside me. Eli's name flashes across the screen along with dozens of missed notifications from an unknown number. I don't have to check to know who they're from.

Golden Boy.

God only knows how he got my number. But I suppose with the connections he has, he could probably get my blood type and a copy of my social security card if he wanted them.

I ignore both Blakelys.

Maybe I should just kill Eli before the wedding, slit his throat with a razor blade and see if my frozen heart thaws. I think I might even feel something when the light fades from his eyes, leaving them as dead and cold as the man who once owned them. But then I wouldn't get the satisfaction of destroying his precious empire too.

I could let his son fuck me first. Wouldn't that be ironic? Saving myself for the father and giving it to the son. If the rumors are true, he's one hell of a fuck. The freak has fan clubs for fuck's sake. They aren't obnoxiously big, but still, fan clubs. *Plural.*

Hell, maybe he'd even scare away the nothingness with his rumored-to-be massive cock.

Maybe I'd feel something again.

Maybe . . . but I doubt it.

I stand, snatching my phone. I walk back to my car, hobbling a little as I do. Then I start the long drive back to campus, leaving the stretch of rotting shit and smoke behind me with every passing mile.

16

LAYNE

I skip my apartment and head straight for campus, abandoning half a Red Bull and a bottle of water in the car. I'm tired, but even more than that, I'm hungry. I have to go to class today. I've missed too much already. I dig a pair of black shorts from my gym bag on the floorboard of the back seat and slide them over my cut leggings. Dried blood still stains the inside of my thigh, though I wipe it from my hands as best I can.

I fish a hoodie out of the backseat too and slide it on, letting it swallow me. Then I grab my backpack out of the back and head across campus to the cafeteria. The world jiggles but doesn't quite wobble as I walk, and my stomach pinches with hunger. The sun is too fucking bright, and I pull the hood of my hoodie up and over my head as far as it will go.

Shit. It's still too bright as everything goes white-washed for a second and fades beneath the light.

I stumble over a bump on the sidewalk and immediately right myself with a few steps forward. The rush of a crumbling wave floods my ears and then recedes. The world teeters again, and I latch onto a nearby light pole to steady myself.

"Fuck," I mutter as a cheerleader passes by, dressed in her uniform and everything. She gives me a wide berth and eyes me like I'm diseased.

Did I cut too deep? This has never happened before.

Or maybe it's the blood loss and my living off liquid caffeine and hate.

Well, the smoke inhalation probably isn't helping matters.

No, it's definitely all the above combined with having to visit my mother's final resting place. I don't care where they dug a hole and threw in her decrepit body. She died in that house long before they put her jutting bones and leathery skin into the ground.

I hold onto the lamppost, trying to blink away the white spots that speckle my vision. The world shines beneath the glow of a flashlight, and I grip harder for support. My stomach pinches hard again, and it's gnawing away at me, whittling through me from the inside out.

I have to eat.

Move, Layne! Move!!!

With a steadying breath, I release my grip on the lamppost and resume my walk to the campus cafeteria. I'm still unsteady, but I manage to not faceplant on my way there. It feels like ages pass before I finally arrive at the cafeteria. It's an enormous building, all modern architecture made of glass, marble, and steel with giant stone pillars that reach for the heavens. I manage the steps and enter the building, following the roped lines until I arrive at a row of card-access turnstiles. I head for the one straight ahead and swipe my campus ID through the machine. It clicks and lets me through, telling me in its automatic voice to have a good day.

It's loud and bustling even for this early in the morning. The promise of coffee and hot food lingers in the air, but the lines are long, ten or more people ahead of me in each one, so I turn to bypass them. The world does a topsy-turvy thing that can't be a good omen for staying conscious. I manage not to fall and beeline for the grab-and-go section, snatching the first two things I reach, a chocolate-chip muffin wrapped in cellophane and a bottled orange juice. I swivel, a little unsteady, and head for the checkout counter when a big body intersects my path.

My nose stops millimeters from crunching against a broad chest, and I step back, taking a long look at the roadblock.

There's a broad chest attached to a big, tall body.

Well, a broad chest attached to a big, tall, *rock-hard* body.

Okay, technically, a broad chest attached to a big, tall, *rock-hard* body owned by none other than my nemesis.

Archie Blakely.

Fuck me.

Golden Boy peers down his nose at me and smiles. He's sporting his football team jersey and a pair of light blue jeans, his thumbs curled around the belt loops. He looks good enough to eat.

Fuckety fuck.

"Layne," he says, my name rolling off his tongue a little too familiar as his ridiculous smile stays in place.

I roll my eyes at his highness.

"Out of my way," I mumble, moving forward and bumping straight into his chest when he doesn't actually get out of my way.

Ow.

I rub my nose and scowl at him. *Both* of him.

Oh God. It's a nightmare come true. I blink his twin away.

"Where have you been?" he asks, his smile faltering as his arms cross over his jersey. The veins in his hands jut out with the movement, trailing up his tan arms.

Holy hell.

Since when does he have such manly hands?

My heart flounders, and I don't know if the culprit is my low blood sugar or his presence, but I choose the former because the latter is just not acceptable.

I glare up at one-and-a-half of him.

"Move," I demand.

He cocks his head—heads—at me and regards me with his crystal-clear blue eyes.

"Sorry," he says, "I couldn't hear you over the sound of you running away again."

"Move!" I snap.

"Make me," he challenges, raising one delicious eyebrow.

I swear to God if I don't eat in thirty seconds, I'm taking a bite out of him. I dart to my left to go around him. I don't have time for this.

He intersects my path . . . *again.*

"We need to talk," he says, arms crossed, frowning.

"No, we don't," I say. "There's nothing to talk about, Princess. I need to eat, and you need to get outta my way."

The corner of his mouth quirks. "Did you just call me Princess?"

"I'm sorry I offended you, *Your Majesty.*" I try to push him out of my way. It's like hitting a brick wall. RIP, my palms. "Now move."

"Aw, pretty girl," he leans down, his arms still folded across his chest, and whispers hot words over my hair, "we both know I'm the king, and it's time for you to kneel."

"Fuck no."

"Why? You'd look so pretty on your knees."

A traitorous flush blossoms across my cheeks, and I feel the warmth of it blistering over my skin.

"Get out of my way," I hiss, talking to one-and-a-half of him again.

So I can think straight without wanting to taste you.

He ignores my command and considers my choice of food.

"What's with the grub? I figured you were a born-again vegan or something as much as you hated on Carter's burger the other day."

What in all the fucking stars is this two-legged vibrator saying?

"Who?"

He. Needs. To. Move.

"My friend, the one whose lunch you deposited in my lap."

Ohhhh . . . that Carter.

"Sorry," I murmur, the world doing that bright thing again as I try to side-step him.

"No you're not," he says, easily intercepting me. "You're not getting out of having this conversation."

"What conversation?" I snap.

"The one we're having right now," he leans in and runs his

tongue across his teeth. "The one where we talk about how you'll marry my dad, but not me."

I nearly laugh, but it comes out as a wheeze and makes me dizzy.

"You're out of your mind," I dash around him, but the movement is too much, too fast, too . . . *bright.* I stumble and nearly fall.

"Whoa," he says, wrapping a big arm around me and holding me upright against his chest. He feels so safe, so solid. I breathe him in and relax a little. I hate myself for it.

"Are you okay, Layne? You look paler than usual." There's concern in his voice, and I don't like it. He shouldn't be concerned. Not for me.

"I'm fine," I try to shoo him away, but somebody keeps turning out the lights.

"Oooookay, time to sit," he says, steering me toward a chair and taking my backpack off my shoulder and depositing it onto the seat next to me. He calls something to the lady at the checkout lane before he unscrews the lid from my juice and slides the bottle across the table at me.

"Drink," he says, and I do until I finish the whole bottle and need to breathe. I'm exhausted but not quite so dizzy when I'm done.

"You look like hell," he remarks, eyeing me with a frown.

I cock my head at him. "You look . . ." *delectable,* "like God ran out of hair dye."

"You love the blond, pretty girl."

Yes. "No, I don't."

He opens the muffin, the wrapper crinkling as he does and pushes it across the table at me. "Want to tell me what's going on?"

"I'm fine," I say, the juice in my stomach rolling. If I eat that muffin, I'm definitely going to throw up on the campus's star running back.

"You don't look fine."

"I . . ." *Why are there two of him again? Isn't one enough?*

"Come on," he says, standing and coming around the table to my side.

"Why?" I shake my head at him and immediately regret the decision.

"Because you like Casper and the color white had a baby."

"White is not a color," I grumble. "It's the absence of color."

He leans in, wrapping an arm around my arms and hoisting me to my feet. Hell, he smells like a burning fire and sugar cookies, and I again have the urge to bite him.

"Everything's a color when it's on you, Red," he murmurs against my ear, grabbing my backpack and sliding it over one shoulder.

What does that mean?

"Where are we going?" I ask as he steers me to the exit.

"My place."

My heart hiccups in reply.

"I'm not sleeping with you, Blakely," I manage, the world tilting.

He chuckles soft and low, the sound vibrating inside his chest.

"Trust me, beautiful, when we hook up, there won't be any sleeping involved."

Heat flares in my middle, incinerating my breath along with it.

"But," he continues, "I'm just dropping you off. I've got class and stuff to do before the game tonight."

"No," I whine, fighting him, though his grip around me tightens. "I can't miss class today."

"Don't worry," he says. "I have a hookup. I'll get the absences taken care of."

Of course he has a hookup.

With his help, I walk to his fraternity, and he helps me up the stairs, passing a couple of tall guys on the landing, who look at me like their eyes have bugged out of their heads. *Fucking weird.*

Then we keep climbing.

"Too many stairs," I complain.

A second later, I'm lifted, one of his arms under my knees and the other around my back.

"Better?"

My whole body purrs at the soft, low word.

"Mhmm," I say, nestling into his warmth, my eyes closing.

He keeps climbing, strong and steady.

"I'm too heavy," I grumble, but I don't put up much of a fight. There's a weight on me, pressing down on my eyelids, slowing my heart rate, and calling me to the darkness of sleep.

"You're perfect," he answers, walking down a long hallway until he stops in front of a stained wooden door, undecorated and completely nondescript. *Also weird.*

He fidgets with the doorknob to his room and carries me inside.

The place smells like him. Vanilla and fire, sweet hedonism. I barely catch a glimpse of his place before he deposits me on the bed, and I give in, letting the comforter hold me. God, the guy knows how to pick his bedding. I snuggle in deeper.

"Shh," his breath tickles my ear as he lifts my legs and slides me into his bed, beneath the smooth, cool sheets.

"I can't wait until I'm old," I say, nestling into the cocoon of blankets.

He chuckles low, and my heart sighs in response. "Why's that, Red?"

I answer to his pillow, my eyes closed. "Because then I can forget you and your beautiful face."

He chuckles again, and I feel the bed dip as he leans over me, his hands on the pillow on either side of my head. Warmth flitters across my back and over my ass as he presses closer.

"Oh, pretty girl," he whispers against my hair, "after we fuck— and we *will* fuck—you'll never be able to forget me."

He presses a kiss to the back of my head as sleep beckons in the distance and guides me home.

17

LAYNE

*W*ake up.

Archie's voice carries to me, sinking down to pillow me in warmth. His rumbled chuckle follows, settling over my skin, and I nestle deeper into the comforter. It's soft and fluffy and smells like him.

Wake up, pretty girl.

"No," I murmur into his bed. I want to stay here, hidden from the world, forever.

Something bangs outside his room, and laughter follows, pulling me from my dreams. I wake up in a foreign bed, alone.

What the fuck?

Where am I?

Oh shit . . . Golden Boy.

The puzzle pieces of this morning slide together as I sit up in bed.

I razed my mother's home.

I cut too deep.

I nearly passed out.

Dammit.

I should probably be skeeved out by sitting in the pretty running back's bed. It feels . . . intrusive being here, in his space, looking across the room at his desk, polished, black-painted wood that looks expensive even from here. There are some loose pens on the desk in a pile in the corner and an empty charging port for his laptop, but not much else. My gaze scrolls away, past his bathroom and the white subway tile that runs up the walls of the shower, to the open door of his closet. I spot his clothes hanging inside on velvet hangers, his shoes on a wooden rack on the floor, and a small dresser tucked at the back.

Everything is neat and tidy, and it's so against everything I would have expected that it throws me for a loop. Where are his smelly socks on the floor and rancid gym clothes? Where are the annoyingly large barbells and the half-eaten bags of chips? Or a trashcan overfilling with crushed beer cans and suspicious tissues? Where's all the gross guy stuff?

I pull myself further out of bed and look around the room. It's actually sort of . . . nice, for a room in a frat house, at least. Golden Boy may live his life lackadaisical and care-free in public, but his space reflects something entirely different.

Control, order . . . restraint.

Interesting.

Now would be the perfect time to rifle through his shit and find an ugly secret to hold over his head, but something stops me. I can't bring myself to do it, not today, not after he helped me. Tomorrow, maybe, but right now . . .

Fuck, maybe Golden Boy is starting to rub off on me.

The thought is unacceptable, so I blame it on the blood loss and shitty day.

My inner thigh aches where I reopened the old scar. I need to clean the area and bandage it. I need a shower and a change of clothes and dreamless sleep too.

My phone buzzes, and I look over the lip of the bed to find Archie left my backpack on the floor. I rifle through the front pocket and retrieve my phone. Eli's name pops up on the screen.

3 missed phone calls.

7 unanswered texts.

Shit! Shit! Shit!

I dial his number quickly, and he picks up on the first ring.

"Layne," he says, and by his tone alone, I know he's clenching his teeth.

"Eli," I breathe back at him. "You're back in town?"

"I landed five hours ago."

Fuck. How long have I been asleep? How many classes did I miss now?

I bite the inside of my cheek to stifle my groan. "Oh okay. Class . . ."

"Meet me at my place," he snaps. I swear I feel the sting of his words as they lash across my skin.

Or I could gouge out your eyeballs with my thumbs instead.

"Of course," I manage. I've come too far to tap out now.

Get it together, bitch!

"Wear what I like," he orders a second before he disconnects the line.

Gouging out his eyeballs is looking better by the second.

Eli knows this isn't a marriage for love, but he still expects me to play the part. That part includes *not* ignoring him. Hell, any reasonable gold digger would have been all over him the moment he touched down back in Cali.

Not in his son's room . . . in his bed . . . secretly wishing he was here too . . .

"Fuck," I grumble, scrambling out of bed. I eye a pad of Post-It notes on his desk and quickly debate scribbling a short thank you note to Golden Boy. I discard the thought quickly.

I don't need him getting the wrong idea. My body may want him, but my brain has other plans. In no world do Archie Blakely and I end up together, and the quicker he accepts that, the better. I'll never forgive his family for the destruction of mine, and he'll never forgive me after I steal his birthright and put a knife through his father's heart, if the elder Blakely even has one, that is.

Fuck, could I imagine it though, giving in to Golden Boy, touching him, being with him. Mouths and hands fumbling every-where, us stumbling to the door to his room while he fumbles with the key, before we tumble inside a moment later, me landing on top of him on the bed.

A hot string untangles low in my belly, burning my breath away with it.

Filthy, nasty slut!

My mother's voice severs the fantasy, and I jerk back into action, swinging my backpack over my shoulder and leaving Golden Boy's space. The hallway, thankfully, is mostly empty, but two guys on the opposite end of the landing stare at me when they catch me leaving his room.

"Come on, boys. Didn't your mommas ever tell you staring is rude?" I say, flashing a grin as I pass.

It's not like I'm the first girl to slink out of Blakely's apartment.

Unless . . . wait, what did the blond man-ho say the first day of class?

I don't invite people over to my room, Red. Ever. It's a once-in-a-lifetime invitation.

Surely . . . I mean no way, right? . . . *Right?*

I choose not to jump onto that crazy thought train and bound down the stairs, not even giving the frat boys a second glance. I walk out the front door of Phi Epsilon Alpha, and I'm feeling a lot better than I did this morning, though I can still smell the smoke from the fire on me and could use a cup of coffee . . . or the entire pot. I beeline across campus toward my car and head back to my apartment. I shouldn't keep Eli waiting, but he can't see me like this, especially not after he told me to wear what he likes, which can only mean *one* thing, to wear what I wear at work, minus the mask, of course.

My first night in the club, Eli snatched it right off my face, breaking the silk ties at the back. Uncovering your face goes against strict club rules for the girls and patrons alike, but even my boss wouldn't question the mighty Eli Blakely, and he knew it. A moment later, he pulled me into his lap and smiled at me, apparently happy with what he saw.

"Now what do I have to do to fuck you?" he had murmured, his tongue sneaking out to taste the line of my jaw, though I barely felt it. It's hard to feel anything when you're dead inside.

In a couple of months, at the end of the semester, we'll be wed, and then I can walk away, my family vindicated, filthy rich and single. Until then, I've gone too far not to keep him happy.

Further down the fucked-up rabbit hole I go.

When I get home, I shower, dress, and prepare myself in record time. Eli's town car picks me up twenty minutes later, and it's a too-fast drive before it deposits me outside his building, the glass and metal skyscraper looming in front of me. I thank the driver and start up the steps, my heels clicking on the concrete.

This is getting too messy, too complicated for my liking, and I frown as I enter the lobby. The security guard knows my face and nods to me before I enter the elevator and hit the button for the penthouse. Golden Boy has become an annoying fixture in my life. Now I'm sneaking out of his dorm room and back to my fiancé? What is wrong with me?

I'm fucking everything up. I have the opportunity to destroy Eli Blakely on his throne of blood, yet I find myself caring less and less about vengeance every day. I think of the son when I should be thinking of the father.

Get your shit together, Layne!

Eli buzzes me into his apartment after I hit the call button, and I open the door, my stilettos clacking on the black marble floor. I hate coming here. Eli's home—and I use that term loosely—feels like a tomb. Everything's black and gray, and despite the huge rooms stretching across the entire first floor of the building, the walls seem to close in around you. Like every minute, they're moving forward an inch or two until, suddenly, you're pinned between them and you don't know how it happened. This is also where I'm most vulnerable, and Eli knows it. He could lock me in here and keep me captive for weeks, and no one would know. Hell, probably the only thing stopping him is a strong survival instinct that warns I'd definitely try to kill him for it.

I make my way through the bare living room and down the long hall to Eli's office at the rear of the apartment. I raise my knuckles to tap on the door but stop when Eli calls, "Come on in."

I walk inside, finding him seated at his desk, a cigar smoking on a solid gold ashtray and a glass of liquor, empty except for a sliver of amber-colored liquid at the bottom of the glass, in front of him.

"How was your trip?" I ask him.

"Strip," he commands, the word razor sharp.

Fuck. He's in one of those moods.

My mother's voice stays away, like it always does for him. Because the bitch can only ruin my happiness, and I am far from happy with Eli.

I undo the buttons on the peacoat and drop my coat on a black leather chair in front of his desk. He stares at me, his salt-and-pepper hair cut short and immaculate, his arctic eyes rolling over me, taking in my white garter belts and stockings, my matching bra and panties. I'm wearing everything he wants, everything but the mask.

He leans back in his big leather chair, tipping his chin at me, and regards me a moment longer, his mouth parting as he does.

"Come here," he orders, pushing away from his desk, his knees going wide.

Does he know I was at his son's place? If he did, would I still be breathing?

I round the desk, and he grabs me and yanks me around and back, sitting me on his lap. One strong arm wraps around my waist, the other runs over my stomach and across my breast, kneading it and pinching my nipple.

"Fuck," he murmurs, the smell of liquor clogging the air, "you look good enough to eat."

"Mmm," I murmur, giving him what he expects, grinding my ass against his crotch and over his dick, feeling his hard cock beneath me. I arch back against him, thrusting my breasts and slide down the front of him, his hands rough and demanding everywhere he can reach.

The air is pungent with the double-barreled whiskey he prefers, pricking at my eyes with his every breath. The room is cold, nipping at my bare skin as he gropes me.

I barely feel it when he tweaks my nipple again, harder this time, and slides a hand around my thigh, digging his fingers into my flesh. His touch is dull and blunted, and that spark inside my chest that Golden Boy brought to life dies beneath his father's fingers.

Eli shoves a hand between my thighs, rubbing between my legs and over my pussy.

His fingers roam over the fresh cut that I covered with a liquid bandage and make-up at my apartment. If he notices the raised scars, he doesn't comment on them.

I doubt he notices.

The phone on his desk rings out of nowhere, and he snatches it angrily as I keep gyrating above him, grinding my ass against his cock.

"Blakely," he barks into the phone.

A voice murmurs through the line, but I can't hear it. Eli slaps the outside of my thigh hard with a smack, then does it again, the sting flaming across my skin before he unceremoniously pushes me off his lap. "We'll finish this later," he says. "I have business to attend to."

He always has business. Thank God, too, because it saves me from dealing with him.

"I can stay," I offer, though it's the last thing I want.

He tells the person on the other end of the line to hold on.

"I'll call you," he says to me before smacking my ass this time. He starts talking on the phone again, and I'm silently thanking whoever interrupted us.

"Pick up the RSVPs on your way out," he calls as I leave his office. "The courier brought them to the wrong location."

I don't need glasses to read between those lines.

Whomever it was had bothered the great Eli Blakely and definitely doesn't have a job anymore.

"Sure," I say, thanking whichever angel oversees business calls for delivering me from him.

I walk through his apartment and find a basket near the foyer. I pick it up to carry with me.

The card on top sticks out to me as I walk, the return address catching my eye.

Ms. Celina Blakely
Thompson Hill Club
Thompson Hill, Barbados

Archie's mother. Eli's ex-wife *six* times over.

I stop walking to the door, my hand freezing on the card.

How did she get an invitation? I didn't invite her. Eli wouldn't have invited her.

Surely the planner wasn't this careless? No. There's no way. I confirmed the invitation list with her personally.

Which means this shit is the work of the only spoiled, blond brat I know.

And I know exactly where to find him on game day.

18

ARCHIE

The crowd in the stands loses their shit, their roar loud and blaring. Hundreds of cameras go off every second, but I just look back at my brothers, smiling and laughing as they run onto the field and surround me, hugging me, high-fiving each other, cheering, and whooping on the gridiron.

Another semi-final win in the books, and damn if this season couldn't be going any better. The buzz from the win bubbles inside me as my brothers start a cheer for Coach. Two of our defensive linebackers pick him up and carry him, one of Coach's legs on each of their shoulders, him holding onto them to steady himself.

I stand there and watch, laughing with my team, and it feels . . . it feels like a dream.

It's pure euphoria when you win, adrenaline pulsing through your limbs, a smile glued to your face that you can't shake. I've never experienced anything like it, not even during sex. Pussy can't compete with the high of the win, the feeling like nothing in the world can bring you down.

Her pussy could.

I'm still smiling as the voice, the incessant little fucker, chirps in my ear, but I refuse to let thoughts of the red-headed succubus ruin this perfect night for me.

14 and 0.

Both defensive and offensive lines kicking ass.

Hell yeah!

"Brought-It-Home Blakely! Brought it home!" the cheerleaders on the sidelines cheer, and the buzz gets louder. "Brought-It-Home Blakely! Brought it home!"

Shit, that one's new, and I love it, even as a microphone is shoved into my face.

"Ella Forrest, WNDO Broadcasting, northern California," a fine-as-hell woman says, her brown hair pulled into a ponytail and two football-shaped rhinestone earrings in her ears. "How are you feeling right now, Number 11?"

I smile at her and watch as a flush creeps across her cheeks and over her skin.

"Fantastic," I say. "Absolutely fantastic."

"Is there anyone you'd like to credit for the win today?" she asks, planting the microphone back in front of me.

"It was a team effort," I say to the camera with a smile. "I wouldn't be here without my brothers."

She smiles, showing her straight teeth, and looks back at the cameraman. "You heard it here, folks. Indisputable MVP of tonight's state semi-championship game, Number 11, Archie Blakely, says tonight's win was a team effort. Congratulations, Number 11."

She holds out her hand to me, and I shake it quickly.

"Thank you," I say as our linebackers lower Coach to the field. A moment later, he's immediately doused in what's left in the water cooler. I laugh as he freezes at the cold water, but even Coach can't help but smile when we win. I give a few more interviews, and by the time they're over, it feels like I've shaken the hand of every person in the stadium before I follow the boys through the tunnel toward the locker room.

"Ar-le-an! Ar-le-an!" my teammates in front of me chant and I join in, fist pumping with my brothers. I follow them into the locker room and walk down the rows until I get to my locker that has my name placarded above it in black-and-white letters.

I place my helmet on the wooden bench behind me, which runs between every row of lockers. Then I shed my jersey and shoulder pads and drop them to my feet. The boys are still rowdy, whistling and cheering and towel-slapping asses, when the door to the locker room opens, and I hear a parrot of *Girl!*

Girl! Girl! Girl, gents!

Hot damn, which one of these unlucky bastards had their girl-friend show up right now, when we are all bare chested and with our cocks out? I laugh, but I don't stop undressing. I don't give a shit who's in our locker room. Well, unless it's my mom. It would be hella weird if it was my mom.

Considering she's still on her tropical escape from reality, I think I'm safe though, so I shove down my pants, peeling off my boxer briefs and thigh and knee pads in the process. The buzz is still there, haloing my head, but it's starting to wear off. I'm sweaty and dirty—thanks to a dirty tackle in the third quarter that hurt like a sonov-abitch. I need a shower and a change of clothes and then I plan on finding Red.

"Holy hell!" Berkley shrieks like a girl as he turns down the row of lockers, fresh out of the shower, and attempts to cover himself.

I'm digging in my locker, trying to find my body wash, when I'm shoved abruptly from the side and into one of our defensive linemen with an *oomph*. It starts a chain reaction in the crowded locker room, and it's like a game of falling football players as we topple into one another. I right myself quickly and look for the culprit, finding my father's fiery-tempered fiancée glaring at me.

"Red," I say as the locker room quiets around us. The boys must want to see how this plays out. To be honest, so do I. I don't know what I did to piss her off, and I almost ask her if she's feeling better from this morning. By the hellfire she's radiating though, I think it's safe to assume she's feeling much better and currently wants to cauterize my balls. Her cheeks are fifteen different shades of pissed, and her glare is glacial, like the tropical oceans in her irises froze over with her fury.

Fuck. She looks so pretty when she's mad.

I turn toward her and give her a good view of what I'm packing. Her eyes flit between my legs despite her best efforts, and her cheeks tint even further with her blush. I've never been in a measuring contest, but I've heard enough from my partners to know I'm big—massive, actually. I consider it part of my charm. And my massive dick definitely affects her, even if she doesn't want to show it. Sure, she might have expected it after feeling me up last week, but now she knows it.

And she'll never forget.

She goes uncharacteristically speechless, her mouth parting, and the left corner of my mouth lifts with a smirk. I give her another moment to enjoy the view before I say, "My eyes are up here, pretty girl."

The team snickers around us.

They all know who she is. It's not like my father wants to keep his arm candy a secret. It's a damn badge of accomplishment among his middle-aged pals—the younger, the better. Red is perfect, just legal enough to be on his arm at cocktail parties.

She glares at me, crossing her arms over her fantastic tits. The gesture does nothing to hide the creamy flesh peeking out beneath the coat she's wearing. The V-neck is low, giving me a view of the freckles that lay sprinkled across her chest. I want to play connect the dots with my tongue and make her beg for mercy. Is she ticklish? I hope so. The coat is weird though, too much for an abnormally warm autumn and paired with glossy white fuck-me stilettos that make her at least five inches taller.

A strange choice for a Friday night.

Almost like she's a . . .

Her snarled words latch around my ankles and bring me crashing down back to earth. "Why the fuck did you invite her, Blakely?"

It takes me a moment before I realize what's she's talking about. The RSVPs must be rolling in by now, though mine is currently wrapped in a new envelope, relabeled, and with my mother in Barbados.

Oh shit! Did she RSVP to their bullshit nuptials?!

"Invite who?" I ask, pursing my lips and one hundred percent fucking with her.

"Your mother to my wedding!" she snaps, and one of my team-mates murmurs, "Oh shit!" The sentiment is echoed across the locker room.

My smirk broadens. Red is white-hot mad, and I love it. It's about goddamn time she stopped looking so confident.

"Why are you upset?" I ask, trying to sound innocent, and I'm pretty sure fucking failing at it. "You're marrying for love, aren't you? Why do you care if my mom comes? It's not like she's a threat to you, right?"

She grabs somebody's cleat off the wooden bench and lobs it at my head. She's too close, and I can't duck it. The smelly, slimy-from-the-field thing lands hard against my left temple.

She snarls as my gaze focuses back on her. "What part of get the fuck out of my way do you not get?"

I lean in, my temple hurting like a bitch, and there's this roaring inside my ears that makes me want to slam her into the lockers and fuck the attitude problem right out of her. Maybe my father would finally call off this charade if I made her scream my name all over my fat cock.

I crowd her space and in typical Layne-fashion, she doesn't back away. Instead, she tips her chin at me and stares me right in the eye, even when I'm sure to press close enough that the heat from my body skims across her skin. She's millimeters away from my dick, and she doesn't even seem to care.

Fuck, she still smells like chocolate and cinnamon, and I suck her scent in greedily. My cock is rock hard between us, and she gasps when I lean in a sliver farther, pressing it against her stomach. Maybe another guy would be embarrassed, especially with all my teammates here, but I think if I cared to look, they're all probably sporting half-chubs too because I can't be the only one that feels the zing of electricity that surrounds her.

Like she took her halo with her when she fell.

Like it glows even brighter on Earth.

I cock my head. "Want me to stop, pretty girl? Then call off the wedding."

"Fuck you, Golden Boy," she snarls. "You have no goddamn idea what you're asking me to do."

"I'm asking you," I bare my teeth, "to choose me instead."

"It's like a disease with you! The silver spoon lodged in your throat must have cut off the oxygen to your brain. I. Don't. Want. You."

I *tsk*. She sneers.

"Liar," I say.

She stretches on her toes, and with the shoes, her lips are a few short inches away from mine.

"Don't act all high and mighty with me, Golden Boy," she snarls. "You're a fucking child, a child having a temper tantrum because you can't get your way."

"What did you say, Red?" I cup a hand to my ear. "I couldn't catch your words over the torrent of bullshit leaving your pretty mouth."

Goddamn, I want to split her open on my cock and feel her insides. She brings her face even closer to mine and bares her white teeth, breathing the scent of cinnamon and sugar across my face, like she just ate a pack of Red Hots on the way here. She rubs against my cock with the movement, but I don't think it's intentional because she swallows when it hits her stomach.

"I said," she snarls, "*Fuck. You.*"

"It sounds to me like you need someone to teach you some manners," I hiss. "How about I wash out that dirty mouth for you, huh?"

Her eyes go wide, but I don't give her a chance to reply. I grab her by the elbow and yank her down the row of lockers and toward the showers. I can feel my brothers watching me, but I don't care. All I can think about is punishing her and that face she makes, that infuriating smirk she gives me when she thinks she has won.

I yank back a curtain, find the stall empty, and shove her inside.

"Stop it!" she screeches. "Stop it!"

I slam her, one-hand around her throat against the tile, and pin her there, cutting off her air. She stops hitting me and starts hitting my arm. I jerk the lever to turn on the water, and it lands ice cold on both of us, but I pull her away from the wall and into the hard stream of it. She screams bloody murder, hitting and flailing against me, beneath the water. It hurts when her nails rake across my biceps and down my arms, but I don't give her the satisfaction of reacting. Instead, I imprison her there with me as she scratches, cutting and tearing at my chest a moment before she tries to bite me.

The annoying jacket of hers is covering too much, and her hair is drenched, straight and flat to her shoulders. The shower continues to pelt us, and when she tries to bite me *again*, I shove her back against the tiled wall, still under the water but not under the main stream. I grab an abandoned bottle of body wash on the shelf above her head.

"Such a dirty mouth, Red," I tell her, flipping the flange cap up with my teeth and tasting the bite of soap.

"Don't you fucking dare!" she tries to raise a hand to slap me, but it's too late. I force her to tip her chin at me and force her mouth open with my thumb. Then I squirt the soap into her mouth, and she gags, flailing before she hacks it right back at me. Greenish-blue streaks hit my chest, but I don't stop there. With one hand, I keep her pinned against the wall, and with my other, I rub the soap off me and onto her, lathering it up and over her jacket and the bare skin I can reach, getting all of her soapy before she slams a shoe down onto my bare toes.

MOTHERFUCKER! It hurts!

"Get the fuck off me!" she snarls, but I keep washing her, rubbing soap everywhere, up and over her coat and across her skin.

"Stop fighting!" I grit out as she continues to wriggle. My foot throbs in time to my heartbeat, and I'm certain she's broken at least three of my toes. "You're only making your punishment last longer."

I tear open her coat with both hands, the buttons popping off as I do.

Then I go completely still.

Delicate white lace hugs her curves, cradling her breasts and hinting at her dusty nipples. Thin lines of white silk crisscross her middle, across the freckled skin and down, connecting to matching white panties.

"Fuck," I say, looking up at her eyes again. I find her already staring at me, her chest heaving, the water and soap dirtying the lingerie.

Did she dress like this for him? Does he make her? Would she do it for me?

My fingers skim across the slight curve of her ribcage and across her breasts. My thumb catches her rock-hard nipple, and she sucks in a sharp breath.

I watch her and the rivulets of water running down her cheeks, across her throat, and over her chest. She pins me with her unreal aqua eyes.

"Don't," she says, the word a plea.

I tweak her nipple again, and her chest rises even faster, all of her quivering in the wet fabric. It's as though time stands still. She looks at me. I look at her. All the while, the shower spills ice cold water onto us both.

I knead her breast, hard but slow, tortuous. Her mouth parts on a moan as I drag her against me, letting her feel every inch of my cock, ensuring she'll know exactly how hard I'll tear her in two.

"Oh," she breathes, grinding against me, her eyes fluttering shut.

"Tell me you don't want it," I whisper against the shell of her ear.

She says nothing as my teeth clamp down, and I run my tongue along her outer ear. "Tell me you don't want me to fuck you right here, Red. Tell me you don't want your tight pussy fisting my dick."

She moans, and it almost has me spilling all over her as precum leaks from my dick and onto her bare stomach.

I lift her chin to force her to look at me. She's breathtaking, cold, wet, and turned on. She's pale everywhere except for two rosebuds, one on each cheek, and lips that are flushed from the curses she's been throwing out of them.

"Tell me," I say.

She says nothing, defiant even now, and that's all the confirmation I need before I slam my lips into hers. She molds to me, and I push the coat off her shoulders and yank her up so her legs wrap around my middle. When my cock presses at her center, pushing and pulsing, she moans again.

"Goddamn, Red," I tell her, whispering hot words against her skin. "You drive me crazy. I've wanted to fuck you from the first moment I saw you."

"You want to fuck everyone," she murmurs on a breath.

I grip her chin because her statement—how easily she discredits us—pisses me off. She locks gazes with me.

"No," I tell her. "Not like that. Never like that. I dream of you, Red. When they're on their knees, putting their lips on me and sucking my dick, it's you I want. You fucking consume me."

I don't give her time to analyze that. I grab her face and kiss her, flattening her to me. She tastes like cinnamon candy and the tart sour of soap. I reach between us and tear off her bra. I'm hard and rough, but I can't help it. I need her. I need her so badly that I'm going to lose my fucking mind. I lower my head and suck one of her breasts, as much that will fit, into my mouth, and she arches against me. Her big tits press against my chest as her legs tighten around my middle.

"Oh fuck me," she mewls, clawing at my back.

I break away from her breast and smirk at her. "Baby, you don't have to ask twice."

I move a finger between us and slide a hand beneath her panties and over her pussy. God, she's so wet already, and when I slide a finger in, she's impossibly tight.

I thrust again, and she arches her back and grinds her pelvis against me. I kiss her again, tasting cinnamon, soap, and desperation. I finger-fuck her harder, adding a second digit. Her teeth clank against mine as the kiss deepens, and I wrap my hands around her ass and line us up, shoving her panties to the side as my cock teases her entrance.

How can she already feel perfect when I'm not even fully inside her yet?

"Boys, listen up!" Coach calls from the locker area.

I don't care who sees, but she goes rigid a moment before she scrambles away from me. She shoves me backward, and I slip on the soap and water, landing hard on my ass, as she scrambles out of the shower, holding her coat shut, and runs for it.

I call her name as she leaves me hard and cold beneath the pelting water.

19

LAYNE

I feel myself splintering, tearing apart on the inside. Again. I did it *again.*

I almost let hit him have me, all of me, taking my virginity unceremoniously in a locker room bathroom.

What's wrong with me?

It's all unraveling, my best laid plans, everything I thought I wanted. I came to Arlean University to get close to Eli. I committed myself to vengeance, pouring over everything I could find on the man who erased all hope in my life before I knew the meaning of the word. I'm supposed to marry him and kill the piece of shit on our wedding night. Then I guess I'll disappear into the sunset and have the lawyers argue over the estate.

I don't know. I don't care about the money. I care about watching the light leave the elder Blakely's eyes when he realizes I'm going to take everything from him. I care that he knows his blood-splattered dominos will topple, and he can do nothing to save them.

There's never been an after plan for me. I haven't even thought about it.

Because killing him was enough. Tormenting him in his final

moments was enough. Knowing that my father finally had vengeance would be *enough*.

But it's all unraveling, and I feel the spin of it as I bolt out of the locker room, skidding across the tiled floor, between football players and a guy dressed in a green half-zip and a pair of khakis who I can only assume is the team's coach. His eyes widen a fraction of an inch when he sees me, and he starts to say something, but I don't stick around to hear it.

I have to get away. Far, far away from Golden Boy and the temptation that threatens to ruin my best laid plans.

I've been given the perfect opportunity, better than I could have ever imagined, by Eli willing to marry me in exchange for my virginity. And I'm ruining it.

Campfires burning low.

Vanilla.

Him.

Flashes of a man I shouldn't want explode behind my eyes.

His devastating dimples and knowing smile.

His crystal-clear blue eyes and the gleam of white teeth.

His hard flesh that scares away the nothingness and warms that cold, dead part of me.

Slickness smears between my thighs and pools in my panties, the lace catching on the sensitive flesh and flaming the fire that Golden Boy ignited with his touch. The voice of my mother, my worst memory, seizes the opportunity.

You piss off all over his name by spreading your legs like a whore!

No! My shouts are loud, reliving again inside my head. *No, mama! Please!*

You nasty, filthy slut!

Vomit clogs my throat, and I cough as I run out of the stadium. I swear I hear my name in the crowd, but I push forward. I want to feel without her torment, to live without her haunting my nightmares. But pleasure isn't allowed, not for me, only pain.

Pleasure brings my mother's ghost and sets a fiery spear straight through the center of me.

Pain brings cold nothingness.

I choose the cold.

I reach the parking lot, hit the key fob for my car, and slide onto the driver's seat. I shiver and turn up the heater to blast away the dead thing solidifying inside me.

I need control.

I need it now!

My thumbs are clumsy as they type out a text.

ME

Can I come in tonight?

My boss's reply is instantaneous.

J

Always for you.

You okay? Thought you were dealing with your mom?

ME

I need to work.

J

You're welcome anytime.

The shivering subsides a little as I shift the car into gear. My phone rings with Archie's number, which I have saved as "Golden Boy" from when he stole my number and texted me out of the blue, but I ignore the call. Then I ignore it again and again, until the screen finally shows a singular text.

GOLDEN BOY

Where are you, Red? Talk to me.

I sniffle, my vision wavering beneath unshed tears as I will myself to calm.

"Don't you cry," I say aloud. "Don't you dare fucking cry."

I repeat the mantra all the way to the club, unshed tears prickling at my eyes, my head aching. I pull up into the lot around back, and the security guard on duty opens the gate to the parking lot and waves me inside. I park at the back of the building, close my eyes, and breathe.

Don't. Cry. Bitch.

I fish for my bag in the back seat and exit my car. I head over to the employee entrance and enter my employee pin number on the keypad next to the door. The black door opens with a beep, and I head inside before it locks again. I've taken barely three steps inside before Jasmine, my boss, brings me in for a hug.

"You look pale! Are you all right?" She flattens me against her generous chest before releasing me enough that I can breathe. She regards me with a frown. "Are you sure you want to work tonight?"

Jasmine has to be the nicest club owner ever. She's in her early 50s, I think, but still in fantastic shape. She's got a motherly protection over the girls and a take-no-shit attitude for the boys. Somehow, she's managed to make a strip club classy. Plus, the pay is great, way better than working at any of the restaurants or shops in town.

"I'm fine," I tell her.

"I didn't think you'd be back so soon," she frets. "I thought with your mother's estate and Eli's proposal, you might slow down a bit . . ."

Her gaze flicks to the chunk of diamond currently weighing down my ring finger. She isn't wrong. I could sell the thing and pay for my entire college career but working for her wasn't just about the money.

It was about control.

Of course, a colossal fuck you to my dead mother helps too.

"I'm sorry I've been MIA," I offer. "I've been . . ." *Planning the downfall of one of your best paying customers? Almost letting his son fuck me?* ". . . busy."

"It's fine, dear. I was just worried about you." Her dark eyes asses me in that matronly way of hers again. "If you want to work . . ."

"I do."

She nods and smiles. "Dressing room is where you left it."

"Thank you, Jasmine," I tell her.

"Anytime," she replies with a smile, and somehow, I know she means it.

I head into the dressing room. There are a few girls inside, getting ready for their shifts, but the others must be on the floor. The room currently looks like a glitter bomb blew up in it, probably because it did, and smells like the bouquets of roses nestled on the floor of one of the girl's stations.

Angel's.

She was Eli's favorite before I showed up, though I'm pretty sure there's no hard feelings. She honestly looked relieved when I took him off her hands. Although Jasmine protects the girls who work for her—I've literally seen her grab grown men by the scruff of their necks until they beg for her to stop—she's also a smart business-woman. Eli pays very well, so she allows him and a couple others to bend the rules, to an extent at least. I don't know how far she'd let them go, and I've never cared to test those boundaries.

Consent is the name of the game here. Some girls allow kisses. Others allow groping. Some even allow undressing and biting or licking. Me, though, I'm all see and no touch, and it drove Eli mad from the moment he laid eyes on me. It's exhilarating knowing a guy is staring at you, watching you, wanting to rip your clothes off, but can't do anything. It's complete, utter control.

I set my bag on top of my station.

My stage name, Lily, is scrawled across the top in gold glittery letters.

Like Lily of the Valley, beautiful but poisonous.

Or Lilith, queen of the demons.

Depends on who's asking.

It's been weeks since I took a hiatus from the club. Jasmine doesn't know the whole story about how I grew up, but she has guessed enough to know dealing with my mother's shit wasn't going to be easy. Still, as I dress into my outfit, choosing a crimson brassiere, garter belts, thigh-high stockings, and matching stilettos, the routine slips back into place easily.

Fake eyelashes applied.

Two coats of lipstick.

Enough eyeliner to make my eyes pop beneath the matching mask that I tie around my head, fastening it into my hair.

It's a methodical process, and it takes a solid hour since I have to dry my hair too thanks to Golden Boy. When I'm done, I spray myself with a perfume that promises to douse you in pure gold, and it does too. All of us wear it. It makes your skin shine on stage like you're coated in a million little diamonds.

When I'm done, I secure my engagement ring with Jasmine, who keeps it in a safe for me, and walk down the hallway to the stage. A couple of girls pass in the opposite direction, drinking bottled water. I arrive behind the stage that looks out at the club. The emcee spots me and gives me a nod.

"Good luck, Layne," he says, before he leans over in his chair and speaks into his microphone.

"Tonight," he announces, his voice uncharacteristically low for his small frame, "we have a very special surprise, gentlemen. May I present a one-of-a-kind angel sure to drive you wild? Her rules are simple. No touching . . . ever. So keep your hands to yourselves and prepare for the dance of your life. As a reminder to our new guests in the front row, rule violations will result in immediate expulsion."

He winks at me as he queues up the music. It's soft jazz, just like Jasmine requires all her girls to perform to, and my heart runs wild in my chest, a flush of sweat creeping across my skin. Anticipation and adrenaline flood my veins.

I walk out onto the black glass stage and beneath the spotlight.

Wolf-whistles erupt, and I can feel eyes I can't see latched onto me as I move, slinking between the poles. I curl a palm around a pole in time to the music and twirl all the way to the floor before sliding back up again. Someone howls, and it's got to be the newcomers the emcee mentioned because they sound young. The mature patrons don't do that. If anything, they throw a hundred at you just to see if you'll bend a rule. If I'm feeling generous, I'll take the hundred and give a lap dance, but that's it. I can make a couple grand in one night from that.

I shimmy down another pole, letting my hair fall across one shoulder before I spread my legs and ride it back up again, breathing in the scent of expensive liquor and the fading perfume from one of the other girls. I dance to the end of the stage, where I can finally see people in the crowd beyond the blinding light. I throw my leg around a pole there, curling my knee and calf to hold myself upright and arch my back, thrusting my breasts toward the ceiling.

A college boy who can't be much older than me smiles from a clothed chair at a table as I do, his gaze heated and hungry. He's got a friend next to him, and they must have paid a small fortune to be here because getting inside the club isn't cheap.

I simper back at him and unwrap my leg. Then I come around to the front of the pole, slide down it, and spread my legs, giving them a show that would horrify my mother.

"Holy shit," one of them murmurs, and I smile down at my murky reflection on the glass stage before I look back at the crowd and lock eyes with the bane of my existence.

Golden Boy is sitting in the front row, dead center of a leather booth, and stares straight back at me, smiling.

Oh fuck no.

20

ARCHIE

One congratulatory talk from coach and a very, *very* cold and single shower later, and I'm still stuck on Layne, wondering where she is, what she's doing, who she's with, and—most importantly—why the fuck she ran . . . *again*. I look down at my phone, willing her to respond to my unanswered texts and phone calls.

Nothing happens. She still leaves me on read.

"Way to go man!" a sophomore offensive lineman says, slapping my shoulder as somebody starts up a chant in the parking lot. "Tigers! Tigers! Tigers!"

We're nowhere near the stadium, yet it feels like I'm on the field again, breathing in the high of the win with my team. Brentley, a kickass defensive lineman, pays the guy at the entrance and tells us to hurry before he pushes one of the studded leather doors open and disappears inside. We follow him.

I haven't been here since freshman year, when the former quarterback got shit-faced on the ride over off fruit punch spiked with Everclear. He threw chunks on two of the girls within three minutes of us setting foot in the place. After which, the team was immediately and indefinitely banned. But that guy graduated two years ago, and money talks. Well, along with the promise of not getting black-out drunk.

We head into the club between walls draped with black velvet. The place smells like leather and money as we enter the main room replete with studded leather chairs and shiny black tables. Soft light falls from the ceiling and shines above a bar tucked away in the corner. A blonde woman in a white lace corset and a matching pair of boy undies appears out of nowhere at my side and smiles at me beneath a matching lace mask that covers the top half of her face. Her bleached teeth gleam when the light hits them just right.

"Archie Blakely," she croons, cocking her head at me with a simper. "You brought it home, didn't you, Number 11?"

"Hell yeah, he did!" one of my buddies says as I tip my chin at her and tell her thanks. She's pretty and the look she's giving me promises me a good time, but I'm not remotely interested. My cock doesn't so much as twitch at her, and the realization tastes like shit when it goes down.

What the fuck is happening to me?

I shouldn't have let the boys come with me tonight. Hell, I shouldn't have come. It's not like my ego can't take a hit every now and again. It can and has happened. Occasionally, committed girl-friends and devoted bible thumpers have turned me down over the years. Hell, not even Brad freaking Pitt can lock it down every time. Well, maybe *he* can. Shit, dude even makes me question my hetero-sexuality, and I'm the guy who, over summer break, had an 18-hour, three-way with a pair of foreign exchange students who *almost* talked me into pegging.

Literally. That's how hot they were.

I should be back with the rest of the team at one of the afterpar-ties letting a sorority girl blow me like she's trying to get an engage-ment ring out of it. I shouldn't be at a pretentious, anti-fun version of a gentlemen's club on a hunch, looking for a girl who runs every time we almost fuck. I mean, where are the G-strings? Where's the glitter? Or the girl that offers you a handjob in the back for an extra hundy?

I'm not here for any of that shit, though. I'm here for *her*,

Red's non-phone-answering ass. Pops has always had a thing for strippers. They played a major role in his first and fifth divorces from my mother and a supporting role in at least two others. I'm hoping and praying he met Red at one of his familiar haunts, and this is my best guess given the outfit she was wearing tonight. God, that fucking outfit. I swallow a groan. I'm going to have wet dreams for weeks because of that outfit, not that there was much of it.

Not many places dress their girls like that, so here I am. If she's not here, maybe I can at least get some info on one of his former favorites and put a roadblock on the way to his seventh marriage.

I'm acting like I can't take a hint.

Like I've gone full-blown creeper.

Like I'm desperate . . . probably because I am.

We are out of place as we walk farther into the club, past men dressed in bespoke business suits and much younger women preening around their tables in lingerie and matching lace masks. I won't leave though, not yet, not without something, anything, to prevent their marriage of convenience. Layne has infected me with her *un*sweet talk and filthy mouth, her aqua-colored eyes and blazing red hair, with each and every part of her. If the sham with my father goes on any longer, I think I'm going to lose my fucking mind.

It's not about the money anymore.

Or the family dynasty.

Or the promised cushy job.

Or the inheritance that will pad the pockets of my great, great, great grandchildren.

It's about *her*, and the way she ignites my soul and sets fire to every plan I've ever had for myself. It's about how she pushes all my buttons and never backs down. And how her body purrs for me while she wears my father's ring.

Goddammit, Layne. Answer your fucking phone!

We take a seat at a booth, and I look at the girls as we do. Brunettes. Blondes. No red heads.

No . . . *Red.*

"What can I get you boys?" a waitress dressed in black lingerie asks, her brown eyes almost black beneath her mask.

"Shots!" Torres says, flattening a hundred to the table.

My phone vibrates in my pocket, and I pull it out, hoping to see Red's name flash across the screen. Instead, my friend's name stares back at me from our shared group chat with my brothers back in New York.

IAN

Saw the game on ESPN. You did good, Blakely.

ME

Thanks, man. Means a lot.

EVERETT

Yo, you all right, Archie? Where are the jokes?

ME

Not feeling it tonight, bros.

CHASE

Quick, somebody call an ambulance. I think Blakely became an adult.

IAN

You okay, man?

ME

I will be.

When I find her.

EVERETT

Ominous...

IAN

Good luck, man.

CHASE

Arch finally got #girlproblems.

I close the chat as a leggy blonde dances across the stage over to us. She's wearing towering glass heels that add at least four inches to her already lengthy frame. Johnson whistles at her, but Brentley shuts him down with one large arm on his shoulder.

"There are rules, boys," he reminds.

Johnson nods hurriedly and straightens the collar of his polo like it'll somehow help him fit in at this place. I wish they had let me come alone, met at a party later, but Torres looked like a puppy being offered a treat when he asked where I was headed on my way out of the locker room, and I told him the truth.

The girl on stage twirls beneath the rotating stage lights as the waitress delivers our shots. I pluck one from the table and swallow it in one gulp. It rolls like liquid fire down my throat and flares when it hits my belly.

A few other girls join the blonde on stage, and a voice from somewhere calls out rules with each new arrival. You can touch the brunette dressed in ivory apparently, but you can only touch the brunette dressed in blue if you ask first *and* receive permission. I can see why father would love this place. Fucker never did learn the meaning of no and definitely takes every rule as a challenge. Slowly, the girls make their way offstage, their heels tapping against the polished black glass as they do, filtering into the growing crowd as more businessmen arrive. A blonde sets her claws in one of my teammates, who smiles at her like he just won the lottery. The announcer says something about another girl—no touching at all with this one, apparently—but I'm half listening. I text Red.

ME

Where r u?

Answer me, Layne.

As has become her infuriating pattern, she doesn't reply. I'm starting to wonder if I got the wrong number, but I doubt it. Student Admissions keeps everyone's info on file current, and it only took me a smile to the receptionist and an excuse about a group project to get it. I frown down at my phone. I'm getting sick of playing just the tip with my father's fiancée.

Click, click, click sounds as another girl walks onto the stage. Out of the corner of my eye, I spot a pair of crimson red, *fuck me* stilettos below long, freckled legs wearing matching lace stockings, garter belts, and garter straps. At my side, Torres elbows me between the ribs. The waitress delivers another round of shots.

Ow! Torres elbows me again, and I start to tell him to cut it out when I look up at the stage and my heart stops beating. Delicate lace the color of blood cradles her creamy skin and hugs an ass I could bounce a quarter off of. Her boobs spill out from the matching bra she wears as my mouth goes dry. Her hair, colored like a blazing sunset, kisses her shoulders with every step. I follow the line of her delicate neck, up to her painted lips exposed by the lace mask that covers the top half of her face, both in the same color as her outfit. Her irises are bright blue beneath the stage lights.

My mouth parts.

Hot hell, it's . . . *Red.*

She doesn't see me yet as she strides across the stage, weaving between the shiny silver poles.

Torres elbows me in the side again.

"Man," he says, "isn't that your girl?"

I wish.

I say nothing, though I doubt he's even listening anymore. Every one of us, all of my teammates, stare at Layne. She gives my boys on the opposite end of the booth a show of her thick ass, squatting all the way to the floor. I have an insane urge to tear off my shirt and throw it over her, before she's in front of me, sliding down the pole and spreading her legs wide, her hands running between her thighs and spreading herself for us.

Pale flesh covered by thin red lace.

Fuck. Me.

I spot a flash of something inside her right thigh. She's covered it with make-up, I think, but it's sort of off colored, and my gaze latches on it.

What is that? A scar?

I want to inspect further, but her legs close as she finally looks up from the floor and directly at me. Her luscious mouth parts as I stare at her and smile. My smile splits even wider as a flush stretches down the column of her throat toward her collarbone.

I don't have to say it aloud. She already knows it.

I won't let you run again, pretty girl.

My tongue traces the bottom of my canine as I curl a finger, giving her a come-hither motion. A brunette chick pockets a bill on the opposite end of the table and starts to give Brentley a lap dance.

I can't see the upper part of Red's face thanks to the mask, but I know it's her. The sharp glare she throws my way just confirms it. That look says she'd rather chop off my dick than come any closer.

Oh, but you'd much rather ride it, wouldn't you, Red?

I cock my head and curl my finger, again beckoning her to come over.

I expect her to take the stairs down to my level. I don't expect her to take one crazy long step off-stage in shoes no woman should be able to walk in and sashay across the tabletop.

"Fuuuuccckkk," Torres mutters, and I want to punch him in the dick for whatever he's thinking right now. Not that I'm not rock hard and ready to ram through this table to rut Red into the next world, but he's not allowed to think those thoughts.

She looks down at me, sneering as she crouches, surprisingly balanced considering her obscenely tall shoes. She regards me with a raised eyebrow, and says, "What are you doing here, Golden Boy?"

What she means is *how in the fuck did you find me?*

"How much for a lap dance?" I ask, sliding two hundred out of my front jean pocket over the table at her.

"Sorry," she says, eyeing my money with a scowl before pocketing it a moment later. "No touching."

She sounds positively happy about that rule, and my cock really wants it to be a challenge.

"Damn girl," Torres says next to me. "Ice cold."

I slowly slide another two hundred across the table at her with one finger, my gaze latched on hers as it arrives in front of her shoe.

"How much?" I repeat. "Everyone has a price. You certainly do."

Torres snorts. One of the other boys laughs. Her flush crawls even lower.

"I don't want your money," she snaps. Yet, she still pockets it.

Is Daddy not treating you right, pretty girl?

I lean in, silently challenging her to look away first. "What do you want, then?"

"For you to leave me the fuck alone."

"Give me a lap dance," I tell her, "and I will."

She frowns, tipping over toward me, pressing the fingertips of her left hand against the tabletop as she does. Her scent slaps me across the face, but it's my dick that aches with the impact.

Chocolate.

Cinnamon.

Layne.

"You know what you are, Blakely?" she says, her words clipped and angry. Her teeth glow stark white against her blood-colored lips. "You're just a scared little boy, afraid Mommy and Daddy are going to leave him all alone, irrevocably fucked up by your shitty parents. You can try to hide behind that laid-back, don't-give-a-fuck image of yours, humping everything you can find until you graduate. But you will never fill that mommy-and-daddy sized hole, Golden Boy, so I suggest you cut your losses and don't even try."

I lean up, my ass lifting off the seat, breathing hot air onto her. "Aww, baby, the only holes I want to fill are yours."

"Get. Out," she hisses, baring her teeth.

"Why?" I cock my head as her flush blots her collarbone. "Afraid you might be one of the girls I hump?"

"No."

I almost kiss her with my whisper. "Liar."

She says nothing, her gaze locked on my lips.

"Let's go somewhere private and talk about it," I offer.

"No," she declines instantly. I swear it must be her default answer.

"Why not?" I whisper to her lips. "You afraid, pretty girl?"

"Never."

I stand, cupping an arm around the back of Layne's legs and

throwing her over my shoulder. A moment later, all hell breaks loose. The security guy at the front yells. One from somewhere behind the stage arrives, and Layne's fists are battering my back. I have no idea where I'm going, but I round the booth and head backstage, opening the first black-painted door I can find as somebody yells at me to stop. I barrel inside, Layne still atop my shoulder. I put her down, and she's yelling and pissed off and still hitting me as I lock the bolt on the door behind me and lodge the nearest chair beneath the doorknob for good measure.

She slaps me. *Hard.*

My cheek stings like a sonovabitch.

"What the fuck is your problem?!" she snarls.

"You're my problem," I snap, my words growled as I grab her by the shoulders and haul her against me. Someone pounds on the door outside, but the lock holds.

"Every second of every fucking day, you're my problem." I continue, stepping forward. She steps back, her breasts heaving against her tiny lace bra. "You're the first thing I think about in the morning, even though I don't want to. You're the face I see when another girl is trying to suck my cock. You torment me. You kiss me and come alive when I touch you and rub your greedy cunt all over me, but then you run! You *always* run! I can't stand it, Layne." Her back flattens against the far wall as I press forward, preying on her. Then I'm in front of her, and she's shaking beneath her mask. I carefully take it off her, unraveling the lace at the back, before I drop it to the floor. Her entire body shivers when I lean in, rubbing my nose and cheek across the side of her face. A moment later, and my mouth follows the same path, licking and nipping at her. The chalky tang of her makeup hits my tongue.

"I . . . I don't . . ." she begins, swallowing hard.

I go lower, sucking and biting and kissing her neck.

"Say it like you mean it, pretty girl," I tell her, "and I'll stop."

"I don't . . ."

I cut her off, chuckling softly against her skin, and relishing when she trembles even more against me.

I lift a hand, skimming it up her stomach and over her breasts.

"Come on," I challenge her, my tongue laving across her throat. "Say. It."

Her heart hammers so fast, I can feel it beating like a rabbit beneath my hand cupping her breast.

"I . . ." she mewls.

"Say it."

My mouth follows the line of her collarbone, licking and nipping, and she moans. I grin against her skin and pull away from her just enough to push her panties to the side. I thrust two fingers into her pussy, and she throws her head back. She stares up at the ceiling, writhing between the wall and me.

"Always so wet for me, Red." I praise with a smile, flicking my thumb over her clit.

She moans.

I slip a third finger inside, my thrusts becoming harder, rougher as I finger-fuck her. She'll be mine before this night is over.

She shakes and murmurs my name before I flatten my mouth down onto hers, our teeth clashing, our tongues warring for dominance before she gives in with a soft whine. She tastes like cinnamon candy again, and I can't get enough.

"You want me to fuck you, pretty girl?" I ask as someone pounds on the door, shaking it on the hinges.

She mewls in response, but I barely hear it. Her gaze locks on me before she brings a hand to either side of my face and kisses me this time. Her fingers weave into my hair as I fuck her with my hand, scraping my fingertips against her walls. She's shivering all over now, and my cock is so hard, aching to be inside her. With one hand still pistoning into her tight pussy, I fumble with my jeans and free my cock.

I lift her up against the wall, her legs going around my waist without hesitation. She whimpers as I withdraw my fingers, but she doesn't have to wait long. I line up the thick head of my dick and slam inside her, feeling something give as I do.

I go completely still, bottomed out inside her as her nails rake across my back with her cry.

She's a virgin.

She *was* a virgin.

I don't fuck virgins.

Yet . . . *you're glad it was you.*

"Oh fuck," she says, going rigid as she shakes against me. Her tight cunt pulses around me, and it takes everything in me to not come right now. She digs her nails into my shoulder blades, and I press my forehead against hers.

"Red," I say to her, the air between us hot.

"Baby, open your eyes." I take two fingers and tilt her chin to force her to look at me. Her eyes are closed beneath the longest lashes I have ever seen, and she's shaking all over, a thin sheath of sweat coating her skin.

I say it twice more before she complies, her gaze wide, scared.

"Just be with me, okay?" I tell her, whispering the words against her soft skin. "I'm right here. Just be with me, okay?" I lift a hand to tap a finger against her temple. "Get out of your head, pretty girl. Let me love you."

"Archie," she says softly, like she's seeing me again.

God, my cock throbs at her saying my name.

"Keep looking at me, Layne. I want to see you when I fuck you, okay?"

She bites her painted lips and nods.

"I'm a virgin," she admits.

"I know, Red. I'm a lucky guy."

She stares at me, her eyes going wide.

What did I just admit?

"You're so beautiful," I tell her, drawing out of her slowly.

"Bet you say that to all the girls," she manages, gritting her teeth and throwing her head back, exposing the column of her throat to me.

"No, I don't," I murmur between us, slowly pushing into her wet heat again. "Look at me."

Her eyes snap to mine again, her irises the color of the ocean at nightfall in the dim light of the room. I start a slow, lazy rhythm. She needs to loosen up before I really fuck her, or it's going to hurt.

"I don't call other girls beautiful, Red."

"Really?" she asks, her mouth parting on a soft keen as I thrust a little faster.

"Really," I tell her, kissing her again.

Slow. Sensual. My tongue twines with hers as I slide my hands beneath her ass and grip her tight. She breaks our kiss to breathe, and we both gulp for air.

"Are you here with me, pretty girl?"

"Y . . . yes," she manages on a breath.

Thank Christ.

I pick up speed, pivoting my hips, my fingers digging into her ass, as I really start to move. Our skin smacks together, the sound visceral, urging me on even further. I hammer into her, impaling her pussy on my cock as my balls rock against her taint.

"Oh . . . oh . . . oh . . ." she starts to chant, her tits jiggling against my chest with every roll of my hips.

Clap, clap, clap, clap.

Faster and faster.

The air grows sweaty and hot as I fill her sweet cunt. My fingers hold onto her ass as I bottom out.

"Fuck, Archie," she cries.

"That's right, pretty girl," I growl. "Bleed on me, baby. Give me everything."

Her eyes flutter closed again.

I grab her by the chin and squeeze until they pop open again. The slap of skin against skin and the scent of sweat and sex fills the room. I ram into her, faster, harder, my breath exploding past my lips, her tits and ass bouncing with each thrust.

I don't slow down. Her back scrapes across the wall, and I tilt her pelvis, hitting her clit just right.

"Come for me, baby," I order.

"A . . . Archie . . ." she mewls, "it's too much. It's too . . ."

"Come for me," I order. "I won't stop until you do."

"A . . . Archie . . ." She starts to shake.

I fuck her harder, faster, ramming into her slick cunt.

Her entire body quivers in my hands.

"Look at me," I roar. "I want to see your face when you come all over my cock."

She stares at me, those beautiful eyes locked on me, as her cunt starts to pulse.

"Oh God," she says, her nails digging into my shoulders.

"Don't say his name, baby," I tell her, ramming into her. "You only get on your knees for me now."

She comes, throwing her head back against the wall and screaming my name. I bottom out inside her and finally come, spilling in her over and over again, for what feels like forever.

We stay there, both of us breathing heavily. She's pinned between me and the wall, her legs wrapped around me, her pussy still impaled on my dick. Her heart batters against me where her chest is pressed to mine.

"Fuck, Red," I murmur against her hair, trying to catch my breath. "That was perfect."

She doesn't reply, though. When I look up, I see that she's staring straight ahead, having gone completely still in my arms.

What. The. Fuck.

21

LAYNE

*B*lakely fucks relentlessly, pounding into me, his breath sweltering against my face as I cling to him. He fucks me like I weigh nothing, like I'm a rag doll in his sculpted, athletic arms. I can't do anything except wrap my legs around his hard muscular waist, crossing my ankles low on his back, latch onto his shoulders, and hold on for the ride.

It feels like his cock is rearranging my insides, impaling me with each brutal thrust of his hips. My pussy burns and feels good at the same time, stinging yet slick. I'm sore already, his pelvis grinding against mine with each bruising drive of his hips, but I welcome the pain.

Pain.

Pleasure.

Something—*anything*—besides the numb.

Golden Boy makes me feel *more*. He makes me feel alive.

My skin smolders against his hot chest, and my core throbs as he bottoms out over and over again.

Smack. Smack. Smack.

The sound of our fucking is fast and loud. He said he wouldn't stop until I came, but it's too much.

It's all too much, my legs shaking, my breath lodged in my throat, my back arching against the wall. I taste the metallic bite of blood, like I've bitten my lip, or maybe he did, and the saltiness of sweat. I'm wrapped in him, in his scent of lingering campfires and sweet vanilla, and in the collision of him, sculpted muscles and sinew, against me.

It's too much.

It's too much!

It's . . .

"Oh God," I say, holding onto his shoulders as molten warmth builds inside me, and I'm spiraling, losing control until . . .

"Don't say his name, baby," Golden Boy purrs from far away, still pounding into me. "You only get on your knees for me now."

Liquid heat detonates through me, burning the world away, incinerating my bones and breath with it. I scream his name as he empties inside me, his cock pulsing, painting my walls with ropes of hot cum.

The pleasure fades in receding waves until it starts to hurt again at the space where we're joined. I'm lost, staring at the wall behind him as someone pounds on the door, rattling the knob and the chair lodged beneath it. My blood and our cum seeps out of me as the stinging swells and the pain returns.

It drags me back to five years ago, and I'm not in Golden Boy's strong arms anymore. I'm back inside my father's shop, my converted bedroom, behind my mother's house. Nathan Mylers from my science class sits on my bed across from me. He's got inky, messy hair that curls everywhere and a gap between his front two teeth that you can only see when he smiles. He doesn't ask why I have an apartment in my backyard or look at me like he's better than me, and I love him for it.

I try my best to wash up in the shop's small sink, even washing my clothes and hanging them out to dry, but I know I'm not as clean as everyone else. I don't like using the washer inside the house anymore, not after last time when I found a dead mouse at the bottom of it. My teacher even had a meeting with my "father" about my cleanliness, or lack thereof. My neighbor—who was paid to be there by my mother—told her I had issues with *personal hygiene* he and my mom were working on. The lady took one look at me and bought it hook line and sinker. Not that I was going to say anything. I don't want to go to a foster home. I've heard the horror stories of handsy foster parents and little-to-no privacy. At least here, I have my own space, and it's all mine. I'm-safe here, even if I made it myself.

Nathan is everything I wish I could have in a friend. Smart. Funny. Nice. He's got a great laugh that makes me smile, and he gives me a gap-toothed grin as we finish setting up our three-dimensional model of a cell, a group project for science class.

"Thanks for inviting me over," he says, carefully picking up our model to place it on a free space on the workbench to dry. Then he turns around and looks at me.

"You're a cool chick, Layla," he says, calling me by the name my mother gave me.

"Thanks," I say with a swallow, my gaze dipping to his lips.

He catches it but doesn't call me out on it. Not like the other boys at school would.

"I gotta get home," he says, grabbing his backpack from the floor and heading the few short feet to the door. He turns back toward me, and the light overhead weaves ribbons of indigo through his dark hair. "You wanna hang next weekend?"

My heart belly flops beneath my ribs.

"Sure," I say with a nod.

He smiles, a blush bridging his cheeks. "Same time? Same place?"

"Yeah."

"Cool." His hand stills on the door. "See you around, Layla."

"See you around, Nathan."

He leaves, shutting the door behind him, but his shadow stays behind.

The scent of his body wash, cardamom cut by caramel, lingers in the air.

The chair he had tried to sit in lays broken and discarded next to my tiny desk.

Our painted model of a cell dries on the top of my father's workbench.

I sigh, my head hitting the pillow as I fall back against my bed, my heart still cartwheeling.

Nathan and I are going to hang out. He thinks I'm cool. He smiled at me.

I am . . . happy? Is this what happiness feels like?

At least I can look forward to something, and that hasn't happened in a long time, not for years at least. I want to stay here forever, in my bed, staring up at the rafters of the ceiling, dreaming about a boy, but my bladder has other plans.

I need to pee, the primary reason I ever step foot in my mother's house anymore.

Reluctantly, I crawl out of bed and head outside as dusk nestles on the horizon. The back door is unusable, barricaded by boxes and trash years ago. I can still climb inside through the window above the kitchen sink, but the latch likes to stick, and I need to pee now, not in ten minutes. I trudge around the side of the house, weeds flattening beneath the high-top sneakers I stole from the thrift shop on Main Street.

I continue to the front door, finding it unlocked, and let myself inside.

My mother's lamps do little to illuminate the den, save for the spot right next to her recliner. Her precious stacks of trash block the windows and press against the broken blinds, preventing most of the outside light from coming inside.

"Layla," my mother croaks from her chair, calling for me.

Like she always does. Like I hate.

"Mom," I say back, walking between the piles, trash crunching beneath my feet. She's gotten worse the past few years, refusing to even let me throw out the garbage, but she keeps a small area beside her recliner clear for a small box television with an old antenna that picks up only a few channels.

She sits in her recliner, reeking of booze, her eyes glassy and pupils blown from the dim light or whatever she's managed to get her hands on, probably painkillers from the neighbor's friend. He's started coming over now too. Whatever she gets from the government each month goes to either our neighbor or to him.

Her hair is more gray than auburn now, and it sits in a messy bun at the back of her head, frizzy and knotted. My nose wrinkles when I catch a whiff of her. When was the last time she had a bath?

Her hand catches my wrist, and she looks up at me and sneers, the white of her eyes yellow beneath the bloodshot.

"We never would have come here," she says, "except for you."

Not again.

Not tonight.

Not now.

"Mom," I say, trying to wriggle free of her grasp. Her grip tightens, her dirty nails digging into my flesh, puncturing my skin.

A hiss escapes between my teeth.

"Your father would still be alive if I hadn't gotten knocked up," she spits, the words running together in her drunkenness. "But he just had to have it all, the fancy job, the fancy house, the fancy fucking life!"

"Mom," I say again, trying to pull away from her, but she won't let go.

"You ruined everything!" she snarls, spittle flying with the words and stinging my face. "Now you piss all over his name by spreading your legs like a little whore!"

"No! No, Mama! Please!" I say, tugging away from her, my back scraping against the tower of newspapers behind me, sending it toppling into the piles behind it.

She stands suddenly, the sour stench of stale beer and piss hitting me head-on. She bares her yellowed teeth, her upper lip disappearing into her gums. An unlit cigarette falls from her lips and lands on the pockmarked floor.

"You nasty, filthy slut!" she spits, slapping me hard across the cheek. The impact makes my eyes jiggle in my skull.

"Stop it!" I shout, trying to pull away from her again, but she's stronger than me.

She reaches blindly behind herself, yanking a brown beer bottle with a peeling label from a pile of filth, and shoves me with both hands down to the floor. Bits of trash nick at the backs of my bare arms and legs, and my head hits something unforgiving, knocking the world away for a moment with the collision. My mother raises the bottle with a sneer, and the glass breaks at the bottom when she hits my ribs. I wheeze, my breath knocked out of me. The world topples over again, as she thrusts a filthy hand beneath my denim skirt.

"Is this what you want?" she screams. "Is that what you let that ugly boy do to you? You spread your legs for him, you dirty whore?!"

She shoves the neck of the bottle between my legs, pushing my panties and the hard glass into me, a fraction of an inch, bruising my pubic bone with her sloppy thrusts. Pain explodes between my legs, and I scream as she rears back to try again. My scream dies in the filth around us as I kick and hit her, scratching against the paper and plastic littering the floor and trying to roll away, the floor crunching and giving way beneath me.

Dead bugs.

Garbage.

Mouse shit.

Her eyes are dark lifeless orbs, and she smells like cheap beer and piss when she raises the broken bottle for another hit. I rake my nails across the thin leather skin of her face, and blood spurts from the gashes. She wails as I dig my nails in deeper, scraping lines down her cheeks. She rears back, jerking away from me and stumbling backward into her chair. The bottle falls to the floor, and she continues to scream. I scramble to my feet, sliding on the floor and knocking over piles of garbage, and run outside, slamming the front door shut as I do.

I can go anywhere in the world, and she wouldn't follow, but I can never go home.

It hurts between my legs in the place where the bottle hit against the bone, the pain deep and bruising. I stumble, sobbing as I head to the back of the house. I cry, snot clogging my nostrils, and tears carrying away my vision.

I can still smell her, urine and fermented beer, sour and rank. I trip over something in the weeds and fall to my hands and knees down to the grass. Vomit rides up my throat, and I puke my guts on the lawn, over and over and over again, until I dry heave. Then I gag against the sunset, ugly noises coming up until my throat is raw and my middle hurts.

I don't know when I get up off the lawn, when I stop crying and finally climb to my feet in the darkness and feel the wetness that soils my legs.

Piss.

I pissed myself. Just like her.

The realization makes me heave again, bile and thick saliva splattering with the piss onto my shoes.

I lurch toward the shed, and a single thought runs through my brain.

I didn't cause her shitty life.

But I can kill the man who gave me mine.

PART IV

NIGHTFALL

— Gil (Years Prior) —

My heart hammers in my ears as I run.

Down one flight.

Then two.

Then three.

My shoes tap against the concrete steps, my left hand sliding across the metal rail.

Tap, tap. Tap tap tap.

Tap, tap. Tap tap tap.

Round and round, I bolt down the stairs, my heart battering away in my throat as the building shakes with the raging fire. Heat permeates through the exit doors at each level as I race for safety. Smoke seeps beneath the doors and pillows the air.

It's sweltering. It's suffocating. Sweat sticks to my skin.

I cough, ash and char prickling at my lungs, and I jerk at the knot on my tie, loosening it. Finally, I spot the ground floor and the exit outside. Thick saliva clogs my throat, and I sputter as I arrive at the exit. I push the bar on the door with both hands, but it doesn't open. My nose smacks against the metal, and I curse.

I rear back and try again, putting my weight into it.

The door doesn't move as the building groans around me and shudders.

"Open," I demand, coughing between breaths. "Open, goddammit!"

I hit the panic bar wildly, over and over and over again, the cool metal in contrast to the rising heat in the stairwell and the smoke dancing in the air.

The door doesn't budge.

Fuck!!!

I gulp for air, making a sound I don't recognize, and the building shudders again as something crashes far above me.

I can't breathe.

I can't breathe.

I. CAN'T. BREATHE.

I start up the stairwell, and I'm nearly to the first floor when a truck of heat slams into me, stopping me in my tracks. Flames I can't see lick at my skin through the smoke clogging the stairwell. My eyes burn, and I back up, down the steps, following the line of the concrete wall until I hit the turn at the bottom of the stairwell. I follow the turn, flattening my back against the concrete, and run straight at the door.

It jitters on its hinges but doesn't open.

I fumble for my phone in my pocket, sliding it out and to my ear, keeping it close to my face to see the screen beneath the smoke. I have to call someone. I have to . . .

I gulp for air, my heart knocking against my sternum. The world tilts and rights itself.

Everything hurts beneath the blazing heat.

My skin.

My insides.

My bones.

I stumble, falling into the concrete wall and dropping my phone as everything shutters for a second. My head swims. I feel nauseous.

"Goddammit," I mumble, the curse sloppy, as I reach for my phone but don't find it. The light of screen is gone, erased with the lights in the stairwell, hidden beneath thick smoke.

I fall to the floor, sucking in soot and ash. It singes my esophagus, incinerating me from the inside out.

It's so hot, so dark, so . . .

The building groans above me again and a thunderous roar shakes the walls.

I gulp in a broken breath that tastes like hot metal and ash, smoke clawing at my throat and splintering my lungs apart. My cheek flattens to the cool concrete floor beneath me, and I'm left with a singular thought as my mouth opens, gasping for air that never comes.

I love you, my sweet girl.

I love you.

I love . . .

I . . .

22

ARCHIE

I say her name like I'm scared. Because I am.

Layne has gone rigid, and although I'm sure she's still breathing—I *triple* checked—she's not responding to me or the commotion outside the door. I carefully untangle her from me and place her on the floor. She stands on her own, but when I talk to her, she gives me nothing except a dazed look that makes the knot inside my stomach wriggle.

A glassy-eyed stare, her eyes dulled to a dusty blue, says everything she does not.

That she's hurting.

That I can't help her.

That I shouldn't try.

Fuck that.

I tuck away my limp dick, feeling like a colossal asshole for whatever hell I've unleashed. Maybe someday, *years* from now, we can joke that I fucked her into another reality, but right now, I can't even manage a laugh at the rogue thought. I'm sweating like it's high noon at summer training and pacing the room like I'm trying to find the damn escape key.

"Layne?" I say again.

She gives no response.

I shuck off my shirt, peeling it off with one hand at the back of my neck, and drop it over her head, moving her arms up and through the short sleeves. She lets me, but she doesn't help. When I'm done, I take a step back and survey her. The cotton tee swallows her, ending mid-thigh. It does nothing to assuage my worry.

"Fuck," I curse, stepping forward again to grip her face between my hands, forcing her to look at me. "Are you okay?"

No response.

She's not okay, dumbass. She's literally gone mute.

The hammering outside the door stops, and I debate moving the chair wedged beneath the knob and unlocking the door. I don't know how to explain *this*, though.

Should I call for help?

Take her to the emergency room?

Fall to my knees and beg her to wake up?

"Talk to me, pretty girl," I murmur, rubbing the exposed skin of her forearms up and down, over and over again. Her skin is cold and clammy beneath my touch.

My heart hurls into my throat and stays there.

Fuck, fuck, fuck!

I'm so out of my depth I might as well be floundering in the middle of the damned Pacific.

"Shit," I murmur, breaking away from her before forcing her to look at me again, squishing her cheeks between my palms.

"Do you want to get out of here?" I ask her.

Again, no response.

She blinks, and I take it as an answer. I grab her hand and walk over to the emergency exit on the exterior wall, hitting the door hard. It smashes into the concrete wall outside, sending bits of black-painted brick down to the asphalt. The dumpster further up the alleyway toward the rear of the building reeks, and I cough as I steer her by the hand to the parking lot.

A car alarm pierces the night air and voices sound at the back of the building. I don't stick around to see what they have to say. I don't give a fuck about them. I don't know what Red needs right now, but it certainly isn't a bunch of fuckers all up in her face.

"Come on," I tell her, picking up the pace. She follows me, jogging alongside me, her heels clacking against the pavement and her legs porcelain pale beneath the city lights.

I auto-start the G-Wagon and help her into the passenger seat, tucking her legs on the floorboard and buckling her in before I slide into the driver's seat beside her. The tires skid on the pavement as I peel out of the parking lot.

"Layne?" I ask, looking over at her. The street lamps illuminate her face, in and out, in and out, over and over again. She looks straight ahead out the windshield, past the cars in front of us, and beyond.

I'm out of my element. I don't know what I'm doing. Shit!

I merge onto the highway, veering into the lefthand turn lane at the last minute, and some asshole honks his horn and gives me the bird. Like I give a fuck.

I hit the gas and follow the merge lane onto the highway. I crank up the heat for her because she has to be freezing right now. She's wearing lingerie and my shirt. I'm cold, and I have a solid fifty pounds, maybe more, on her, and I'm wearing pants.

"Layne," I say to her again as we ride, "where do you want to go?"

She doesn't respond. She just stares straight ahead at the red taillights cresting the hill in the distance.

The knot in my middle wriggles again, going crazy, and I sit up straighter, trying to get rid of it.

What do I do?

Where do I go?

How do I deal with . . . this, whatever this is?

I thrum the leather steering wheel, tapping a fast beat against it. I can't take her to my place. Game nights are packed, and after a win? Hell, the party will be going until at least sunrise. I don't know shit about what she's going through but putting her in front of a bunch of drunk frat boys and sorority chicks screams bad idea.

"I'm going to take you home," I announce to the car.

If she was lucid, she'd probably ask—demand to know—how I got her address. I'd tell her it's from the same place I got her phone number, but in fairness, I didn't ask for the location of the place she calls home. The receptionist at admissions gave me that one for free.

Now I probably shouldn't have saved it into my phone like a total stalker, but Red and I can have that argument another day, preferably when she's talking.

I map directions on my phone, and it broadcasts through Bluetooth to my in-screen navigation system. The wriggling mass at the pit of my stomach relaxes a little as we drive, or maybe it's some perfume she's wearing. Chocolate and cinnamon and all things slightly sweet.

We pull up to her place twenty minutes later, and I find a spot on the curb in front of the building. I hate to do it to my baby girl, but Red needs me more right now, so I park my car and pray my wheels stay firmly on my vehicle. Red's place isn't a shit hole, though. She's done well for a college kid, holed up in the revamped, bourgeois area of the city with art galleries and pet daycares around every corner.

We walk up to her building, and I let us inside, holding the door for her. I lead her up two flights of stairs to the third floor and stop outside what I hope is still her apartment.

Number 311.

As soon as we're in front of the door, I know I've fucked up. Her keys are at the damn club, with the rest of her stuff, I'm guessing.

You're a fucking moron, Blakely.

I look over at her. "Any chance you have an extra key around here?"

She doesn't reply, and I start skimming the top of the doorframe.

No key.

I pick up the plain front door mat.

Still no key.

I hear a double knock and look over to find her in front of the next-door neighbor's apartment. *Whoa. When did she unfreeze?* An older lady with blue hair answers a minute or two later, dressed in a housecoat and bleary-eyed from sleep.

"Hello?" she says with a yawn before she goes still and has, what appears to be, a small heart attack.

"L . . . Layne!" she manages a moment later, her eyes hitching on Red's beautiful bare legs and stripper heels, probably horrified by her lack of dress.

"I'm so sorry to wake you, Ms. Potts," Layne replies with a small smile, "but could I borrow the spare key?"

The lady looks out of her doorframe and glares at me. I tip my chin at her and give my best approximation of a look I hope conveys *I didn't do that to her. Well, I did, but it's complicated. Can we start over?*

"Are you all right dear?" the old lady not-so-quietly whispers.

"I'm okay, promise, just embarrassed." Red offers the old lady another small smile, and I feel like I'm spinning through the Twilight Zone.

"I remember those days," I swear I hear the lady mumble before she disappears for a minute and returns with a key.

"Here you are," she says. "And don't worry about it. You aren't the first tenant to lock themselves out in the middle of the night. Have a good night."

"Good night," Layne replies, turning on her heel to walk to her apartment. Her face falls, and she looks like she just shed a second skin as she unlocks the door and lets herself inside. I follow her, shutting the door behind us.

"You okay, Red?" I ask, but she doesn't reply.

I watch as she undoes the straps on her heels, dropping them to the laminate floor. A moment later, she peels off my shirt and drops it a few feet away before she turns and disappears into another room.

I follow her, chewing on the inside of my cheek. I don't know what to do, but I sure as hell am not about to leave.

Her place smells like her, chocolate and cinnamon, but it feels unloved and clinical, like a showcase home without a soul. There are no photographs or push-pin boards with two dozen notes on the walls. There's not even a television, just a tufted gray chair with a blanket thrown over the back and an empty matching loveseat that looks new.

I shove my hands into the pockets of my jeans and wait a beat, trying to give her space. She can talk. I heard her talk. Maybe she just doesn't want to talk to me. It hurts a little.

Since when do you care if they talk to you?

I listen as water starts to run and rock back on my heels. I wait a minute, maybe longer, and peer out the windows on the wall facing the street to look at the light traffic driving past.

I walk over to the room where she disappeared, seeing the footboard of a bed and the open door to a bathroom.

Water splashes softly.

"Layne," I say again.

No response.

Fuck it.

I walk through her bedroom and into the bathroom.

I find her in the tub, her hair in a messy knot on top of her head, stray copper strands tumbling down her neck and to her shoulders. No bubbles, just Red, naked and beautiful beneath clear water.

"Can we talk about it?" I ask, sitting on the tile floor next to the tub. It's cramped and my legs splay on either side of her toilet, but I make it work.

She doesn't respond.

"What are you thinking?"

Again, no response.

I watch her. She doesn't even attempt to wash herself. She just lays there in the tub, her breasts peeking out of the water, her freckled legs stretched to the end of the basin.

"Are you scared?" I ask, reaching over to tuck a loose strand of hair behind her ear. Her skin is hot beneath my fingers as the tub steams around her. At least she's not cold anymore.

"Talk to me, pretty girl," I murmur, tucking another rogue hair behind her ear again. "I never meant to hurt you."

There's a beat of silence before her aqua eyes find mine, flaring with blue fire.

"You didn't hurt me," she replies.

"She speaks," I say, before I add, "what happened back there?"

Because it felt like you broke.

She doesn't answer my question. She just blinks at me, erasing the fire in her gaze as her expression turns cold and detached. "You can go, Golden Boy."

"Is that what you want? For me to go?"

"Yes."

The word *liar* catches on the tip of my tongue, but I know she'll just double down. She's so fucking stubborn, my Red.

"Okay," I shrug my shoulders, pretending it doesn't sting. "If that's what you want."

I climb to my feet and look down at her. Her dusky nipples crest the bathwater, quivering slightly with every breath. It takes my breath away too.

Get it together, man! You've seen hundreds of chicks naked.

"You sure?" I ask her.

No response.

"Okay," I nod to myself. "See you around then?"

I know I'm feeding into whatever this is, but I don't care. I have no intention of actually leaving. There's repression, and then way above that, somewhere in the stratosphere, is Red. She may have it together now, but she didn't half an hour ago, and I'm not buying whatever tough girl image she's selling.

I walk out of the bathroom, through her bedroom, into the small living room, and all the way to the front door. I open it, give it a beat, and then shut it loud enough for her to hear.

I wait another minute, trying to give her space, giving her the best approximation of what she asked for. I rock back on my heels and stuff my jittery hands into my pockets. I stare at the wall. I stare at the floor. I stare at the ceiling, too, before I grab my phone out of my back pocket and find twenty-seven missed phone calls and fifty-six unread texts. I go to the first name on the list.

TORRES

Where tf you go, man? There's a crazy lady here screaming about calling the cops for kidnapping that red-headed chick.

Man, she's gonna call the police.

Answer me, bro!

There's a security camera in that room? Guess they count the $$ there.

Cops watched the vid. They are arguing with crazy now. Heard one of them laugh and say it was definitely consensual.

They still want to talk to that chick, though. CALL. ME. MAN.

I shove that shit down in the deal-with-later box.

Water splashes, lapping against the porcelain tub, and fuck, I've probably been out here like two minutes, but I can't stand it anymore. I stride back down the hallway, past the kitchen, into the living room, through her bedroom, and into the bathroom.

"Red," I begin before the rest of the words die in my throat.

Everything in me freezes, my heart, my breath, the unspoken question.

The water is pink, colored like someone dipped Red in an Easter egg kit. Blood swirls, twisting and turning, before it dissipates.

The stench of rusty iron overpowers her chocolate. Metal washes away the cinnamon.

Layne has a foot dangling out of the tub, dripping pink water to the floor, a razor blade in one hand, and she's staring down between her thighs as she draws the blade across her skin.

No, pretty girl. Why? Why?! FUCKING WHY?!

"What the fuck?" I roar, and she startles, looking up and locking gazes with me.

"Get out!" she shouts.

"Never," I growl, grabbing a hand towel off the counter of the sink and wrenching the blade from her hands. I throw them both, and they land against the wall a second later, the towel and blade sliding down and clattering on the tile.

She shrieks and tries to slap me. I pin her wet wrists between one of my hands and yank her up, flattening her chest to me.

Wet. Hot. Pennies.

"Get off me!" she hisses.

"Not until you fucking talk to me!"

She jerks away from me, freeing her wrists and shoving me away with both hands. She steps out of the tub onto her floor mat, dripping as blood runs red rivulets down the inside of her leg and across her ankle to the floor.

"You don't know me, Blakely!" she snarls. "Stop trying to save me!"

"Then tell me!" I shout as she squeezes past me, disappearing into her bedroom.

"You couldn't handle it." She looks back at me, her upper lip retracting over her teeth with her words. "You stand there in your rich boy clothes, with your fancy car, everything you ever wanted at your fingertips, but you don't know shit about the real world."

"I know you're fucked up," I clap back. "I know you hide behind a bad attitude and . . . and fucking *cutting*. Goddammit! Talk to me, Layne!"

She cackles, the sound ugly and jarring.

"You wanna know, Golden Boy?" she says, her voice going low and calm, though I hear the anger sifting between her teeth. "I grew up surrounded by filth and shit, the child of a hoarder too scared to leave her damned house."

She takes a step forward. I stay where I am.

"I would pray for the towers of shit to topple over and crush my mother to death. I would *dream* of it. Because when she wasn't collecting all her precious trash, she took it out on me."

I swallow hard. She takes another step forward, naked and bleeding on the cream-colored carpet.

"When I was sixteen, the bitch tried to rape me with a beer bottle." She slides a hand down, over the curve of one breast and between her legs, touching herself. I feel sick. "Does that make you hot, Golden Boy? Wanna fuck?"

"Layne . . ." I warn.

"I felt the glass for *weeks*. I threw up and pissed myself after. What about that? Is that big cock of yours hard?"

My stomach somersaults. Bile chars the inside of my throat.

"Don't push me away, Layne," I manage with another swallow.

She keeps walking until she's right in front of me and pins me with her stare. "Do you know, Blakely, what's worse than your own mother assaulting you, hmm?" Her lips curl with the taunt. "Being so weak, you don't even leave when she does."

"That's not your fault," I whisper, choking on the words. "You were a kid."

"I had to wait for her to die. I was *pathetic*."

"You were a child."

"I was weak!" She spews the word like it disgusts her to even utter it. More blood follows the lines painting her leg and down her ankle to darken the floor.

She reaches out and plants a hand dead center of my chest, skin against skin. There's the fetor of wet, hot pennies again, mingling with the bite of vomit scuttling its way up my throat.

"I had to wait for her to die," she says, "before I could finally get my revenge. Then I burned all her precious treasures, all the useless trash she loved more than me."

"You weren't weak," I tell her. "You were human. You were afraid."

"I wasn't afraid," she scoffs. "I don't feel anything."

"Everyone feels something."

"I feel nothing! I am cold and dead on the inside, Golden Boy. The only thing I care about is vengeance."

"And you got it, Layne," I murmur. "Let yourself live."

"No," she shakes her head and droplets of bathwater fall to the carpet and across my shoes, "there's still one person left who has to pay. He killed my father, and my father's death killed my mother. And my mother killed what was left of me." She cocks her head at me. "Come on, Archibald. You're smart. Figure it out."

I blink at her.

When she said, *Just stay out of my way, and I'll stay out of yours?*

After I kissed her and she murmured, *I can't do this. We can't do this.*

When I told her she didn't have to marry my father, that she could marry me instead, and she replied, *You don't know what you're talking about.*

She was saying it all along, and I didn't listen.

Oh fuck.

"Eli," I murmur, shaking my head. "I don't know what you think . . ."

"I don't think, Golden Boy. I know. My mother told the story every time she was too drunk to stand. Your father and mine were in business together almost two decades ago, co-owners of Throxium Enterprises. And when that business started to fail, your father burned it to the ground with my father inside."

"No," I shake my head again, "there has to be a mistake."

"No mistakes, just cold hard facts. Gil Gallagher dead at twenty-seven years old, victim to a freak fire no one could explain."

"They would have charged my father if he did that."

"No one cared!" she spits. "Don't you get it? My dad was a poor kid from the wrong side of the tracks. Yours came from old money."

"I don't believe it," I say.

"I don't care."

"They would've found evidence of arson. Insurance wouldn't have paid out."

"There was nothing concrete," she snaps back. "My mother spent the last of her savings trying to find proof. She hired a personal investigator. He found nothing except a million-dollar life insurance policy taken out by your father against mine."

"No," I shake my head once more. "My father's a lot of things, but he isn't a murderer, Layne."

"The building was only in Eli's name, Golden Boy, and the business was worth nothing. Don't you get it? Eli used my father as an exit from bankruptcy."

When I don't agree, she sneers, "Jesus, you're just like him."

"Don't make me the villain," I say, my fists balling at my sides. "Not everyone is out to get you."

She cackles. "But you got what you and your daddy wanted, right? You fucked me."

"Don't pretend it was just sex."

She cocks her head at me. "But that's what you do, right? Fuck 'em and leave 'em?"

"It was more than that."

"Why? Because your ego can't handle that I see right through your bullshit? You wanted one thing and got it. You're fucking *excused*."

"I know you feel it," I tell her, erasing the last bit of distance between us and gripping her by the shoulders. "It's *all* I think about. Don't pretend you don't feel it, Layne."

"The only thing I feel is this." She reaches between her legs to her cut thigh and the blood still seeping from the gash and slaps me hard on the chest. Blood smears across my skin.

"Stop," I tell her.

"Why?" She cocks her head again before she reaches between us, gathers more blood seeping from her wound, and lands a second blow, leaving another bloody handprint next to the first.

"Are you afraid?" she taunts. "A sad little rich boy dirtied by the poor girl's blood?"

"I don't give a fuck about your blood," I snarl. "Stop pushing me away!"

She slaps me again. Another handprint joins the first two.

"Stop it."

Again.

She smears it, painting my chest sanguine.

"Stop it!"

Her lips curl, and she stands on the tips of her toes, her mouth inches away from mine. "Make me."

"Fine," I snarl, yanking her against me and slamming my lips down onto hers.

She goes wild, clawing at me, pushing me away only to bring me back. She bites my bottom lip hard, drawing blood, and then shoves me away again, her hands landing on my pectorals with a loud *smack*. I capture her by the wrists and tug her back to me. We collide in a teeth-clattering tangle of limbs and flesh.

She shoves me down onto her bed, so that I bounce on the mattress and then climbs on top of me to straddle my hips.

She kisses me, and it tastes like blood from my busted lip and salt. I wrench my lips away.

"You're bleeding," I breathe.

"I don't care."

She climbs off me, yanks off my jeans and boxers, and sends them to the floor, freeing my cock. Then she crawls back between my legs and puts her gorgeous mouth around my dick.

I should stop her. I should tell her we still have shit to deal with, to talk about, but fuck, it's warm, wet velvet as she flattens her tongue against the underside and drags her hot mouth up my shaft.

"S . . . stop," I manage with a tight swallow.

"No," she answers around my dick.

I curse, my hips bucking when she hollows her cheeks and sucks fast and hard. My hands tangle in her hair before she tears away from me abruptly, straddles me, and impales herself onto my dick, sliding all the way down to the root.

She goes rigid for a moment before she arches her back and moans.

Blood smears all over my thighs and legs, across my chest and up her stomach. She looks down at me and drags an index finger through the blood smeared across my chest and thrusts it between my lips.

It's dirty and wrong and . . .

She starts to move, rolling her hips and thrusting her breasts to the ceiling as she takes my cock. She slides up and down, my dick glistening with her wetness as she rides me.

"Fuck," I say on a moan as she finds a rhythm. I grip her hips, helping her, and her hands latch onto my forearms as she rolls her hips.

Up and down, round and back, her big tits bouncing with every thrust, she grinds her clit against me. She's wild, riding me like I'm a bull, her red hair falling from her ponytail clip and brushing against the top of her breasts. It's the hottest thing I've ever seen as our skin claps together, the headboard hitting the wall each time she comes down.

Thud.

Thud.

Thud, thud, thud, thud.

Faster, harder, the entire bed shaking and creaking as she fucks me.

I sit up, grabbing her ass as her legs crisscross at my back. I take a nipple into my mouth and suck the tight bud. She bucks, the smell of blood and cum and sex in the air around us.

"Oh God," she moans, my lips still latched around her nipple, before she goes wild, bouncing hard and fast, riding my cock like she's a porn star. My fingers dig into her ass as the *thud* of the headboard hitting the wall picks up a notch. She's making sounds I've never heard before, keen cries spilling from her lips before she suddenly goes rigid and comes, her pussy fisting my dick. I grind her against me one more time, my fingers biting into her ass, and thrust home, jetting ropes of thick cum inside her and finding her lips to kiss her, swallowing her cries.

23

ARCHIE

*L*ayne is still asleep in bed, naked and half hidden beneath the thick, quilted comforter. Her room smells like her— dark chocolate and snickerdoodle cookies—but it's cut by the tinge of drying blood, sweat, and cum. Her bedroom is a mess, her bathroom probably is too, but I haven't checked. Blood is on me and her sheets, dirtying them with ugly dark brown stains. It's on the carpet and on her, though at least she stopped bleeding hours ago. My gaze lowers to her long leg, which has slipped out from beneath her silky sheets, and the blood drying there turned to a ruddy brown on her freckled skin. I stare at the mess of scars inside her thigh, tiny white and pink lines crisscrossing back and forth, some thick and raised, others not.

A hundred tiny Xs, maybe more, mar her skin.

My chest splits in two as I continue to stare, unable to look away. She hurt herself to feel, because she thought it was the only way to make everything better, to feel safe.

But she is safe with *me*, goddammit!

She feels with *me*.

She is better with *me*.

There's no undoing what has been done, but I'll be damned if I sit idly by and watch her implode her life, blowing up her future to smithereens in some misguided quest to make her childhood make sense.

She's been asleep for hours, but I've been awake, listening to the soft lull of her breathing and the dull whir of the cars passing outside her building. I never stay, but I will for her, even if it scares the shit out of me and makes my skin shiver on my bones. I won't abandon her. Not like everyone else in her life did in one way or another.

My mind drifts back to the name she uttered hours ago in her attempt to scare me away.

Throxium Enterprises.

I've heard of the company, and Layne may be a lot of things —gorgeous hellion being front and center—but liar doesn't strike me as one of them. She was so adamant, so certain, that my father killed hers. She even went down this insane path, implementing a colossal plan for revenge because of her conviction in that belief. Hell, if I was in her shoes, I would've probably just killed the guy I thought murdered my father, but not her. Holy fuck, she went all out. It's both impressive and a little terrifying, if I'm being honest.

At least the charade of an engagement with my father can be over. She doesn't have what he wants anymore—virginity—I made sure of that. Her blood is all over my cock to prove it, and as fucked up as it is, it gives me a sick satisfaction to know he can never have it. She was mine from the moment she stepped foot on campus. She just didn't know it yet.

I look over at her, quelling a crazy desire to reach out and trace the mess of scars inside her thigh, to follow the line of each one. But then she'd wake up, and she looks so peaceful when she's sleeping.

Throxium Enterprises.

Throxium . . . my mind mulls over the name.

I know my father had a business partner years ago. I know they went through financial trouble of some sort, but in no way do I think he killed anyone. My father's an asshole of epic proportions, but he's not a murderer. I don't blame her for hating him. She had decades with a shitty mother, her only fucked-up source of affection in the entire world, to convince her of his guilt.

Still, I need to fix it. I *want* to fix it for her.

I tap the screen on my phone on the nightstand next to me and check the time. It's nearly four in the morning, but my father has always been an early riser, so I climb out of bed and put on my jeans, stealing my t-shirt from where Layne left it earlier in the living room. I scrawl a note onto a notepad I find in a drawer in the kitchen next to the fridge. I leave it on the counter for her.

I'm going to fix this for you, for us.
- Archie

Then I head straight for my father's penthouse, although I hate going there. It always feels like a big ass jail—everything neutral, painted gray and black and, occasionally, white. I prefer our old home in New York, though last I heard, my mother got that in the most recent divorce and is redesigning it into her, quote, *pink palace.* Well, there goes that place, I guess.

Half an hour later, I pull up at the front of my father's building and parallel park. I hit the button for the lock, and my car horn beeps twice as I dart up the steps and into the building. When I enter, I give a nod to the security guard at the front desk, who is sitting reclined in his chair and tips his chin at me as I head for the elevators. I ride an elevator up to the penthouse, entering the code for access to the top floor. The elevator door opens a moment later, and I walk the short distance to my father's place and use my key to let myself inside.

"Dad?" I call, but there's no response, just the low hum of the refrigerator and the soft darkness of early morning. I walk through the den and go to his office. A cigar still burns on the glass ashtray on his desk, sending tendrils of smoke and the heady aroma of cloves lazily swirling into the air, but he isn't there. I walk further into his apartment, cutting through the library, before I hear giggles from somewhere up above.

"Bingo," I mutter to the empty space.

He's on the upstairs deck, and by the sound of it, he has company. Neither is unusual, even at this hour, for him. I pass through the dining room, walking around the untouched table, and climb the metal stairs to the roof of the building. When I reach the landing, I let myself out onto his personal patio, and the giggles grow louder.

"Dad?" I say again, the wind whistling as it runs invisible fingers through my hair. There's no answer, and I walk beneath the sleek steel veranda and across the stamped concrete, passing a row of manicured hedges that sit in giant white pots. I find my father on the other side at the far end of the roof, a king in his oasis. The sauna bubbles across from him, steaming in the cool morning air alongside the heated pool.

He loves it up here, but I hate it. The wind sounds unnatural this high up, like it's whispering at you to walk over to the glass railings and look down. It makes me shiver.

My father is reclined in a black pool chair. He's already dressed for the day with a red-headed woman on his lap, though I can tell even from here that she isn't natural, not like Layne. Her color is more cherries than burnished orange, and she giggles again as he slaps her naked thigh, just below a black silk thong that barely covers her pussy. He raises his hand to run lazy circles around her pierced nipple before he pulls the silver ring there, and she yelps, not laughing anymore. He smirks as he reaches over and takes a sip of his drink, probably tonic water this early, and finally spots me.

"Son," he says, somewhere between annoyed and confused. "To what do I owe the pleasure? Shouldn't you be holed up in a sorority girl's cunt right now?"

Great. He's definitely annoyed.

"Can we talk in private?" I ask, eyeing the woman.

He slaps her thigh again, hard enough to leave a welt, and tells her to get out. Despite saving her from God only knows what, the lady tosses me a nasty glare as she heads for the door. She probably lost out on a big tip because of me, not that I care. I did her a favor.

"Now that you've ruined my fun," Eli murmurs, gesturing to a chair beside him.

I walk closer but stay standing. He takes another sip of his drink.

"What is it, Archibald?" he demands. "You didn't knock some bitch up, did you? Spit it out."

"What happened to Gil Gallagher?" I ask with a swallow.

He sips his drink again and cocks a brow at me. "That's a name I haven't heard in a long time. Where did you hear it?"

There's no point lying. He'll never tell me the truth, not unless he knows it will benefit him.

"Layne is Gil's daughter," I answer.

My father stills for a moment and blinks at me. He's not a man accustomed to shock. It takes him another moment before he laughs wryly.

"That explains why the PI couldn't find anything on her," he says. "I guess I have an engagement to call off. Your mother will be *thrilled*." He refills his glass out of the decanter on a side table next to his chair. Then he sneers at the pool and the steam rising against the horizon. "What a conniving little whore."

My fingers clench into the fabric of my jeans to avoid them going around his throat.

"Gallagher was the co-owner of your first company," I offer for him, "Throxium Enterprises."

My father nods. "Yes. Yes, he was. He was also a coward."

He glowers at the water, his gaze darkening with every passing second. But I need answers, and his temper tantrum can wait.

"What happened to him?" I push.

My father sighs as though our conversation is physically tiring him. "He died in a fire at the business."

"Layne thinks you killed him," I say.

My father stares out at the pool and the waves softly lapping at the sides.

"You've been talking to her?" He cocks an eyebrow at me before he sets his drink down on the table. "That figures since you've fucked everything else with two legs on campus."

"She thinks you killed him," I repeat, ignoring the jab.

"Gil wanted to stop before we had even begun."

What is he saying?

"That's not a no," I remark.

Deny it, motherfucker. Deny it! I need to hear you deny it.

My father sighs again. "What answer would best suit your delicate sensibilities, Archibald? Here, I'll make it easy. No, of course, I didn't kill the cunt's father."

What. Is. He. Saying?!

"Say it," I murmur.

"You're going to have to speak up, son. I can't hear you over the bitching."

"Say it!"

His sharp gaze hooks on me. "Who do you think paid for your fancy clothes and your fancy schools and your fancy fucking car?" he spits, stabbing a finger against the dead-center of his chest, standing as he does so. "I did."

"You killed him," I breathe, the words clogging my throat, cutting off my air.

"I had to," he hisses, "and I'd do it all over again. Gil Gallagher was a pussy. He wanted to pull the plug and throw away all the years we had devoted to the company, the *millions* in investments your grandparents made. He wanted to close the doors!"

"So you killed him?!" My stomach heaves inside me. I'm going to be sick.

"I did what had to be done." He scoffs. "We would have lost everything. Our name would have been ruined, a generational legacy destroyed," he snaps his fingers, "just like that."

"Because of you!" I spit back at him. "Because you invested everything, and you failed."

"I fucking succeeded!" he shouts, raising his arms. "Look around you, boy! Who do you think built all this?"

My stomach rolls again. I'm going to be sick.

She was right.

He killed Gil.

He murdered her father.

Fuck!

Bile scalds my insides, and I cough at the rotting taste. I stumble toward the door, my feet sliding on a loose bit of concrete.

My father laughs, derision leeching into the sound.

"Stop the hysterics, son, and grow the fuck up," he calls to my back. "The bitch can't prove anything. If she could, I wouldn't be sitting here."

I continue away from him, desperate to not be here.

My father's a lot of things. A liar, a cheat, an asshole, and a philanderer to name a few.

I guess I can add murderer to that list too.

Layne wants to kill him, and I'm not sure I want to stop her, not for his sake anyway.

24

ARCHIE

y feet hit the metal steps, and I race down the stairs, each of them rattling as I do.

Clang. Clang. Clang, clang, clang.

I'm going to be sick.

I'm going to be sick.

I don't want to be sick.

My father's laugh haunts me as I descend, running so fast the entire staircase shakes with each pounding footfall.

I arrive at the landing, my shoes skidding on the polished stone floor. I take two more steps and knock a vase off its tall pedestal, sending it toppling down to the black marble. It shatters loudly on impact, sending countless tiny bits of stained glass flying everywhere. Bile tastes sour and rancid on my tongue, and the smell of chlorine from my father's pool lingers in my nose.

"Fuck," I stay stumbling away from the mess.

My father's words echo in my ears.

If she could, I wouldn't be sitting here.

If she could, I wouldn't be sitting here.

If she could.

He's right. She couldn't prove it, so she resorted to killing him instead.

She accepted his proposal with plans to end him.

She devoted her goddamn life to destroying him, ruining her own in the process.

The wound inside my chest splits open even farther.

I barrel through his apartment, stampeding through one empty room after another. My father's admission shadows me, stealing all the air and squeezing my lungs. There's a tightness clawing at my chest now, tunneling in deep, and I can't breathe. I gulp air, but it doesn't seem enough as I slam the door to his apartment behind me.

I start to pace the hallway.

Up and down across the black-and-gray argyle carpet.

If she could, I wouldn't be sitting here.

Surely, I misunderstood. I heard wrong. I . . . I . . . I know what I fucking heard.

He murdered her father, and I don't know what the fuck to do about it. She can't prove it. He won't go to jail or be punished or . . . or pay in any way. I can't make it better for her! I can't fix it like I fucking promised! I can't do shit!

I fumble for my phone, my hands shaking and the movement jittery. I nearly drop it before I manage to dial my mother's number.

She answers on the second ring, laughing as she does from somewhere across the globe. The sound is a small comfort to my rising panic.

"Hello," she says, her laugh lingering with the word.

"Mom," I manage, coughing and choking.

"Archie," her voice softens immediately, "are you all right, darling? Did something happen?"

"Gil Gallagher," I manage.

"Who?" she laughs and the phone rattles as she murmurs away from the phone. "You're incorrigible. Go get us another drink, dear."

"Gil Gallagher of Throxium Enterprises," I spit into the empty hallway.

"Oh my gosh," she says a moment later, "it's been years since I heard that name."

"He killed him."

"What, darling?"

"He. Killed. Him. Dad killed Gil Gallagher."

"Excuse me," she murmurs to someone on the other end of the line. I hear rustling followed by the tap of shoes.

"Darling," she says a moment later, even softer this time, "I'm sure there's been a misunderstanding."

"He fucking admitted it to me!" I snarl, hitting the wall at my side hard, leaving an indent in the plaster and busting my knuckles. Blood seeps between them and down my fingers to the carpet.

"Sweetheart," she says with a concerned sigh, "are you sure you're okay?"

"He got away with it!" I say. "Gil's family suffered and he . . . he . . ."

"Let's not jump to conclusions." My mother titters nervously. "We don't know that."

"His wife became a hoarder too afraid to leave the house. She assaulted their daughter. She . . ."

"Oh okay," she interrupts. "Well, I am very sorry. I wasn't close with his wife. I didn't . . ."

"Are you sorry?" I snarl. "You don't sound like it!"

"Well," she titters again, the pitch even higher this time, "Archie, it's very complicated. Your father and Gil had a business arrangement. You see, Gil was very good with numbers, and . . ."

"He got away with murder!"

"Sweetheart," her tone is sharp, enunciating the word, "I'll be on the first plane to California. We can talk about this."

I don't respond.

"Are you all right, dear?" she asks.

Still, I don't respond.

She repeats her question as I continue to pace the hallway.

Up and down, up and down, as the gray diamonds sewn into the carpet blur together.

The realization comes to me slowly.

"I need another minute, Tony," my mother says to someone, her words leaving no room for argument.

"Why are you not upset?" I ask her, coming to a stop in front of the row of elevators.

"Darling," she pauses, breathing into the phone, "are you all right? Talk to me."

"I've been talking to you, but you don't seem to be paying attention, *Mother*," I snap, staring at a metallic elevator door. "Why are you not upset? I said your ex-husband murdered someone, and you aren't upset."

"Well . . ." she trails off.

"Why?" I demand, gripping the phone tight.

There's a pause as she breathes into the phone again.

"Darling, your father has done a number of things over the years," she answers eventually. "He saved us when the company folded. He poured every last bit of his trust fund into that company until your grandfather, God rest his soul, cut him off. We were broke. We were struggling and the insurance money allowed your father to rebuild, to create what he has today. He saved us from ruin, baby."

Her words pierce straight through my chest like a cold dagger to my center.

"You knew," I breathe.

"No . . . I . . . I . . ." she laughs nervously.

I imagine her across the globe, standing on a concrete patio in a tropical paradise overlooking the beach as the water rolls onto shore. I see her as if she's right in front of me, fiddling with the thin, gold bracelets that she always wears on her tan wrists, spinning them back and forth. It's her one and only nervous tic.

"Darling, let's not do anything rash, hmm?" she says eventually, her tone soft and placating. "Gil wasn't like us. He didn't grow up in our world. He would have understood his sacrifice was necessary for our happiness."

The dagger in my chest drives deeper, and a tremble worms its way down to my bones.

"So because he wasn't rich, he deserved to die?"

"Son . . ." she sounds offended.

"You're delusional!" I hiss.

"Archibald, listen to me!" she begs. "Let this die, son. It was years ago. No one is around to remember. You will just hurt the family if you bring it up now."

"Yeah, no one's alive except Gallagher's daughter."

The line goes quiet. I hear the moment she stops breathing.

"What did you say?" my mother whispers.

"Gallagher's daughter, you remember her, right? She's alive. She remembers."

I back up against the wall opposite me and slide down it until I crouch on my knees. Vomit scalds my throat.

"Is this girl asking questions?" my mother asks after a long moment. "We must be careful, son. We must distance ourselves."

I laugh, the sound bitter. It echoes in the dead hallway. "Distance ourselves? When Dad asked her to marry him?"

My mother gasps. Panic slices through the line, and something in me relishes hearing it. After everything Layne went through, my mother knew the entire time and did nothing. She stayed with my father. She *remarried* him, over and over again, divorcing him for much more petty reasons. For most people—for good people—I think infidelity would be a minor concern compared to murder.

"Your father's weakness was always his dick, darling," she says after a long moment. "What's he going to do about the situation?"

She doesn't have to open her mouth again for me to hear the words.

Is he going to kill her too? Maybe burn her to a crisp like he did his business partner? Take out a life insurance policy and collect the hard-earned proceeds while he's at it?

I stand abruptly, the movement clumsy, before I stride to the closest elevator. I punch the button hard as my mother repeats her question.

I don't answer, letting her words die in my ear, before she repeats it, then again, and again. Each time she utters the words, they're more panicked than the last, her voice turning shrill and demanding, her tone rising higher and higher.

The line goes quiet, and I swallow hard.

"I don't know what he's going to do," I answer as an elevator arrives with a ding and the door opens. I step inside, turning to punch the button for the ground floor. "But I hope he fucking hangs for it."

With that, I throw my phone. It sails the short distance through the elevator and across the hall. It shatters against the wall, the screen cracking and pieces scattering, before the doors close, and I start to descend.

A singular thought ruminates in my head as beeps count each floor.

Layne wants to kill my father.

And he fucking deserves it.

25

LAYNE

I wake, naked in the darkness, to the sound of silence. With a yawn, I stretch my arms up to the headboard, my fingers skimming across the wood. There's a wonderful soreness between my legs, and I blindly reach for Archie, finding the opposite side of the bed empty and the sheets cold.

I open my eyes and blink over at his side of the bed. My heart flops at his absence, but I push the feeling away, ignoring it, and look to the window. Dawn hasn't crested the horizon, and the lights from the street lamps pass through the glass panes and shine onto the carpet.

My needy heart flounders again, and I swallow hard before the words come out.

You don't need him. You just want him. It's different.

"Archie?" I say to my room.

There's no answer, and I climb out of bed, stretching on the tips of my toes, trying to relax my sore muscles. Golden Boy was right. He may not be a god, but he certainly fucks like one. I lost count of how many times he made me come—four, I think—until my battered pussy was too sore, and he licked me clean, laving my sensitive flesh with his tongue. A shiver darts up my spine at the memory, igniting a delicious heat between my legs.

My mother sneers in the back of my brain. I'm going to need a metric ton of therapy to deal with that shit, but for now, I tell her to shut the fuck up.

I am allowed to feel.

He makes me feel.

And there's nothing she can do about it now.

My bare feet pad across the carpet, and I check the bathroom for Archie. I find it empty. I continue into the den, and a knot ties itself in my middle when I see he's not there either. My gaze scrolls, looking for him, before I spot a note at the end of my bare kitchen counter. I snatch it from the fake granite countertop and quickly read it.

I'm going to fix this for you, for us.
- Archie

I frown at his messy scrawl.

Fix it? What does he mean *fix it?*

The realization punches the breath from my lungs. Surely, he didn't. He wouldn't . . .

He went to confront Eli.

Fuck, fuck, fuck!

Eli is *mine!* Mine, dammit! Mine to punish! Mine to torment! All mine! What the fuck is he thinking?!

I stare at the note.

For you.

He's trying to fix it for you.

Panic blends with my rage until I shake with it, making the note tremble in my hands. Golden Boy can't take on his dad. Not for himself. Not for me! Not ever!

He's sweet. He's kind. He's . . . he's golden. His father, on the other hand, is as black as they come. Eli will tear Archie to pieces and set the scraps on fire while his son is still trying to find the good in him.

Goddammit! WHAT ARE YOU DOING, ARCHIE?!

I scramble, tripping over my feet and nearly falling to my ass as I race back into my bedroom and to my nightstand, looking for my phone. Panic slices through my chest when I remember it's at the club in my locker.

Shit!

I dress quickly, snatching up a pair of undies and leggings from my dresser and the first t-shirt I can find. I throw them on before I cram my feet into my running shoes without untying them, then I snatch some cash for the cab from the emergency stash I keep in an empty coffee container in the cabinet next to the fridge. I grab a knife from the drawer below it, pausing just long enough to find the right one. It's stainless steel, long, and serrated, perfect for cutting out Eli's black heart.

I slide the blade down into my leggings, the metal cool against my heated skin. The knife follows the line of my upper thigh, and I cover the handle with my shirt before I bolt out the door and down the stairs into the building's foyer. I wave for a cab and hop inside a moment later, giving the cabbie the address for Eli's apartment.

The driver doesn't make small talk as he drives—thank Christ. I couldn't even pretend to pay attention to him if he did. I stare out the window at my side, watching as we pass through the thin traffic. My knee bobs wildly, my fingers tapping against the cracked leather on the backseat.

An itchiness creeps across my flesh, sinking its teeth in, poisoning me with the need to cut, to regain control. I look down and find myself absentmindedly rubbing the scars hidden beneath my black leggings.

Back and forth, back and forth, faster and faster, like if I do it quick enough, my fingertips will sharpen into small blades and pierce my skin, satiating the need.

Pull it the hell together, Layne!

We arrive at Eli's building, and it snaps me back to the present. I toss the driver the cash I grabbed from the coffee tin and dart inside.

I don't give a fuck about the change. He can keep it, burn it, or take a shit on it for all I care.

Archie, Archie, where's Archie?

I bolt through the front door and into the building. My sneakers squeak on the shiny marble, and the morning shift guard raises his eyes from his newspaper and looks over his desk at me.

"Have you seen Eli Blakely's son?" I call to him, stopping in the center of the massive foyer. "Tall, blond, blue eyes?"

"Yeah," he answers with a nod. "Went up about twenty minutes ago."

Fuck, fuck, fuck!

I dart for the elevators, punching the button, and the one to my left opens a moment later. I hurry inside and punch the button for the penthouse. The metal sarcophagus feels like it's moving too fast and too slow at the same time, and when it finally arrives, I tap in the floor passcode. The door opens to let me into the hallway.

I step out of the elevator and freeze. There's a dent in the wall directly in front of me, breaching the sheetrock with bits of paint and plaster littering the floor. I spot Archie's phone among the damage, the screen shattered, bits of metal and glass on the carpet around it, his glossy Arlean University phone case cracked to bits.

Did they fight? Did Eli win? Did Eli hurt him? . . . FUCK!

My heart skips into my throat, and my hands shake again as I spot the open door to Eli's apartment and dart inside.

"Archie?" I call to the quiet, but there's no reply. I continue down the hall, past the kitchen and into the den, darting into the rooms.

I come to a halt when something crunches beneath my shoe. I look down to find bits of stained glass peppering the floor.

"Archie?" I say again, louder this time.

There's no reply except for the jittery wheeze of my own breath. My gaze scrolls past the glass and up to the staircase to the rooftop deck.

They're on the roof.

I bound up the stairs, the metal clanking beneath me, and out onto the deck. The promise of sun kisses the horizon. No Archie, though, just the whistle of the wind and the knoll of my pounding heart.

"Archie?" I say.

There's no response.

I walk forward, following the line of sculpted hedges toward the corner of the infinity pool that pours into the city skyline. Around the hedges and onto the open deck, I find Eli stretched out in a chair in front of the pool, sipping from a tall glass.

Reflexively, my hand finds the blade beneath my shirt. My gaze flits across the roof, over the stamped concrete and to the edge of the rooftop, past the mini-bar and to the hot tub. My mind whirls with questions as I swallow Archie's name.

How much does Eli know?

What has his son told him?

Is Archie okay?

Eli side-eyes me from his chair, and his jaw ticks. His cold blue eyes assess me.

"Layne," he says, my name sliding slowly off his tongue.

"Eli," I manage in return, inching forward to look around him, past the matching row of hedges on the opposite side of the roof. I can't see anything except the green sculpted bushes.

Fuck. Where are you, Golden Boy?!

I inch closer with no other choice but to walk straight past Eli to see if Archie is on the other side. Is he hurt? Unconscious? Worse?

It's either walking past the Blakely king or jumping into the pool and swimming past him. I'll take my chances on dry land.

Eli sips his drink again as I pass, careful to keep him in my peripheral vision. Chlorine pricks at my eyes and stings the inside of my nose before all my hopes and fears are extinguished in one blow. My breath leaves me in a long exhale and is carried away by the whipping wind when I turn to find the concrete pavestones opposite the hedges Archie-less. I stare at the empty space. No blood. No signs of a struggle. Nothing out of the normal at all.

"He's not here," Eli murmurs a moment before his fingers scrape across my middle, just below my breasts.

Fuck, when did he get up?

I go still beneath his touch.

"Why are you here, Layne?" he murmurs against my hair.

Worried about your son, I think, *who I just fucked.*

I'm not dumb enough to say it aloud. Eli's got fifty pounds of lean muscle on me, maybe more, and stands a foot taller. With him at my back right now, he also has the advantage.

"Eli," I say instead and move to pull away from him.

He doesn't let me go. He's fast, too fast, as he grabs me around the middle and pinches hard enough to bruise my insides. His hot breath blows across the side of my face as his other arm snares me.

"You've been a very naughty girl," he hisses with a low chuckle.

Shit! He's going to kill me, probably just like he did his son.

My chest hews open at the thought, my heart stuttering. The vile fucker. *What did he do to Archie?!* I'll make him bleed for it, for me, for my father, for the golden son he doesn't—*didn't?*—deserve.

I snatch the knife tucked into my waistband and twist free, throwing a wild slash, and catching Eli across the middle. The blade slices through his white dress shirt and nips at his middle. It's a shallow hit, and we both know it.

Eli stands there a moment, assesses his damage, and smiles. It's not nice, though. If anything, it's a predator's smile, his teeth too white, his canines too sharp, his arctic eyes too pale. That look promises death. Too bad for him, I'm going to kill him first.

He lunges for me, and he's quick, too quick. He knocks the blade from my hand with a jab of his forearm, and it skids across the floor to stop in front of another pool chair.

"You bitch!" he sneers as his hands clamp around my middle, pinning my arms flat against my sides. I buck against him, trying to break free, but he's too strong. I yank an arm free with an *oomph* and dig my nails into his forearm beneath his rolled-up dress sleeve. He howls and jerks backward, taking me with him.

We tumble into the water.

Warm. Suffocating. Wet.

Water shoots up my nose and clogs my throat as I claw and kick at him, desperate for air. He gives it right back at me, and I take a foot to the middle, knocking what's left of my breath out of me before I manage to get away. I come up for air, coughing and choking. Water washes away my vision and drags my hair into my eyes. Then he's on me again as I swim to the shallow end, over to where I can stand. He grabs me by the hair and searing pain rips through my scalp before he gets in my face and sneers.

"Is this what you want?" he snarls before he pushes my head beneath the water.

I gulp in water and cough, but I can't get it out. It's lodged in my throat, and it hurts, halving me down the middle.

I try to scream, but I can't. I reach up and try to claw Eli's hands, or anything I can reach, but he's too strong. He yanks me out of the water, and I cough and splutter.

Eli cackles before he shoves me under again, water washing the world away. Everything is muted. His dark pants, his black belt, his Rolex, all of it bleaches beneath the raging churn of the water and bubbles I create with my thrashing.

It burns in my middle.

It hurts.

It . . .

He yanks me up by the scalp again, and I cry out as he tears out a clump of hair this time. He pulls my head back, exposing my throat to him. I'm dizzy and unsteady as I cough up spit and chlorinated water, feeling it pool in my mouth to leak down my chin.

"Let me tell you a secret," Eli hisses through clenched teeth. "I will always win, little girl. *Always.* People like you will always serve people like me."

I spit in his face.

"Fuck!" he snarls as I rear back for an uppercut to his jaw. Before I can land the hit, he slams me into the wall behind me. My skull hits the concrete hard, and a ringing blasts through my ears.

The world turns off for a moment, and I wake to the warmth of blood matting my hair at the back of my head.

Eli jerks me around, capturing my hands in one large palm and planting them on the concrete. With his other, he tears down my leggings and my panties to below my ass.

"Time to pay up, little girl," he snarls behind me. "I earned this cunt."

"No," I try to say, but it's gargled, drowned by the blackness rolling over me. My head lolls forward, and I startle awake, my forehead pressed against the concrete. I cough as blood seeps between my lips and drips to the porous stone.

Eli knocks my legs wider with his knee and shoves the blunt tip of his dick inside me.

Everything in me breaks, shattering at once.

It hurts. I scream.

I choke on the blood and the lingering chlorine as he rams deeper.

"That's right," his hand cinches tighter around my wrists. "Take my cock like the whore you are."

No, no, no, no, no, no, NOOOOOOOOOO!

I'm so raw already, and the feel of him grates my insides like thick shards of glass. I vomit, coughing and choking on bile and blood, but he doesn't stop. If anything, my suffering spurs him to go faster.

My head pounds in time to my heartbeat, and the world goes black again.

The world relights with his hard, frantic thrusts.

The fire that the son ignited extinguishes with his father's every impale.

I choke, bile burning my teeth, tendrils of blood stretching across the concrete.

He comes on a groan, pulling my ass against him. I am ice cold as the world fades to black again.

26

ARCHIE

I grind my molars as I step off the elevator and into the lobby.

My father's a murderer.

My mother knew and apparently didn't care, not when my father's arrest would have jeopardized the family fortune.

Layne suffered.

My fists open and close, clenching and relaxing, as I run through the lobby.

I promised her I would fix it. I can't fix it. If anything, I just made it worse.

Shit!

Faraway, someone says something, but the sound dies before I make sense of it. I have to get back to Layne. I have to protect her. I have to . . . do something.

Shit!

I bolt outside and into the low buzz of early morning traffic. I start down the steps, ready to run for the car when a security guard catches my shoulder.

What?

I startle and nearly hit the guy before I stop myself. He's older, his short beard more gray than black, and out of shape, with a big round belly that jiggles when he breathes. He's totally out of breath when he manages to wheeze, "Girl," *gulps air*, "looking," *gulp*, "for you."

He gestures back to the front of the building with a clumsy hand.

A girl looking for me? What?

It slams into me like a freight train.

Layne!

I bolt back into the building, leaving the security guard behind. The guy grumbles something, but I don't know what it is. I'm back inside the cool air conditioning, my sneakers skidding and squeaking across the floor as I come to a screeching halt in front of the elevators and press the button. It lights up, but the elevators are all gone. I watch as the lights above the doors mark them as on the thirteenth floor and above. A moment later, the one closest to me descends one floor, stopping on the twelfth.

Fuck! I can run the stairs faster than this!

With that thought, I bolt to the emergency stairwell, down the hall, opening the door and climbing up the concrete steps. My footfalls echo in the small space, and my arms piston at my sides.

I'm on the seventh or eighth floor when my thighs start to burn, then my calves, and finally, even my breath. I suck in stale air, fear and adrenaline surging beneath my skin.

One flight passes after another, my sneakers squeaking, making it sound like I'm on a basketball court instead of in my father's building. My legs are on fire when I reach the top floor. I try to throw open the door, but it doesn't move before I notice the keypad beside it. I jab in the code for the penthouse floor, and the keypad beeps as the light on it switches from red to green. It takes another excruciating second for the door to unlock with a click.

I slam it open and shout her name.

"Layne!" echoes through the hall, but she doesn't answer.

My heart batters furiously in the hollow of my chest. Every part of me is on fire. My legs, my arms, my face, my middle. It's not the fear that burns through me, though. It's something meaner, nastier.

Desperation.

I sprint down the hallway, calling her name again, but there's no reply. I spot my phone still shattered on the floor in front of the elevator, and I bolt into my father's penthouse, shouting her name.

It reverberates in the hollow space, but again, she doesn't answer. The silence sends my pulse skyrocketing.

I run through the kitchen, calling for her again, darting between rooms, but they're still dead, empty and asleep. There's only one other place she could be, one other place my father could be.

The roof.

I bolt through the living room and up the stairs. My heartbeat skitters even faster with each rapid breath.

"Layne!" I yell to the wind as I barrel onto the roof. There's no answer from anyone, and I don't see her or my father. There's just the hum of traffic waking up in the morning and the first glimpse of early morning sunlight.

Two hurried steps later, everything in me goes cold. The wind carries soft whimpers to me, and I lurch forward to the pool. What I find glues me where I stand. I'm abruptly freezing and on fire. I smell blood and chlorine and the death of *everything* I care about.

My father is soaking wet, water darkening his hair an ugly brown and plastering his white dress shirt to his chest. He's bleeding from a cut in his middle, or at least I think he might be. There's so much blood, *too* much blood.

On him. On her. In the water. On the concrete.

He stands behind a broken and battered Layne. Her right eye is nearly swollen shut, her bottom lip fat and bleeding, her nose scraped and busted. Blood pools in the water beside her, on the concrete in front of her, and runs from her nose down to her chin. Vomit puddles on the concrete next to where he has her hands pinned, and tears paint shiny rivulets across her bruised face as he . . . he . . .

Rapes her.

A strangled, dying sound explodes past my lips as my father moans and thrusts even faster, tipping his head to the heavens. Like he's taunting them to send him straight to hell where he belongs.

Layne's bleary eyes roll back in her skull, and a switch inside me flips.

I want his blood.

I want his pain.

I want all of it.

Then I'm going to kill the fucker.

My father thrusts even faster, his movements jerky. Layne isn't there, though. She's gone, her fiery gaze utterly erased. If it weren't for the tears streaming down her cheeks and the choppy exhale of her breath, I would think she was dead.

I rear forward as my father stills behind her with a final groan. It takes one step to commit the look of a living corpse to memory. And three more to be forever haunted by the expression of pure ecstasy on my father's slack-jawed face. And six more to reach them.

I yank Layne out first, making sure she's on dry land, before I reach down and grab the bastard by the front of his dress shirt. I heave him out of the pool with both hands, his eyes popping open in shock as I drag him across the concrete. His dick flops between us, limp and wet, as I slam the bastard onto the floor.

"You fucking piece of shit!" I roar.

He cackles up at me wildly before I hit him hard, directly on the face, hearing the satisfying crunch and feeling the give of his nose beneath the unforgiving line of my knuckles. His nose immediately spurts blood, and it runs across his cheeks and into his mouth, painting sanguine lines across his teeth.

My father laughs again, the sound somehow both cocky and unhinged, and I hit him. I don't stop. I don't pause. I barely even breathe as I pummel the bastard as hard as I can, knocking the wind from my lungs with every punch. Bones break with pops and cracks that spur me on harder, faster, further.

My knuckles split open, but I barely feel it. White-hot fury sears me from the inside. I want him to pay. To suffer. To *die*.

I can't see his face anymore as I continue to wail on him, hitting anywhere I can reach from my position on top of him. His face, his neck, his chest, his shoulders. Until all I see is the blood and snot and spit, but somehow, he's still laughing, even as he gurgles on his own blood and chokes on it beneath me.

The pungent odor of piss and shit slams into me, and I realize he shit himself. Still, I don't stop, not when both of his eyes are almost swollen shut, or when his jaw juts out at an unnatural angle with a sickening crack that tells me it's dislocated, or when he starts to suffocate.

I don't stop until I'm dragged off him, howling for revenge, my father still breathing.

Warm water presses against my back, soaking my shirt, and I turn to push whatever it is away when I lock gazes with Red. Her face is bloodied and broken, and it's even worse up close, where I can see the busted capillaries around her eye and her split lip still oozing.

She reeks of blood and pool water.

"Stop," she says, her busted lip making the word thick and slow. "Stop, just stop it."

I want to kill him for her. I will kill him. *For her.*

"Stop," she says again, wincing as she tugs on me, her leggings not even pulled all the way back into place.

I don't move, and she grips my face between her hands and stares at me. She pins me there with her one aqua eye that isn't swollen. My father gurgles on the ground below me and convulses.

"No," she manages, starting to cry again, her eye swelling even further with her tears. "No, not for me."

But everything is for you, I want to say.

"Please," she begs, and I feel my resolve start to melt before I finally nod at her. My fists burn from the hits. My eyes sting from angry tears. All the while, Eli gurgles on his own blood on the concrete.

Layne moves suddenly, crawling on her hands and knees, beneath a pool chair to snatch a big knife. I watch as she crawls back to my father, and I step out of her way.

I should stop her.

I should tell her no. I don't do either.

Instead, I watch as she kneels in front of him, where he now lays, his face swollen and disfigured, blood seeping from every orifice I can see.

Layne draws the blade against his limp dick and presses. He doesn't stir. She presses harder, piercing the skin and drawing a fat drop of blood. Still, he doesn't stir. She drags the blade up and over his chest, across the line of his torn shirt and over his heart. He chokes and spits, nearly unconscious.

Back and forth, she runs the knife across his chest and over his heart. A couple of inches deeper, and it would be over.

I want her to do it.

I want to do it for her.

Yet, I just watch.

Layne suddenly leans back on her heels, raising the knife in front of her between her clenched hands. I hold my breath, but the blow never comes. Instead, she sneers down at my father.

"You aren't worth it," she hisses before she raises the blade and draws a line through the one that already marks his chest, branding him with a giant X across his middle.

He's hers. He's property. Unless he dies from the beating I gave him.

He winces at the fresh cut and stirs but doesn't fully wake. She tosses the blade into the pool, and it sinks beneath the pink-tinted water to the bottom.

She stands and I climb to my feet too.

"Do you need to sit?" I ask, my voice cracking between the words.

She shakes her head, wincing with the movement, and I hold on to her as we walk toward the stairwell to leave the roof.

She grimaces and then whimpers. A moment later, when her legs give out beneath her, I pick her up and carry her down the metal stairs into the apartment, leaving my father writhing on the floor above. We walk through the penthouse and into the hallway where I pull the red fire alarm mounted on the wall. Then I collapse to the floor, exhaustion getting the best of me. The alarm wails, and we hold each other as we wait for the police to arrive.

27

LAYNE

*I*t's cold in here. I'm freezing, all of me shivering as my fingers pull the thin woven blanket up my stomach and toward my chest. A chill leeches from the waterproof mattress and through the bedsheet beneath me and onto my back, where my skin is exposed by the hospital gown.

I hear my teeth rattle in my skull, clattering together, and I grip Archie's warm hand tighter, hard enough to crunch his bones together, yet he doesn't pull away. If anything, he scoots closer until he's right at my side. The doctor pushes the speculum further inside me, burning me from the inside out. The painkillers they gave me do nothing to stop the daggers shooting through my pelvis and up into my abdomen.

The speculum is cold, hard, and foreign, and I desperately want this to be over with. It scrapes inside me, ripping me apart.

1,035.

I hiccup on a sob I refuse to let out, and unshed tears prick at my eyes. The white ceiling swims beneath them, and when I blink, the tears fall, trailing from the corners of my eyes and down the sides of my face to the flat pillow beneath my head. I continue staring up at the paneled ceiling, counting the little holes in each white panel.

1,036.

The doctor adjusts on his chair at the end of the bed, where he's seated between my legs. The pungent stench of iodine hits me, and my eyes water even more beneath the stench.

1,037.

The swivel chair squeaks as the doctor adjusts again. Cold air hits my exposed flesh, and I shiver even harder in the bed.

1,038.

Please be done.

Please be done.

Please be fucking done!

1,039.

A moment later, the doctor slides the speculum out of me, and I exhale at the relief as the pressure finally abates. My insides still burn, though, as my knees fall together. The nurses move to help me move up in the bed and to cover myself.

"All done," the doctor says as he stands, taking off his gloves and throwing them in the waste bin. I barely hear his words.

1,039.

That's how many dots it took to perform the rape kit.

1,039 tiny black dots.

1,039 dots for the hospital staff to gather their evidence, to examine me, to take pictures and collect samples, to poke and prod, to scrape beneath my fingernails and inspect my wounds.

1,039 dots of pain.

The dull ache at the back of my head starts up again, and my swollen eye and busted nose throb in time to my heartbeat. I wish I could give myself to the cold nothingness, but it never saves me from the bad. It only steals away the good, just like my mother did.

I need sleep but everything hurts.

The doctor says something, but I'm not sure if it's to me before he leaves, his two nurses following him.

Warm fingers flatten against either side of my face and turn me gently. I look up to see Archie staring down at me. His touch shoots slivers of sunshine straight through my center, erasing the shivers, and I close my eyes beneath his brilliant warmth. His touch is pure light peeking through the snow, and my eyes open once more as he says something to me.

"Look at me," he murmurs again, and I do. His stare pours liquid warmth into my middle, straight through me. It flutters in my belly and rises, scaring away the last of my shivers.

"There you are," he says, peering down at me.

I've been here the whole time, I want to say, but someone steps into my room. He releases me a moment later. His sunshine retreats, and my shivering starts again.

"Hi, Ms. Steele," a middle-aged man with a potbelly and a goatee too dark to match his brown hair says before he flashes his police badge. "I'm Detective Stewart. I just need to ask you a few more questions if you're feeling up to it."

"She's not," Archie says at the same moment that I nod.

The detective looks to Archie, a frown crossing his thin lips. "I'll just be a minute."

"She's been questioned and examined for *hours*," Archie says.

"It's just protocol, sir."

"It's okay," I tell Archie, and his brow pinches as he looks at me before he nods.

We begin, and I answer the detective's questions, recounting almost everything for what has to be the fortieth time at this point. I'm unemotional, my voice monotone like I'm telling a story that isn't mine.

"So you brought the knife with you?" the detective interrupts eventually, eyeing me over the notepad he's been using.

"She was scared of him," Archie snaps in my defense.

The detective shoots him a sharp look before his gaze slips to me and softens.

"By the looks of it, you had every right to be afraid, Ms. Steele," he says after a moment. "You're lucky to be alive."

"Are we done?" Archie asks a moment later.

"Yes," the detective closes his notepad, "for now."

"Where is he?" I ask, hating how a dose of desperation laces the words.

"You're safe, Ms. Steele," the detective replies.

"Where is he?" I repeat.

He frowns. "I'm afraid I can't . . ."

"Just tell me!" I nearly shout, my voice cracking before I soften my next word. "*Please.*"

The detective sighs. "Your alleged attacker is in surgery at a different facility. That's all I can say."

He eyes Archie's busted knuckles, covered in cuts and dried blood. "From what I understand, he took a hell of a beating, dislocated his jaw, even fractured his orbital socket."

"He deserved more," Archie says, the words low and still.

The detective looks to me again. "Try to get some rest. The DA's office will handle it from here. They'll probably stop by in the morning."

"That's it?" I ask with a cough that hurts from the top of my head to the tips of my toes.

"That's it," the cop replies, like it's just over, like I can move on now, like it never happened at all.

The nurse arrives with a knock on the door and walks inside. Her blue scrubs match the surgical gloves she pulls from a pack hanging on the wall. She smiles at me as she walks over to my IV pole and starts pressing buttons on the machine.

"The doctor wanted to give you something extra for the pain," she explains.

Thank God.

She digs into a pocket on her shirt and takes out a needle filled with clear liquid. She clears the bubbles from the syringe and inserts it into the IV line. A moment later, she adds, "He wants to keep you overnight for observation. It's standard procedure for the hairline fracture at the back of your skull and your concussion. Normally, only family members are allowed to stay overnight, but I won't tell if you won't."

"Thank you," Archie says, and I repeat the sentiment.

I sigh, all of me relaxing. The pain finally recedes as whatever she gave me hits my bloodstream.

The detective excuses himself, and the nurse leaves a minute or two later after checking my vitals. Archie pulls up a chair next to my bed to sit beside me. He holds my hand in silence, his fingers threading around mine, until a cafeteria worker brings in a tray and places it on my bedside table. Archie opens the lid in front of me, exposing chicken tenders and green beans, and my stomach rolls. I push the tray away, trying not to vomit.

"You need to eat," he tells me gently.

"You eat it," I say with a gag. "If I eat, I'm going to throw up."

He frowns but sneaks a chicken tender off the plate as the hum of the machines lulls me to sleep.

I'm jostled awake by Archie climbing into the hospital bed beside me, his big hands moving me slightly to the side, readjusting my IV line, and keeping me covered by the blankets.

"What are you doing?" I mumble through the grogginess as he struggles to fit his large frame beside me.

"You were whimpering in your sleep," he murmurs to me with a shush.

He settles beside me, and his scent—vanilla cookies and campfires—cuts through the smell of bleach lingering in the sterile hospital room. I nuzzle in closer as he lays on his side and gently pulls me toward him so I can feel the steady rise of his breath.

"I thought you left," I admit.

He goes still before he brushes the hair out of my eyes and says, "Never, pretty girl. You can't get rid of me."

I snuggle closer, seeking his warmth, his comfort, his sunshine.

"Thank you for saving me," I murmur as the painkillers beckon me to a dreamless slumber and my eyes flutter shut once more.

"Shh," he tells me, smoothing my messy hair. "I didn't save you, Layne. You saved yourself. I just came along for the ride."

28

ARCHIE

It's been less than seventy-two hours since the *incident* occurred, as the police kept calling it. I'll call it what it was, though, rape. Layne and I are back on campus today for class, though I wish she had let me keep her home for a few more days at least. My hands are worse for wear, busted and bruised, my knuckles in various stages of healing. Layne, though, looks like she's been through hell. Her right eye is rimmed in black, almost completely swollen shut. Cuts and scrapes mar her pretty face, across her nose and over her forehead. Her bottom lip is busted, but the swelling's gone down. Glue mats the hair at the back of her head where they had to stop even more bleeding and put her scalp back together.

I don't give a shit how she looks, but my father's arrest is out there, plastered across every mainstream and minor media outlet. He doesn't have a mugshot yet because of his continued hospitalization, but the details of the charges are there, an arrest for the rape and assault of an unknown woman. I was at least able to save Layne from the reporting vultures, thanks to an emergency call with my father's old public relations team, who won't touch him with the world's longest pole anymore. As soon as someone sees her face, though, they're going to suspect—if not know—she is the *unknown woman*, and I won't be able to stop them.

I look over at her across the seat and say, "Are you sure you want to go to class? You can take a couple more days."

I've already suggested this at least a thousand fucking times since last night. The knot in my stomach tightens with her expected answer. She'll tell me she can handle herself. My response? She sure as fuck can, but that doesn't mean she should.

This time, though, she doesn't utter the same words. Instead, she side-eyes me with her one open eye, and says, "I'm not a doll, Blakely."

"I know you aren't," I placate, reaching over the center console to tuck a stray lock of copper hair behind her ear. "You're the strongest person I know, Layne, but it's only been a few days. You can miss some time. It's taken care of. The absences are already excused."

She frowns and shoots me another look for good measure, one that says we aren't talking about this again. But I want to tell her that she hasn't even cried yet, not really, just an occasional tear when the pain got to be too much.

Not in the hours we spoke with the police.

Not at the hospital as the doctors put her back together.

Or when they had her lay back on the examination table and put her legs in the stirrups.

Or when the nurse gave her the morning-after pill and STI preventatives, and she took them with water from a paper cup.

Shouldn't she have cried?

Shouldn't she be grieving?

Or mad?

Or something besides . . . besides *this*?

"You don't have to go to class today," I say to her, watching as students pass outside the car, talking to one another.

"No, I do," she looks at me again. "I always shut down, one way or the other, and I won't do it anymore. I won't allow it."

"You need to deal with it, pretty girl," I plead. "You need to recover."

She glares at me, and if looks could kill, I'd be smoldering in my seat. "Are you mansplaining getting over rape to me, Golden Boy?"

Her words hit deep, and I wince. She sighs a moment later, running a hand across her bruised face.

"I'm sorry," she murmurs. "I didn't mean that. I know you're just trying to help."

"I'm worried about you," I say.

She gives me a small, reassuring smile. "There's nothing to worry about."

Then she climbs out of the car, and I quickly follow her, grabbing our backpacks out of the backseat. I catch up to her a few feet ahead on the lawn and say her name. She turns around, devours the short distance between us, and captures my face between her small hands. She leans up on the tips of her toes and presses her lips to mine. My hands go around her waist, and I tug her into my arms, letting her lead though, careful of her injuries.

Her tongue swipes inside my mouth, and she tastes of the round peppermint candies she's been munching on all morning. She keeps on kissing me through wolf whistles from guys I want to beat the shit out of, while some twat nearby claps, and until my chest aches for breath. Only then, sucking in air, does she finally break away.

"What was that for?" I manage, looking down at her, my lips hovering over hers.

"For caring," she says. "You want to help?"

"Absolutely. Anything."

"Then don't treat me any different, okay? I need you to just be yourself."

There are so many things I want to say, but I swallow the words, gulping down the question that's been scratching inside my skull, trying to claw its way out. I'm afraid to learn the answer because that question leads to so many others.

What if you're the reason she hasn't grieved?

What if you're hurting her?

What if . . .

"What is it?" she asks, her gaze darting between my eyes as she tries to read my face.

"You're perfect," I deflect, capturing her hand in mine and tugging her forward to the building. She stops walking a moment later, pulling me back to her.

"What did I tell you the first day of school, football star?" she asks me. "That flirty diversion thing won't work on me."

"Come on," I laugh, pulling her toward our Statistics class again.

We're getting looks—well, Layne's getting looks because her face resembles a human punching bag—but I don't care. Fuck 'em.

"Tell me," she says, leaving no room for debate.

"It's nothing, Red," I say.

She yanks her hand from mine. "Tell me."

Even more people are staring now, and I give them all a glare that sends the smart ones scurrying for cover. Morning sunlight hits her back and makes her hair sparkle like spun copper.

I shove my lonely hand into the back pocket of my jeans.

"I'm just worried . . ." I say, licking my lips, willing the words to slide out. "It's fucking stupid. I'm sorry. This isn't about me."

Fix your shit, man!

"You were there too." She steps closer, her brow furrowing. "You saved me, Archie. Of course it's about you too."

I swallow, hard. "It's nothing, Red."

"Tell me," she whispers, concern weaving between each letter.

Now is not the time, Blakely! Never is the time!

"Say it," she pleads.

"My father hurt you, Red," I answer, the words choppy and broken like they went through a meat grinder before leaving my mouth. "And you haven't cried, and I'm worried. I'm worried that you look at me, and . . . I don't want you to . . . I would understand if you look at me and see him." I swallow again, the words poisoning the air between us. "And I can't hurt you, Red . . ." I clear my throat. "I can't be the reason you are in pain, so just promise me, okay? Promise to tell me if I hurt you."

Her brows knit together, and she stares at me for a moment before she shakes her head.

"I could never see your father when I look at you." She steps forward, gripping my face between her soft hands. "I see you. You shine, Blakely, just like gold."

The weight squeezing my chest lifts a little as she offers her hand to me. I accept it, our fingers cinching tight.

Am I this guy, the hand holding guy?

The exclusive guy?

The boyfriend type?

I don't know, but I don't think it matters. I am whatever she needs me to be.

"Walk me to class?" she asks.

"My pleasure," I say, hitching our backpacks up my shoulder.

"Hey," she says, looking over at me, "we're going to be all right, Archie."

"I know," I agree, though everything is in shambles. My father's company, my family, my . . . Layne.

"We're going to be all right," I agree, and for the first time in days, I actually think we might be.

29

LAYNE

SIX WEEKS LATER

I sit in the district attorney's office across from one of their lawyers. The guy looks too young to be an attorney, but he at least seems to know his stuff. He adjusts his bowtie across the table from me. This one is eye-scalding pink with white polka-dots. He wears the most hideously adorable bowties with matching pocket squares, and I wonder to myself if he lost a bet. Everything is seersucker with this dude or disturbingly bright. It's an affront to those of us with eyeballs.

He keeps talking, and I will myself to listen, though he's undoubtedly covering the same shit we spoke about twenty minutes ago. Is that like a requirement of being a lawyer or something? Does their pledge or oath or whatever include some bullshit about boring others to death?

"We have more than enough to convict on the rape and the assault," he says, flipping through Eli's fat file on his desk, papers poking out of it. "Between the rape kit and the eyewitness testimony, I feel confident he will be found guilty, but Ms. Steele," he sighs —*ugh*, it's never good when he sighs. He leans back in his chair, tipping it back. "I have to say again that as to your father's death, we cannot, at this time, ask the grand jury to indict. Everything our office has been able to piece together is circumstantial at best, and flat out inadmissible at worst. Going back that far, nearly two decades, and with most of the evidence long destroyed, it's challenging."

"I understand," I say.

He frowns at me and then down at the file and then back at me again before he straightens in his chair.

"I have good news, though," he says, flipping through the file again. "Eli Blakely's bond was denied, so he'll be sitting in jail until his trial. He fought hard at the bond hearing, even asked the judge to reconsider his decision, but the judge entered an order denying his motion for reconsideration this morning. She deemed him too much of a flight risk to be granted bond."

"Good," I agree with a nod. "Is there anything else you need from me?"

"No," the attorney shuts his file, "thank you for coming in today."

"Thank you," I say, standing and exiting through his door before he can give me his spiel for like the fiftieth time. He joins me and walks me down the hall to the lobby. I'm headed through the door when I nearly collide with six-plus feet of tall, lean, blond man.

Golden Boy grins down at me, and my heart jumps for joy in response.

"Want to get out of here?" he asks.

"Fuck yes," I murmur as he grabs my hand and steers me to the exit. He holds the door for me as we walk out into the early afternoon sun.

"I thought you had finals today," I tell him.

"Didn't you hear? I'm super smart. I got out early." He winks at me, and I swear one wink is hot enough to melt me. I nearly collapse into a puddle onto the asphalt.

Calm your coochie, bitch!

He auto-starts his car with the push of a button on his key fob.

"There's something I want to show you," he says over to me, his fingers warm around mine, "if you're feeling up to it."

"Okay," I agree.

"Shit," he stops in front of his car and looks over at me. "Did you drive?"

"No, I took an Uber from campus."

"Good," he opens the passenger-side door for me, and I climb inside. He hops in beside me a second later, and I turn on the radio as we pull out of the parking lot.

"Where are we going?" I ask as we merge onto the highway.

"It's a surprise," he says.

"I hate surprises," I reply.

"It's a good surprise, promise," he offers with a wink.

"You all right?" I ask him.

"You starting to feel something for me, Red?"

I scoff. "Never."

He grins at me, running his tongue across his upper lip as he does.

"Don't get cocky," I say. "I'm just saying you look like shit, Blakely."

"Hot shit," he retorts with a snort.

"Yes, hot shit," I agree, "but still shit."

"I'm just tired," he says with a yawn. "Between finals and the company and . . ."

"Me?"

"I'm never too busy for you, pretty girl."

"I'm serious," I say.

"I'm fine," he shrugs. "Don't worry about me."

He glances over at me. "Shit . . . Wait." He shakes his head as he changes lanes. "Okay, it can't be a surprise. Are you okay with going to the office?"

"Yes," I answer. "It's going to take more than a building to scare me off."

"You sure?" he offers. "We can turn around."

"No," I shake my head. "I want my surprise."

He nods, smiling to himself, and drives us to the headquarters of Eli's company. We park in the downstairs parking garage and take the employee elevator into the building.

"Come on," Archie says as we arrive at the top floor. He grabs my hand and steers me inside, but it doesn't look like how I remembered. There's no more black and gray or boring cityscapes on the walls. Everything is soft, almost feminine, and the photographs of cityscapes have been replaced with giant paintings.

Roses. Rubies. Sunsets. Flowers, all in soft oranges, pinks, and reds.

"What is this?" I ask him as we walk past employee offices.

"Doing a little renovating," Archie answers with a lopsided grin.

We arrive at Eli's office, or what used to be his office at least, only it looks nothing like it. The desk for his receptionist—and the receptionist—is gone, replaced by two tall wooden doors with sleek silver handles. He opens a door. A thick sheet of plastic hangs from the ceiling immediately behind the doors, and we duck beneath it as we step inside.

Nearly everything of Eli's is gone as well. The gray floor has been replaced with a thin cream carpet woven with filaments of gold. The domineering bookshelves that lined the wall behind his desk have been removed, leaving an empty wall behind them. The only hint of Eli that remains is his giant glass desk, still standing where he used to sit. My heart lurches into my throat and stays there.

"What is this?" I ask Archie.

"The Board voted him out," Archie answers, releasing my hand to let me explore the giant room. It has been expanded into the conference room that used to sit on the other side of the wall, making it even more massive than before. "After they found out about the charges, they held an emergency meeting and forcibly sold his shares."

"Oh my God," I say, my mind whirling.

Everything he had built on the back of my father's death sold out from beneath him.

Archie runs a finger across the back of a lone metal folding chair. "It's too bad someone had to buy the shares and become the primary stakeholder."

My heart catches in my throat once more.

"You?" I breathe.

He slowly nods, gauging my reaction. "With the help of a few very generous friends."

A laugh bubbles out of me.

"Of course the rich boy has rich friends," I tease.

Archie smirks. "I mean, well, yes, but . . ."

"Thank you," I tell him, looking around the room, taking in the erasure of Eli's legacy.

"Oh, pretty girl," he says, walking toward me, his white Henley hugging his broad chest, "I'm not done."

"What?" I say.

"This," he waves a hand at the large room, "will be the charitable donations division of the company. Going forward, half of all the profits—representative of my father's share in the business—will be donated each year. I want you to run it after you graduate, Layne. You can donate to whatever you want. Unsolved crime nonprofits, children's rescue organizations, anything at all, completely at your discretion."

His kindness hurts, incinerating my breath away and starting a pinch in my middle.

"Bring in whomever you want to help," he tells me. "Staff, whatever you need, but this space has your name on it, Red, along with all my shares, if you'll take them."

I shake my head furiously, trying to not cry and failing miserably.

"What's wrong?" he steps forward, his shoes grazing the tips of mine. "I will raze this building to the ground if you want me to."

"I can't accept," I manage, coughing on the words.

He cocks his head at me, concerned. "Which part?"

"Your shares." I laugh with a wet sniffle. "I'd be a terrible board member. I'd never show up on time. I'd dress entirely inappropriate. I'd tell everyone to fuck off."

"I hope so," he grins. "I can't wait to see it."

"I can't . . ." I begin, and his grin falters a fraction. "I can't do it alone." I reach between us to grab his large hands between mine. "Partners?"

"You deserve all of it and more."

"I don't want it," I tell him, "not without you."

I reach up, my hands planting on either side of his face, and bring his lips to mine. He tastes like salt and sin, and I climb his tall frame, wrapping my legs around his waist, my hands circling the back of his neck.

He breaks us apart.

"Are you sure?" he murmurs, his Adam's apple bobbing with his swallow.

"About everything."

"That's not what I meant."

"I know. Make me forget."

He lowers his mouth to mine, stopping to hover just above my lips.

"Pretty girl," he growls, carrying me over to the desk, "I'll make you forget everything before me."

Then his lips crash to mine.

30

LAYNE

*A*rchie carries me over to his father's empty desk and places me on the edge of the glass. His hands find the straps of my tank top and pull them down my shoulders, his calloused fingertips gentle against my skin.

"Is this okay?" he murmurs, his hot breath fanning over my face.

I put two fingers under his chin and steer him to look at me.

"Don't treat me like a doll, Blakey. I won't shatter beneath your touch."

"No," he murmurs against my lips, "I think you'll shatter me instead."

He's been careful with me. He hasn't pushed for sex, for intimacy, for anything, and I haven't wanted it. We've kept busy. He's worked all hours, trying to balance the company, school, and football. I've met with the district attorney's office, studied my ass off, and attended the survivors of sexual assault group sessions the hospital referred me to, though I haven't spoken during them yet. Right now, I'm okay to just sit and listen. It's enough.

Archie stands in front of me and stares, and I know it's another opportunity to back out. It ignites a spark of anger inside me.

I want him, dammit!

I want him to make me feel again, to incinerate the scars left by his father.

I reach between us and peel off my tank top, dropping it to the floor, taking my bra with it. I lift my ass and slide off my skirt, letting it fall with my panties to join my shirt and bra. I kick off my shoes too, letting the warmth of the carpet tickle my bare feet before I lift myself back onto the desk, propping my elbows behind me and thrusting my breasts front and center.

I watch him as he watches me.

He goes very still, his mouth parting as sunlight from the windows scatters diamonds across the room.

I spread my legs wide, letting him see *everything*.

"Holy fuck," Archie breathes, taking a step closer. The cords of his neck jut outward as his fists ball at his sides. Still, he doesn't touch me.

I dip a finger between my legs and touch myself, slow and gentle. The look he's giving me spurs me on. It's absolute captivation, complete control. I run a finger down my pussy and over my clit, and his mouth parts as he cocks his head, bites his bottom lip, and stares at *me*.

It makes me even wetter.

I don't need Eli's company or to command a bunch of old men in a boardroom.

Why would I when I can control the man who burns as bright as gold instead?

I slide my finger up and down my slit, rubbing faster, harder, thrusting my fingers in and out of me, showing him everything. I spread my legs wider across Eli's desk, the glass hard against my ass as I defile the last reminder of him in this room. Fire coils in my belly and my breasts heave as Archie steps forward, sunlight weaving through his blond hair.

"You're fucking gorgeous, Red," he murmurs. "Always so pretty, so wet for me."

He sinks to his knees in front of me and withdraws my hand.

His thumb traces the scars inside my thigh. It tickles, but it doesn't hurt. He kisses my flesh there softly, and it's the hottest thing

I've ever seen. His blue eyes are blown to black as the bristles across his chin tickle my ultra-sensitive flesh.

"You okay, pretty girl?" he murmurs, his hot breath rolling across my skin.

"Yes."

"Then keep touching yourself, baby," he commands.

I do, running my fingers back along my slit as he peppers kisses inside my thighs and between my legs. He puts his hands on my knees and spreads me even wider before he leans forward and licks a line from nearly my asshole up to my clit.

I jerk away, and he nips at me.

"Don't hide from me." He looks up at me, pinning me where I sit, and pops his pinky finger into his mouth. He curls his other fingers until only his thumb and his pinky are exposed. Then he blesses me with a lopsided grin that shows one dimple.

"What are you doing?" I breathe.

"Lay back and be a good girl, Red," he tells me, and I do as he says, leaning onto my elbows on the desk, watching as he lowers his face between my legs and laves his tongue flat against me.

Fuck!

I arch my back, my hair going behind me to scrape across the desk. He thrusts his tongue in and out of me, over and over again, and fuck, it feels so good, but so slow—tortuously slow—as I wind my fingers through his hair.

He suddenly breaks away, his hot breath fanning over my slick skin.

"I thought I told you to keep touching yourself," he murmurs.

"Isn't that what you're for?" I whine.

He chuckles and dips between my legs again, and my grip tightens in his hair. I am shaking, so close, on a precipice.

"That's it, pretty girl," he growls, his thumb thrumming my clit, his little finger nudging my forbidden hole. "Be good and come for me."

I can't stop the fall, and I tumble over the edge as he shoves his pinky in all the way, and heat explodes inside me, all of me spasming. When he lifts his head, his mouth and chin are wet with my cum.

"What do you want now?" he asks, licking his lips.

He's giving me one last chance to back out, but I don't want it.

"You," I tell him.

He stands, discarding his shirt and undoing his jeans, letting them drop to the floor with my clothes until he's naked, all lean sinew and muscle and his thick cock.

"Shit," he murmurs, reaching for the floor. "Condom."

"No," I say, and he goes still.

"I'm on birth control now. I started after . . ." I don't want to talk about this anymore. "Fuck me, Blakely, and don't be gentle."

"Layne," he warns.

"Fill me up, Golden Boy. Fuck it all away."

His jaw ticks.

"Do it!" I say, reaching forward and grabbing the head of his dick. He steps forward with a hiss as I line us up.

His cock teases my entrance as he takes his sweet time.

"Fuck me!" I shout at him, not caring if the employees outside hear.

"I am," he growls, sinking in an inch.

"No, you're not," I snarl.

He draws out slowly, the veins in his forearms bulging as his hands clench around my waist.

"What's wrong with this?" he asks, teasing me with his cock again.

I glare at him. "Fuck him out of me, Archie. Incinerate his goddamn memory. Fuck me like I'm begging you to!"

Something in his gaze detonates, and he grabs my hair and brings me in for a bruising kiss before he impales me, his big cock bottoming out inside me.

"Is this what you want, baby?" he growls, rocking forward. "Want me to split you open? Tear you apart on my dick?"

"God, yes," I mewl.

He chuckles, and the sound ignites a fire across my skin. "You're such a good girl when you're taking my cock."

"It's the," I suck in a breath as he pulls out, all the way to the tip, and slams into me again, "only time I'm a good girl."

My boobs jiggle, all of me shaking with the ferocity of his thrusts.

He scoots my ass up to the edge of the desk and ruts me like an animal. Sunlight spills across his back and into his hair as I cling to him, his fingers digging into my ass.

Smack. Thrust.

Smack. Thrust.

Smack.

My wetness smears between us and across the glass desk.

"I'm going to come," I say when the heat starts to build again.

"You better," he growls, the sound low, vibrating through his chest.

"Oh fuck." I quake beneath his brutal thrusts as he slams inside me over and over again.

"Scream my name for the people outside, pretty girl," he commands. "Let them know how good we fuck."

His dirty words are my undoing, and I come, throwing my head back and clinging to him as he pounds into me, his hot breath tickling my skin. It's so fast, so hard, until I can't take it. Finally, he empties inside me, his hips jerking as he fills me, before he collapses on top of me, pinning me between him and his father's desk. I hold him against me, gently running my nails across his broad shoulders as our breath steadies and our cum stains his father's ugly desk.

EPILOGUE
LAYNE, FOUR YEARS LATER

I sit at my desk and reach for my iced coffee, taking a sip from the ridiculously large clear cup. Papers litter my desk, covering every available inch. I lean back in my chair and sigh to the ceiling. A door opens, and Archie arrives, dressed in a navy-blue bespoke suit with tan loafers. Every time I see him in a suit, it steals my breath away. Running a company looks damn good on him.

He's fucking gorgeous, and everyone in the company knows it, especially the interns, whom I tease him about mercilessly. He strides over and drops a chocolate chip cookie on my desk.

Uh oh. That only means one thing.

"Are you bribing me?" I ask.

"What?" he gifts me a toothy grin. "Can't I do something nice for you?"

I snatch the cookie and take a bite. It's orgasmic-level good, and I've told him that many times. He's taken it as a challenge *every* time.

"You only bring me cookies from the break room when you want something."

He leans against my desk, half-sitting, half-standing.

"Come with me?" he asks, offering his hand.

"I can't," I groan, though the thought of a quickie in the car or a closet or anywhere sets me on fire. "I have all these proposals to go through."

"It's our company, baby," he whispers to me with a wink. "We can do whatever we want."

"No," I complain, though the offer is tempting. "I have to finalize charitable contributions for the quarter."

"Well, then," he picks up an application packet and looks at it before tossing it back to the pile, "let me help. What do we have?"

"This one is for the survivors of domestic abuse in Sacramento," I pick up a proposal in a black three-ring binder and flip to the front page. "They want to build temporary housing."

I comb through the pile, selecting a spiral-bound packet this time. "This one helps fund the processing of sexual assault kits in jurisdictions with limited resources and funds."

"And this one," I find another, "works against human trafficking."

I select another from the chaos. "This one works to end global hunger."

"All noble causes," he says, as I reach for another proposal. It's not as pretty as the others, no clear protective pages or spiral bound notebooks.

"This group provides housing for runaway kids."

He nods, grabs my drink, and takes a sip.

"Well," he clucks his tongue after he swallows, "why not all of them?"

"What?" I look at him like he's crazy because he has to be to suggest that. "These are ten-year grants. That would be an astronomical amount of money. The Board will never approve it."

Archie shrugs. "I think they will, especially when we leak to the press what they're voting on."

"Really?" I breathe, my eyes going wide.

"Really, Red."

I stand and throw my arms around the back of his neck with a squeal.

"I love you," I say, kissing him. He tastes like my iced coffee and a golden heart.

"I love you too," he says to me. "Now that it's decided, come on."

He grabs my hand and leads me out of my office and to the elevators. I expect us to stop, hit the button, and wait for an elevator to arrive, but he keeps walking, right past the stairwell, and then further still, to the service elevator. He calls for the elevator, and when it arrives, we step inside. He hits the button to the roof.

"Where are we going?" I side-eye him.

He shrugs like he has no idea what I'm talking about. "What? Nowhere. Someplace new. You don't know."

We arrive on the roof, the elevator slowly lurching to a stop before Archie inserts a key into the override button, and the door opens.

We step out into a garden—no, an oasis—with plants I don't know the names of and a bubbling fountain in the center.

"It's yours," he says to me.

My breath catches in my chest as my hand skims the petals of a massive tropical flower.

"Don't worry," he murmurs as I take it all in. "You can't kill anything, unlike the poor orchids you murder every few months. It's all auto-irrigated. The engineer says it syncs with the weather or something."

"It's beautiful," I murmur.

He grabs my hand and steers me toward him. "Like someone I know."

He kisses me quickly, and then releases me to explore. Flowers in every color carpet the rooftop and stretch thin veins up and across a massive pergola. There are outdoor wicker sofas and matching chairs with apple-colored cushions. It's everything I've dreamt about, exactly as I imagined.

It was a fantasy, a someday dream whispered in the early morning hours before we climbed out of bed. It was for whenever I learned to not kill every plant I tried to care for. But he's made it into a reality, and it's absolutely perfect.

Unshed tears prick at my eyes as I lean down and breathe in the soft flowers of a rose bush. My mind drifts to Eli, and although I try not to think of him, I can't help it. Just like my mother, thoughts of him carry me away on a whim.

He rots in a jail cell down south, ineligible for parole for the next four years due to the brutal and violent circumstances of my rape. He would hate this beautiful thing his son has created, and the thought makes me love it even more.

"What do you think?" Archie asks, drawing me back to him, like he always does when I need it most.

"It's perfect. It's . . ." I turn around and stop talking when I see Archie in front of me, dropped to one knee, a ring in a black velvet box in his hand.

My heart belly flops all the way to the ground floor. Diamonds in a platinum band, a gorgeous rectangular ruby in the middle.

It's beautiful.

"What are you doing?" I whisper on a breath.

"What I tried to do four years ago, Red," he says. "What scared the hell out of me back then and scares me now, but not as much as the thought of not having you. Will you make me a happy man and marry me, Layne Anne Steele?"

I suck in a breath and the unshed tears spill over.

I look at him and then at the ring and back at him again.

"Come on, pretty girl," he says after a long moment, lifting a hand to run through his hair. "Don't make me beg."

"Or what?" I breathe, teasing him, already nodding my answer.

He stands, slipping the ring on my finger as his other circles around my waist. His lips tickle my forehead with his words.

"Or I'll fuck you up here and let the entire world see what's mine."

"Promise?" I breathe.

"Always," he says a moment before he kisses me.

A WICKED EMPIRE UNIVERSE

<u>Voclain Academy: Ian and Harlow</u>
Beautifully Wicked (Book One)
Beautifully Wanted (Book Two)
Beautifully Yours (Book Three)
Beautifully Mine (Book Four)

<u>Standalones</u>
Vicious Love (Everett's book)
Brutal Hearts (Archie's book)
Delicious Lies (Chase's book) — coming spring 2023

ABOUT JORDAN

Jordan Grant is a lover of all things romance! She likes to write about edgy bad boys and romances that delve into the blur between love and hate. She is an avid fan of all things sweet including red wine and cupcakes (red velvet, please!).

Want free romance books? Check out freebies by Jordan on her website, www.authorjordangrant.com.

Printed in Great Britain
by Amazon

26272817R00150